FIRST CHORUS

CARDINAL SINS
BOOK 2

HEATHER LONG

BLAKE BLESSING

For our spouses.

Yes, they are very well aware that we know what to do with the bodies. They manage to be both impressed and irreverent in equal measures.

FOREWORD

Dear Reader,

Squee! Blake and I are over the moon to share with you book two of Cardinal Sins. If you have not read Kill Song, we highly recommend that you pick it up and read prior to this book.

This will be a four book series filled with action, adventure, crime, passion, betrayal, darkness, and the fine line between justice and revenge. Sounds like a lot? But the simple truth is, we fell in love with our characters and really hope that you enjoy them as much as we do.

One of the best parts of co-writing a book is the shared journey you take. A lot of people ask how we write and assume we break up parts of the book. We don't. Every single scene begins or ends with one of us working on it. Do we take some rather dark glee in dumping the other in the middle of mayhem and letting them sort it out?

Absolutely.

Not only is that one of the joys of working together, it also shows just how fleshed out these characters are in our minds. Decisions can be made on the fly during the creative process and we bat it back and forth easily because these characters become real to us.

We would like to add just a small warning for those who need one. There is violence, mystery, darkness, torture, sex, and laughter in these pages. Yes, laughter. There is also a woman on a mission, a man chasing his future, another racing to escape his past and a third who just wants to know the truth.

Each of our characters struggles with the emotional connections they want, don't understand, but need and are learning to forget the path ahead. The shared journey will be dark at times, that's inevitable.

There are some references to sexual assault (not of the main characters). One flashback includes references to a school shooting that may be disturbing for some readers. Please use caution and protect yourself.

You know how they say be careful what you ask for? Well, don't worry about that. Just dive in and revel in the madness. We love these characters and can't wait to share them with you.

Now for the short bit of business. This is a reverse harem which means the heroine is not going to have to choose at the end of the story.

Oh—and since this is a series, there will not necessarily be an HEA at the end of each book, but we do promise to sort out one by the end.

Probably.

Mostly.

Well, you know what? Just trust us!

xoxo

Blake & Heather

PROLOGUE

RICK

HOURS THEY'D BEEN GONE. The wait for Vienna to come back was always hard, even when I found ways to occupy myself. Fletcher accompanying her, however, added a whole new element of despair to my already heightened worry.

Or was it jealousy?

Yes, it was definitely jealousy cramping my muscles and leaving me aching. I prided myself on being so in touch with my emotions that I could recognize that. It didn't mean I had to like it.

Sighing, I finished off the dusting so not even a spec of unwanted dirt lay anywhere in the house. Originally, I planned to squeegee the windows. When she brought one home the other day, excitement burst in my chest at how fun it would be to use it.

Satisfying.

Taking care of Vienna was a bone-deep satisfaction and watching the results of my work just added to it. The ability to remove the dirty, soapy suds from windows and leave behind a glass pane so spotless you couldn't even tell it was there was about to be my new favorite chore.

Before she'd left, she'd ask me to continue a different kind of work. So, instead of going down my cleaning checklist, I went to her room and retrieved the laptop, careful to follow her explicit instructions on how to get it out and set it up.

Instead of staying in her room, I carried it down to the living room. Her scent surrounded me in her room. I didn't want to disturb it, saving it for later when I needed to remind myself. Some background noise would also be welcome right now. If it was too much and I couldn't multitask, then I'd go back up to her room, but for now, I'd like not to be alone with the silence.

Flicking the TV on, I settled into my favorite spot on the couch, logging in to the dark web. I didn't bother changing the channel from what it had been on, since I had no desire to actually watch it. Whoever was the last in the living room had been watching the I.D. channel.

I snorted, betting on Fletcher.

Vienna knew everything there was to know about her world, and I couldn't see her trying to get ideas or inspiration from the crime channel. One, she didn't do that type of crime. Two, this channel was focused on the past, and she had much more important things to do than this.

The few times we had watched a show together, she had picked comedies. Something mindless but entertaining. Well, there were the times she decided to watch the news, but that served a different purpose.

For a solid hour, I conducted research on the names on the list, both looking up new information, and checking for any changes on existing intel, when something caught my attention on the TV.

A deep, soothing voice of commentary complemented the reel of society pictures on the TV. "The Judge is arguably one of the most notorious serial killers outside of the Zodiac Killer. The hunt for their true identities remains ongoing.

"What separates these two, however, are the victims they choose. The Judge, with over fifty alleged kills and several more assumed, is a vigilante killer. While not all of the victims were men, they always appear guilty of some type of crime relating to women and children. While the nature of the crime may not have been known at the time of their deaths, these rich playboys," a series of dated pictures showed men on yachts, jets, and parties in mansions, "well-respected politicians," this time the pictures told a different story of men and women in expensive suits posing during red carpet events, shaking hands, or in one, kissing a baby on its fuzzy head. "Or community philanthropists, all hid dark, sometimes depraved secrets." The final set of photos was almost sickening to see, knowing the people in those pictures had some kind of guilt under their grand exterior. "Further investigations following their deaths uncovered some shocking and heinous acts perpetrated by the Judge's alleged victims."

Vienna never shared if there was a name attached to her father, or even if the police knew of him, but fierce pride sizzled in my chest. This was the type of work her family did. Saving people when the law wouldn't or couldn't. Like Noel Warrick. She looked like someone's grandmother, and she sold kids. That they would associate someone like the Judge or Vienna with the Zodiac Killer seemed kind of insulting. My perspective had changed entirely from the moment I saved Vienna, and I was happy for the new light of truth shining on the world.

"Sandra Jane, an investigative journalist, who likens herself to a Sherlock Holmes of the digital age, has been compiling the life and crimes of many of these victims. With her new insight on all the pieces of the puzzle known as the Judge, she believes she'll finally be the one to uncover the highly sought after identity of this vigilante killer. Some may seek their own form of justice, and some may thank them for their efforts to keep society safe, but one thing is for certain… The days where the Judge is unknown are numbered. Here's Sandra during her latest interview on Inside Cold Crimes."

A clip of a young, slender woman appeared on the large screen. Whether it was her solemn expression and tenacious gaze, or the size of the TV hanging on Vienna's wall, she seemed larger than life. Striking in an unconventional way, but exuding an iciness that chilled me.

Even when Vienna was working, she never felt cold to me.

"Thank you for having me." She nodded toward the host off camera.

"We're glad to have you join us, Sandra. Jumping right into what viewers are eager to know, we're told that you have new information that could lead to finally identifying the Judge?"

She leaned forward, as if ready to impart a secret of epic proportions but had no smugness in how she obtained it. This woman was all business. "I do. From an anonymous source, I recently gained access to the journals of the late Casey Morgan, the lead FBI agent whose hunt for the Judge has been likened in some circles to Ahab's obsession with finding Moby Dick. Only his white whale was the Judge. The data he gathered was never released to the public, and I believe with the technology available today, this is the key to everything…"

CASH

KRYSTLE'S WORDS had replayed in my head as I followed the directions to Terrence Bailey's place. It was a warehouse down at the docks. That didn't cry shady at all or like some rip off from a horror film. Bad enough the drive had taken me half a day to get to the city, then I managed to hit a traffic snarl that trapped me on a bridge for two hours. Still, the delays didn't matter.

The Judge was active again. I could have told them that. In fact, I'd tried to tell them that, but they cut me out. *Burn out. Mad dog. Losing his mind.* Those were the polite comments. Not that I gave a damn.

It didn't stop me after my first suspension, or my second. The fact they were putting together a new team now? That could probably sting—if I actually gave a fuck. The Bureau was gonna do what the Bureau was gonna do. I'd decided a long time ago to do the exact same. Pops let them dictate his cases, no matter how many times he circled back to this one.

That wouldn't be me. I would find her.

Her.

The more I turned that pronoun over in my head as I reviewed Krystle's report, the more it fit. The Judge had to be a team. No two ways about it, a man and woman were a surprise. Or maybe not. While female serial killers were rare, they weren't a myth. Pops postulated that there could be more out there, but they were never caught. Misogyny was finally doing women a favor in that department. People didn't think they were "capable" of it. Not even the so-called experts.

In fact, the only statistics they possessed came from the ones who had been caught, or at least identified. DNA helped in that department, so did crime scene forensics, but the truth was—women made a substantially smaller statistic when it came to serial killers. Men were the default.

Partners could skew those numbers, so did that make the male partner the dominant? I tended to think so, if only because he had to be the older one. That wasn't misogyny or sexism. The woman on the video surveillance had been younger.

Around and around it went. Terrence Bailey, however, was one of Pops' informants. Off the books and definitely on the down low. I'd only found references to him in Pops' files *after* he died. They weren't in the files he kept in the office either, but his own copies. Copies we weren't supposed to make, but not like I planned to tell anyone.

Once I found a reference to Bailey as the pirate, it didn't take me long to realize Pops had been using him for information for a while. But he kept him listed under the codename Pirate. Probably for confidentiality. Fine. Whatever.

But Bailey worked out of a warehouse on the docks and one phone call told me he would be in tonight. He hadn't been thrilled about me dropping in, but I told him it would be a couple of days. I didn't want him bolting before I got there. Let him think he had time. It was dark and late by the time I followed the GPS's instructions and parked.

The sound of the water lapping against the pilings accompanied a bell ringing in the distance. Cars on the highway sounded a lot further away. The air was cool, humid, but cool when I stepped out. Everything down here was dark, shuttered, like they were closed. The muddied pools of light cast everything in shadow.

A couple of parked cars were my only company. Hopefully, that meant Bailey was still here. Most guys like him weren't going to bolt if they had time to get their shit together. Hence, the "two day" warning. Still, I'd be a fool to not take some precautions, even if I wasn't worried about the guy. What was he going to do? Shoot me?

Hardly.

I checked my gun, old habit, then headed for the doors. The description of the warehouse fit the information I had. His office was on the main floor. He probably needed it close as he handled a lot of cargo, offloading it from ships then sending it out by truck or delivery. All of it private.

Probably not a nine to five job, then again, I wasn't an expert on imports and exports. Inside, a cut hallway led to an unoccupied half-window while the other went only to a set stairs.

Fine.

His office was on the first floor. The stairs went down, so that was the way I went. I supposed it made sense. The warehouse was huge, and it was parked right on the bay. They could probably offload right into it from the larger cargo ships.

The scent of mold, dust, and old dirt tickled my nostrils. But there was a heavier scent just below that. A scent that hit like a sucker punch as soon as I made it to the bottom floor.

Blood.

It was hard to mistake that smell. Blood and just below that, death. Death had a way of stinking that didn't wash out easily. Slowing my steps, I used my jacket to wrap around my hand and unscrewed the light at the base of the stairs. When I opened that door, it was probably a good idea to not announce it to everyone.

As soon as the hallway plunged into darkness, I pulled the jacket back on and then edged to the door. I tested it with a quick, soft push. It didn't latch all the way and the hinges didn't squeal. Good. The moment I got the door open, I had a view of the main, floor. There were a handful of shipping containers in the otherwise wide-open space.. At least two stood with their hatches wide to reveal a lack of contents.

The smell hit me hard. Yeah, it definitely smelled like blood and death down here. My first sweep damn near missed them, but I caught motion in the corner of my eye even as a heavy sigh carried.

"You had to make this more difficult than it needed to be." The warm, husky tones in that disappointed voice wrapped around my cock like a fist. It had to be her. Even before I eased out further and found the blonde woman of my dreams standing in a circle of pale, fluorescent light like some vengeance demon, I prayed it was her.

That voice *had* to be hers.

She had just risen from where she'd been working, her hands stained crimson. The disemboweled body at her feet twitched. Holy shit, the fucker was alive. Check that out. It took real skill to do that to a person and not kill them right off. It was also an ancient punishment, reserved for traitors.

Terrence Bailey had earned a spot on the Judge's list. Even better, the Judge was right here. One half of them anyway. A thrill went through me, even as the fist on my cock tightened. She was *right there.* Everything I'd believed and worked towards for months, and there she was, giving Bailey a traitor's death.

Had they found out he was an informant? Did I care?

Unwilling to let the moment pass, I applauded as I made my way out of the dark little corner the staircase opened. The beautiful demon lifted her gaze and stared right at me as I approached. Goddamn, she was even more lovely in person than on that shitty video.

"I was right," I told her. "You have no idea how long I've been looking for you."

She didn't have a weapon in her hands right now. Excellent, we had time to talk.

"I love that I was right!" I told her. "Now I've got you! You have no idea how long I've waited for this." Real delight unfurled within me. "I have a thousand questions."

Her expression never changed, but something in her eyes did. Ten feet away from her, I paused. Probably better not to crowd her. I mean—I had interrupted her after all.

"I can wait," I offered. "If you need to finish."

Bailey twitched at her feet, But I didn't take my eyes off her. I didn't dare. I'd waited too long and worked too hard. No way was I letting her disappear on me.

This gorgeous wicked genius of a woman tilted her head and pressed her lips together. I almost laughed at her reaction. Damn, what must be going through her head right now?

I was fucking giddy this moment had finally come. A grin crawled over my lips, and I tried my damnedest to wipe it away, but it was stuck. Oh well, this was too much of a breakthrough to put on a professional façade.

Pulling a cloth from the back of her slacks, she wiped her hands off before she tossed it on the body as she continued to study me. I'd never felt like such a bug under a microscope. To be on this side of the fence for once was a novelty. I couldn't even say I hated it. The anticipation of waiting for her first words slowly chipped away at all of my usual self-control.

Drinking in the sight of her, I let my arms hang loose, just in case she were to go on the offensive. I let my gaze rove over every square inch of her.

She was the stuff of wet dreams.

A strong, solid body encased in the simplest outfit of jeans and a black T-Shirt. Both tight enough to highlight her feminine curves that just begged a man to grab on. Shit, my cock twitched.

Her honey-colored hair was braided away from her face and she barely had on a trace of make-up. A natural beauty, too. Her entire ensemble screamed normal, as if she could ever blend in with the masses. Maybe she could, using her body language and choice of clothes to match that of her setting, but anyone who caught a look at her confident expression, those pouty lips, and daring eyes, would not soon forget her.

So, what was her role as the Judge? Solely carrying out executions?

Clearly the woman was skilled in the art of death, but that didn't quite ring true. The more I returned the favor by studying her, the more questions popped into my head. I would revel in the opportunity to find out everything about the Judge.

And this woman.

I must have surprised her, because she still hadn't spoken, although she was too well-trained to let it show. Shrinking in on myself, I tried to appear smaller, less threatening, despite my tall lean frame. Just in case that was a trigger for her, although I doubted it. I made an effort to set her at ease.

Bailey took one last gasping breath at her feet. She hadn't needed to finish him off after all. In the mind of a serial killer, would she be angry with me for sullying her kill?

No, there was no disdain in her expression. I took a few steps closer to get a better read on her. I'd interviewed several high-profile serial killers in my career, and this woman fit none of the usual outward signs. There was no insane gleam to her eyes, no bloated sense of self-importance like she was curing the world of disease, or manic twitches.

On the contrary, she was calm, collected, and intelligent. Ah, the intelligence that shone in her eyes as she tried to figure out a way to most likely kill or incapacitate me.

Hm no, probably kill to avoid leaving any witnesses.

"Who do you think I am?" Her voice was full-bodied like the best wine, with an underlying huskiness. The sound nearly pulled a groan from my throat.

I knew she'd sound like that.

One side of my grin hitched higher as I moved a few paces closer. Now, only about seven or eight feet separated us. The rancid smell of Terrence Bailey's guts almost overpowered the coppery scent of blood, but I barely paid attention to it.

Who cared about that piece of shit? Yes, he had been an informant for Pops, but not a very good one, or bright. I was much more interested in the target in front of me.

"Why, you're the one I've been looking for my entire career." I thought about playing it out, making her guess if I knew who she was or not. In the end, the desire to see her reaction was too strong. "One half of the Judge."

The quick widening of her eyes and her shallow inhale were the only signs that my announcement affected her. Then like the pro she was, she evened back out until she stared back at me with a bored expression. Her left eyebrow even quirked. I struggled against crowing my delight.

"Why would you believe that?" She cracked her neck as her wrists rotated at her sides. There was absolutely zero tension in her body. Other than her slightly dark, pink-stained hands, she could have been standing at a work happy hour. On the wall, not engaging or social, but still calm enough to be in that type of setting.

Who was this fascinating creature?

"Let's just say, I've been an avid follower of your work for years and years. You might call it a family tradition." I smirked. Let her decipher that.

The ghost of a smile appeared, then it was wiped away. "And who are you? Cop? Killer? Rabid fan?"

I scowled. I was a decorated FBI agent. Well, I *had been* decorated, before the Bureau tried to rein me in and hamper my passion. What about me would give this woman the idea that I was a stalking fan?

Outside of the applause and grins. But the beauty of finding this woman in the middle of a kill was epic. It deserved the appropriate appreciation. The respect. The reverence.

"I'd much rather discuss where your partner is." I crossed my arms and shifted my weight between my feet.

A darkness slithered through her gaze. Interestingly, this time she didn't attempt to hide her reaction. "No, I think you're the star of the show now. Care to tell me how you found me here?"

That stupid grin made another appearance as I shook a finger at her. "I don't think that's how this is going to work. What's your usual process? How will you dispose of the body?" My curiosity was eating at me.

I glanced down at the body. A black plastic sheet had been spread out to catch the pool of blood. How had I missed that? Understandably, I'd been preoccupied when I walked in.

"Final chance. Who are you and how did you know to come here?" A coldness blanketed her entire demeanor.

Whistling, I scrubbed my jaw. "That's some threat there. With no weapon and an empty warehouse, you believe you can take me?"

"I don't make threats."

Chuckling, I straightened back up to my full, imposing height. Trying to set her at ease did nothing to further the conversation, just as I suspected it wouldn't. It had still been worth a try.

"Let me guess, you make promises?"

Her lips curled up and if I wasn't mistaken, a flash of amusement entered her tawny brown eyes. "You could say that, yes."

"You're fit, but I'm a good eight inches taller than you with probably fifty or seventy pounds more on my frame. How will you overpower me? Is there a secret pa—" I turned to give the empty warehouse a pointed look.

I barely turned my head a quarter of the way around when my gaze snapped back the other way.

Fucking hell. There was another person here. Too bad I hadn't taken the time to scope the place out.

On that final thought, darkness closed in until I lost consciousness.

VIENNA

"YES!" Fletcher's expression filled with an insane amount of glee as he shot me a look. His cerulean eyes sparkled with a kind of shimmer that belied his blown pupils. "I got him!" He held up the tire iron in triumph. I'd barely managed to catch the intruder after Fletcher launched at him like some mad Viking on a mission.

My little pincushion, who knew he had it in him? Torn between affection and amusement, I set the man down. The blow from the crowbar could have cracked his skull. As it was, I shouldn't have indulged the man's conversation for so long.

"Are you okay?" Fletcher asked, turning his wild gaze on me. "I got down here as fast as I could, but he didn't touch you right? You're fine?" Then as if drawn of their own accord, he turned his gaze onto Bailey's body. The twitching had stopped, and the last little death rattle said he'd given up his last secret. "Holy shit, that's gross as fuck."

"Don't," I said before he could take another step forward. The mess of eviscerating someone was spattered all over me and the black plastic I'd spread out before Bailey and I began our little chat. Ignoring the bloody prints I left on the intruder for now, I stripped him of his weapons and his wallet. There were car keys in his pocket too.

Not good.

"He got here a few minutes ago," Fletcher roused from the

stupor of staring at Bailey's corpse. "You said you would have your phone on silent and I couldn't warn you, so I followed him inside."

"That was very brave of you."

"Well, you don't have to patronize me." Some of his excitement bled away and he wiped a hand against his sweaty face. He'd pulled his long hair back into a single tail at the base of his neck. Tendrils of dark hair escaped and clung to his damp cheeks.

"Fletcher." I didn't add anything else, just waited for him to focus that manic gaze on me. His expression cracked a little as he sucked in a deep breath. "I meant it was very brave. You had no idea what you were walking into and you came anyway."

That meant something.

"Oh." He straightened and his chest puffed out a little.

"Was he alone?"

"Yeah," he said. "Who is he?"

"I don't know." As it was, I flipped open his wallet. The first thing was the driver's license for Channing Cash Morgan. The name tickled something at the back of my mind, but I tabled it for now. A couple of credit cards, a gas card, a loyalty card for some restaurant. There was about three hundred in small bills in his wallet. A second wallet was tucked into his inner jacket pocket.

One look at that and I sighed.

"Holy shit. I knocked out a fucking Fed?" Panic edged back into Fletcher's voice.

"Unfortunately." That was a problem.

Between the intruder's charismatic smile, bizarre applause, and stunningly captivating turquoise eyes, I'd let him get really close. I hadn't missed the fact that he was armed or that my own gun was in the bag behind me. Still…

"Okay," Fletcher said, blowing out another breath then sucking in one noisily. He glanced at the metal bar in his hand like he just remembered he had it. For a second, it looked like he was going to throw it down, then he paused. "Shit. Right. No evidence behind."

Finally, his wild eyes settled and he looked at me. "What do you need?"

I smiled. Letting that emotion out, when this job was far from over and I had to decide what to do with Mr. Morgan along with disposing of Bailey, was a bad idea. Then again, Fletcher didn't surrender to his panic, and I was so proud of him.

"Also, I get that I'm probably looking really good to you right now, but I'm going to require liberal amounts of alcohol later or I will be freaking the fuck out. Okay?"

"Noted," I said, then tossed him Morgan's keys. "You're going to have to drive his car. But move mine closer to the doors and out of the lights."

I had work to do.

Fletcher walked out with a purpose as I grabbed rope from the bag. Terrence was no immediate threat since he was dead, but Channing Morgan was a different story.

He'd been hit hard and should be out for a while, but I wasn't going to give him an opportunity to surprise me. I bent down and rolled him onto his stomach. He'd be easier to contain with his arms tied behind his back.

Looping the rope around his wrists, I finished it off with a double constrictor knot. Once tied, it was nearly impossible to undo without being cut. Where he was going, he'd have little access to sharp weapons. Next, I moved onto the ankles, then the knees.

After he was secured, I started working on the other body. That was much slower work. I finished up the last knot holding the body as Fletcher came strolling in. With the exception of constant swallowing, he was a pro.

I had to tell him again how proud I was of him. To

continue to remain calm during cleanup was a valuable skill. One I was pleasantly surprised he had.

"That's done. What now?" He avoided looking at the floor, keeping his attention solely on me.

"I need to bag this shirt and clean my hands. Terrence's office is on the first floor in the back right corner. He also has a secret room on the second floor, over the office. Can you go grab any servers and look for any evidence of cameras?" While he was doing great, he still needed to have a mission to occupy his mind. He could break down later, but for now, he would stay busy. No idle hands for Fletcher.

Pulling my shirt over my head, I folded it and stuck it inside a small plastic bag, along with the agent's belongings. Then, I grabbed a fresh black T-Shirt from the side pocket. Terrence owned the lot, and the rest of the buildings close by were either condemned or abandoned with no one to see us coming or going. Especially during the dark hours. Chances were, even if there was someone lurking around, they wouldn't notice the blood stain on the black fabric, but I refused to take unnecessary risks.

Everything was packaged up all nice and neat with the agent still peacefully unconscious when Fletcher came back carrying a couple servers.

"There was a panel of security cameras, but I took them offline and grabbed the accompanying system, along with this server from his secret room. He was set up pretty sparse, an amateur." He shook his head in disgust.

Well, Terrence Bailey was never known for being the smartest man in the room.

"Here, put them in here." I held open the black bag for him to stow away the machinery. Zipping it up, I secured the strap across my chest. "Alright, Fletcher. This is going to go a bit different than when we left Dion's. That was easy, we just had to walk out to the car. This time, we have two bodies to take out with us."

As soon as the words left my mouth, his eyes widened and he swung around to look at the agent.

"Sorry, he's still alive. I only meant we'll need to carry him out. Terrence is light, I can grab him. The agent is stockier than you. Do you think you can carry him?"

"Can I carry him," Fletcher mumbled as he bent down to slide his hands under the man. With a grunt, he lifted him over his shoulder and struggled to his feet. I lurched forward to catch him in case he tumbled over, but he staggered back to a firm position. "I got it. This bastard is heavy though, fuck."

"When we get to the doors, I'm going to pop the trunk on the agent's car. I'll also do the same to mine. Then you'll be placing Channing Morgan in my trunk, while I place the other in the car you'll be driving. Understand?"

I kept my gaze steady on Fletcher, watching for any sign he was about to crack, but he remained steady. He nodded and turned toward the door. He didn't leave, but waited for me to get Terrence over my shoulder, and then we were out.

"You need a break? I asked at the entrance to the warehouse as I grabbed the keys from his pocket and unlocked both trunks.

"I'm good."

"Good." With quick steps, we got the bodies in the trunks and I stuffed my bag in the backseat of my car.

"Now's probably not a great time to tell you, I think I'm going to be sick." Fletcher belched as he clutched his stomach.

Rather than make a huge production of it, he grimaced and clamped his lips together tightly. "Hold it," I ordered, twisting to reach into the backseat and under it. I had plastic bags for a reason. Whipping one out, I passed it to him. "Vomit into this."

The pained expression he wore as he took the bag pulled at me.

"I know, it's not pleasant," I assured him. "I'm sorry. Better to keep all the DNA in there."

He made a face, then turned away before he hurled into the bag. I grimaced, but I stayed with him. As disagreeable as the experience was for me, it was far worse for him. More, Fletcher had kept it together. Not only had he come in and followed the agent, he'd helped with clean-up and removal. I could stand here while he vomited and watch his back.

It took him two more attempts before the retching ended. Gloves still on, I took the bag from him and sealed it closed. Then I handed him water to rinse out his mouth. When he went to spit, he gave me a pained look and I handed him a take-out cup. It was basically a styrofoam cup for coffee.

"You good?"

He held up two fingers before he rinsed his mouth a second time then took a long drink of the water before he nodded slowly. "Drew?"

"Little Pincushion?"

The pained expression dissolved into one of surprise and a startled grin stretched his mouth at the comment. Even in the dark, the gloomy yellow pools cast by the lights, his eyes seemed to brighten. "I—" He hesitated and then a laugh broke out of him, it was a little bit of a deep sound that danced up high then came back down. One breath. Then another. Finally, he exhaled with an element of relief. "I just wanted to know what was next?"

"Next, take this," I said, handing him a new bag. "And the water. I'll get you a fresh bottle. Take his car and follow me. We're going to get away from here, then we'll take care of everything else. If, for any reason, you think you're gonna get sick on the road, pull over. We'll take care of it."

"I'm not going to have to do anything with the body in the trunk, right?"

I didn't clarify which body, because Fletcher didn't have to do anything. "Not a damn thing." It was a promise. Then because he deserved it, I rose up on my tiptoes and kissed his cheek. "Thank you, Fletcher."

I swore he straightened and even the air around him seemed lighter. He took the proffered bag and water bottle, then headed for the agent's car. I studied the vehicle for a moment. Then carried the bag Fletcher had used back to my car. Thankfully, I had a cooler in there, where I stored the bag after pulling out the water bottles. Better to deal with later.

Once we were on the road, I kept my head on a swivel and scanned our environment. I hadn't noticed anyone watching us at the docks. There was no one following us now. Fletcher had seen the agent arrive and said he'd been alone.

Maybe he was crooked. Maybe he was there for a payoff. Bailey did a lot of work for a lot of people, and he really didn't care how dirty he got. That was an avenue worth exploring, a thread to pull. Once we were thirty minutes from the docks and on a back road that paralleled the interstate, more or less, I called Reuben.

We needed to meet. There was no love lost between Reuben and Bailey, fortunately. Reuben could also deal with the agent's car, after I emptied everything useful out of it and wiped it down. Then I would take Fletcher and our guest home.

My stomach rumbled. It had been a while since I ate. While wholly unexpected, the agent's arrival might prove useful. I certainly hoped so. That, or we could find out he was dirty. I'd have Fletcher do a deep dive as soon as we were back.

I didn't relish the idea of killing an innocent.

Then again, he'd known enough to identify me with the Judge and that was… unsettling.

Deeply unsettling.

A little sigh escaped me as we closed in on the rendezvous with Reuben. My passenger in the trunk had been quiet so far. Would that last? One could hope.

Fletcher hadn't needed to pull over, thankfully. The meet point, drop off really, because Reuben didn't need to see

Fletcher, was a small abandoned and ramshackle church on the outskirts of a next to nowhere town that had apparently fallen off the map.

It matched the coordinates. Fletcher pulled up next to me after I parked. We didn't spend a lot of time on conversation. I was glad to see he looked a lot better and apparently, he hadn't been sick again. Also an improvement. Then again, bodies in trunks were out of sight and out of mind.

We stripped everything personal out of the agent's vehicle including files, an overnight bag, an unsolved Rubik's Cube, a couple of skin magazines, a beat to death journal in the glove box, and a second gun. I checked under all the seats, and in the engine. While Fletcher waited with my car, I also checked the trunk.

Once I was certain there was nothing else to find, I made sure to wipe everything down, before I sent a text to Reuben that the package was ready for pickup and disposal. The usual fees would cover it.

On the road again, I gave into the urge to rub at my eyes. It had already been a very long day.

I still needed to tell Rick.

FLETCHER

NOW THAT I was in the car with Drew again, I could breathe. The drive to drop off the agent's vehicle had been uneventful, but that didn't stop my heart from raging in a mosh pit the entire way there.

Fuck! I still couldn't believe I knocked someone out. And then he had to go and be an *FBI agent?* I was halfway between being jazzed and shitting myself. I mean, I'd already thrown up.

Shaking my head, I tried not to smell the remnants of puke. Vienna had given me water to rinse my mouth out, and I hadn't gotten any on my clothes. Actually, I glanced down just to make sure. No, nothing that I could see. I smelled sour, but it was most likely fueled by my humiliation rather than reality.

Vienna turned her head away from me as we took a slow left turn. I snuck a peek to see if any disgust played over her features, but there wasn't any. During the entire…event…she didn't grimace, twitch, or show any emotion other than practical compassion.

My face flamed in embarrassment. Shit.

We'd shared a scorching hot kiss at the storage unit. I'd

just started to hope Vienna saw me as more of a man than a usable nuisance, but now? I shook my head again.

How could she find anything sexy about me now? Between offering to help me piss while I was falling down drunk, and the fantastic privilege of holding the puke bag because I lost it, whatever was between us was a lost cause.

At least I could say I was gaining lots of new experiences with my sexy death angel.

An errant chuckle escaped, dispelling some of the darkness that had started to hang over my head. I tried to stop it with my hand but the laughter only got stronger as it crawled up my throat.

Drew tossed a suspicious glance at me, like she thought I'd need to whip open another bag at any moment. I winked to let her know I was okay.

I *winked*?

Now?

What the hell was wrong with me? She didn't have to speculate that I was off my rocker, I was doing a bang-up job of showing her how horrible I was under pressure all on my own. I needed to bring a bit of normalcy back between us.

"What do you think Rick made for dinner?"

This time she shot me a confused look, though one tinged with indulgent amusement. That was something, right? Or she knew exactly what I was attempting to do.

"He texted a little bit ago asking when he thought we'd be home so he could time dinner right." Surprisingly, the obvious adoration in her voice didn't get my hackles up like it normally would. Probably because I was emotionally spent from having the most exciting, or frightening, evening in my life. Did it have to be one or the other? Maybe both? No, definitely both. "He's going with comfort food tonight. Figgy glazed pork chops with mashed potatoes and roasted carrots. Oh, and garlic confit for the bread."

I blew out a breath. "When you all asked me to add culinary schooling in his history, you weren't exaggerating about his abilities, huh?" Fancy garlic spread sounded good right now.

We'd left all the streetlamps behind as we got closer to her place, but the dim light of the dash was enough to see her soft smile.

"Rick's an excellent cook. I'm glad he's able to do something he loves." A pause. "What about you? Are you happy with your life as a hacker?"

If she'd asked me that yesterday, or even earlier that morning, I'd have made some ridiculous come on, but currently I wanted to be truthful without all the fluff.

Being in high-intensity situations really did fuck with me. I swore my emotions had gone through the entire spectrum in the last hour or so, leaving me drained.

"Absolutely. This is what I was made to do. And it's allowed me to distance myself from my prat of a family." I slouched back in my seat, getting more comfortable.

"Is that who you're hiding from now?"

I tensed. Had I said anything other than I needed to lay low for a few days? I didn't think I had.

"You're thinking very hard over there. I know you're running from something. Why else would you essentially move in with us?"

Drew and I, we got along okay. Rick wasn't so bad either, when he wasn't being a raging OCD ass. That didn't mean I wanted to lay all my secrets at her feet. Not right now, and maybe not ever.

Since I wasn't willing to share the truth, I wracked my brain for something I could tell her. Or maybe I should just keep it vague. She already suspected it was my family anyway.

Damn it. I should have been looking on her servers to see

if she had a file on me, like she alluded to keeping on all her associates. How much did she know? Most likely, she knew the basics. I wouldn't be surprised if she knew who my family was and potentially even ran in the same circles on occasion.

Hell, she might even know about…

Nope, not going to think about *that* right now. That was a recipe for disaster.

As a hacker, I couldn't even begin to be offended, but I would have preferred to not have her call me out on my lies. I wouldn't lie to her now, would I?

"Let's just say, in my business, I've made a lot of friends, but where I've always excelled is pissing people off. Sometimes unintentionally, and sometimes on purpose." I shrugged. "It means I need to lie low on occasion. And yes, the Reed family is also a bag full of dicks."

"A bag full of dicks." The way she repeated the phrase made me smile, despite the topic at hand. It was like she needed to test it out and wasn't entirely sure what she thought of the words.

"I mean—most of them just aren't worth knowing." Most, as in 99 percent. The one percent (and percenter) for that matter who I liked was my cousin. Well, I guess it was cousins now. But that wasn't the point. This generation. That worked. My generation was all right. Everyone else? Fuck 'em.

"A bag full of dicks," she said again, but the corner of her mouth curved upward into this sweet little smile.

"Like that, did you?"

The little smile turned into a full-fledged grin that stole every ounce of my oxygen when she flashed it at me. "I'm trying to imagine the person who cut off enough dicks to fill a bag, and then decided that was an accurate description for unpleasant people."

And just like that, my breath returned with an almost painful whoosh and I tightened my thighs. "Yeah, pretty sure they just meant dickish people, not actual dicks. Or I sure as fuck hope not." 'Cause cutting a dick off was not high on my list of experiences I needed to have, or witness. Nope.

Her laughter flooded the interior of the car. Despite the subject matter, it was impossible not to at least chuckle with her.

"Glad I can entertain you." While it might have come out a little snarky, I did actually mean it. I liked it when she smiled.

"Thank you," she murmured, then brushed a hand on my thigh. It was a light touch, there and gone again. "For both the humor and for what you did earlier."

"No problem, as long as we're talking about the stellar rescue. Not that you couldn't have taken care of it yourself. In fact, I know you could have." Hell, I'd had a front row seat to just how badass Drew could be. "Do you mind if I enjoy the fact I saved you?"

"Not at all." Once more she patted my leg, then returned her hand to the wheel. "I appreciated what you did. It was a risky maneuver. And you're not a man who enjoys any kind of violence."

"It depends," I admitted. "This was less about the violence and more about watching your back." She didn't explain why we were there or who that man was. Only told me to wait and to stay outside. While I enjoyed ferreting out knowledge and information, I also appreciated a good need to know.

I did not need to know why she eviscerated that guy. Protecting her had been more important than staying away. Of course, now I was also a witness, but—guess what, let's just file that thought into the trashcan and leave it there.

The guy could have been like that when she got there. I saw nothing. Technically, she didn't even touch the FBI agent.

"Fletcher," Drew seemed to sum up everything about me in the two syllables of my name. "You need to take a deep breath."

"What?"

"You're hyperventilating. It's going to make you pass out if you're not careful, or you'll get sicker. Take a deep breath, slowly, hold it for a moment, then release slowly. Be deliberate." She demonstrated by taking an audible breath. A flush warmed my face but I followed her lead.

For five minutes, we didn't do anything but *breathe*. The wild hammering in my ears and the skittery sensation all over my skin abated. Fuck me, had I been having a panic attack?

I might as well just turn in my goddamn man card.

"Better?"

"Much." Maybe she should just cut me loose. It might be better for her overall. Twisting in the seat to face her, I braced myself to suggest that when a banging came from the trunk. My pulse rabbited at the noise. Goddamn Fed, he kept interrupting.

For her part, Drew just sighed. "Well, I suppose it was too much to hope he'd be asleep all the way there."

"What do you want to do?" Because I hadn't really thought about what we were going to do with the guy.

"Go home, take a shower, have dinner—maybe talk Rick into a massage or sex." She glanced at me. "You?"

Yeah, what I said about cutting me loose just evaporated in my brain. "Can I watch?"

Not what I meant to say, but what the fuck. Apparently, this was a night for new things. Behind us, the thumping continued.

She didn't immediately answer.

It was dark and we'd long ago left behind the road with streetlamps. We weren't far from her place now. The only light in the car was from the dim glow of the dashboard, but I could have sworn there was a heat to her cheeks.

Was she *blushing*?

I grinned. Drew blushing was like an early Christmas present of skin mags and conditioner as a tween. She was so composed and hard to read most of the time, that this little reaction from her was like crack.

Fuck, I couldn't even be sure she was as affected like I thought she was, and my dick went from zero to sixty real quick. I shifted in the seat to avoid the stinging press of the zipper.

The corner of her mouth curled up as she glanced over at me, and my grin turned into a shit eating smile. "That's not a no…" I teased.

She laughed, her head tipping back, highlighting the delicate column of her throat. My avenging angel was soft right now, and as soon as we made it back to her place we were going to lose this moment.

I'd just have to do everything I could to bring out this side of her as often as possible. She could be a cold-faced killer to everyone else, but I craved her amusement. Craved *her* really, but this openness and innocence—honestly, innocence really did apply—it awoke a hunger inside of me. In fact, I preferred that she reserved this side of herself for me.

And Rick, I guessed. The admission came grudgingly. She cared about him and for him. I couldn't change it. I knew when to accept defeat. Defeat, however, didn't mean loss. It just meant I needed to change the game—and thus, the rules.

"I'll make you a deal. You convince Rick to let you watch, then you can join us. As a voyeur only," she said as her voice dropped into a husky purr.

That was a challenge. One that had me squirming in the seat. "Rick won't agree," I complained. Not willingly, anyway. But there was no way I'd pass up a challenge like this. If I had to blackmail him, or hold his favorite cleaning supplies over his head, I'd make it happen.

Ever since I'd met Drew, I knew I wanted to fuck her. She just made it within my reach. Well, almost. I'd figure it out.

The thumping stopped. Shit. I'd gotten used to the constant noise and vibration and now it was gone, it was slightly alarming. Was this like children? When they were quiet you needed to worry?

"Is this an 'oh shit' moment? Should we be concerned that our friendly neighborhood Fed has gone silent?"

Drew glanced in the rearview mirror, then shrugged. "He won't be able to get out of that trunk. The latch that opens from the inside has been welded over. We're almost home anyway."

Home.

It wasn't my home, but the word on her lips sounded fucking fantastic when she included me in the same sentence. "Wait. What about the back seat? Does it lay down?"

I twisted around. Sudden visions of this guy kicking in the seat wasn't filling me with the warm fuzzies. If that happened, I had a feeling I'd be doing the girly screaming I was so afraid of earlier.

"You're hyperventilating again." Drew started breathing in and out on a slow steady rhythm as I mimicked her.

"If I have nightmares, can I sleep with you?" She laughed, but I was only partly kidding.

Whoever this man was, he was dangerous. I wouldn't be able to sleep very well knowing he was locked in the house. He seemed resourceful.

"You shouldn't have any nightmares, Fletcher. The monsters can't hurt you, not when you're with me." Her words could have been said in jest, but holy shit, her tone was serious.

I found myself nodding, because I had no idea how to respond to that. She must not have found anything strange in my reaction because she fell back into a comfortable silence as she scanned the road.

Our conversation kind of died at that point, but it hadn't mattered. We were back at her place within minutes. She backed into the garage, waiting for the door to close before she turned off the car.

Rick opened the door, filling the frame like the psycho puppy he was as Drew said, "We're here."

RICK

WITH THREE MINUTES TO SPARE, the external garage door opening told me she was home. I checked the food, already out of the oven and resting. Everything would be hot. There was bread in the warmer too. Drying my hands on a dish towel, I headed out to the garage to meet them. They'd ended up being gone *most* of the day.

Longer, I suspected, than she'd originally planned, or maybe that had been me. Even with work to do for her, the house to clean, and the meals to prep, I'd found myself watching the clock more than I care for. She was out there alone, with only Fletcher for backup.

Not my favorite part of the whole plan.

The automatic lights in the garage were on when I opened the interior door. Vienna had just backed in, the red taillights bright as she engaged the brakes. The external door hummed as it rolled closed. The only noise coming from the motor on the garage door opener. She kept it all oiled and smooth.

The lights on the vehicle cut off along with the engine. I went to open her door when a sudden mad thumping came from the trunk. Smile fading, I narrowed my eyes. A quick look showed Fletcher climbing out of the passenger seat.

So, she didn't shove him in the trunk.

The sound of banging came from the trunk again in the silence of the garage, the muffled complaints climbed in volume. Vienna glided toward me with a smile. I scanned her from head to toe. She'd changed since she left that morning, but I found no evidence of bruises or injuries.

The soft pressure of her hand on my chest stilled the shiver of anxiety that had been vibrating beneath my skin since they departed that morning. I dipped my head to hers as she rose up to brush her lips to mine. The air whooshed out of me, and my heart thumped just a little harder.

"Welcome home," I greeted her. The tawny golden brown of her eyes seemed so much darker under the yellow light of the garage, like shadows shifted in them. "What's wrong?"

The ease in her presence seemed strained. Fletcher approached slowly, like he'd done something wrong or—no, not wrong, he looked pale and washed out.

That only confirmed my opinion that something had happened. The banging from the trunk escalated just as she opened her mouth. A faint frown tightened her brow and she glanced at the trunk. I slammed my fist against it. "Be quiet and don't interrupt again."

"Holy shit," Fletcher said with a chuckle. I met his gaze and his humor only seemed to ramp up, even as his cocky grin widened. "Gonna welcome me home with a kiss? Cause if you're worried about it, I can assure you, I'm good."

Before I could shut that down, Vienna let out a breathless little laugh. Like falling into a gravity well, my whole being focused on her. "Fletcher, don't tease Rick, it's not nice." Though her own humor seemed to betray that sentiment, it didn't bother me in the slightest. If it made her smile, I was all for it. "And yes, we're home, very busy day."

At the offer of another kiss, I let out a sigh. "What can I do?"

"You two should probably go inside while I deal with…"

"No," I told her firmly. "You've had a long day, if you need me to put him in one of the basement cells, I can take care of that. The wine is chilled and it's been opened to breathe for you. You could even go take a shower if you'd like."

Surprise flickered over her expression. "The basement?"

"Cells?" Fletcher's shock echoed in that one word.

I gave a little shrug. I'd found the dungeon set up during one of my first days cleaning. It appeared to be in use and useful. Since Vienna hadn't given me permission to be down there, I'd left it as I found it and didn't open the door again.

"Fletcher," Vienna said without glancing away from me. "Go inside, shower, and change. Then come down for dinner."

"Yes ma'am," Fletcher said, some of his cockiness fading away.

I sympathized with that feeling. I couldn't read Vienna's expression at all. She'd gone so still and neutral, worry exploded to life within me.

Then Fletcher paused to press a kiss to her cheek. "Thank you," he said softly before he darted around me and through the open door to the house, leaving us alone.

A thump from the trunk interrupted. Again.

Well, almost alone.

Still, I waited. If I'd fucked up, then I'd take my lumps. I still wasn't leaving her to carry that person downstairs. Not conscious. Not when I was *right* here.

Vienna rested her hand on the trunk as she studied me. My heart pounded against my ribcage. She'd never been upset with me before, and I couldn't say I enjoyed the feeling. That was, if she was upset. There was no way to tell under the dim lights in the garage.

Maybe under the bright light of day, where I could see every nuance of her expression, but not right here, right now.

"How did you know about the basement?"

I released a slow breath. Her question hadn't been accusatory, more like curious.

"One of the first times you left, when I'd been cleaning. I thought there might be supplies stocked up down there when I ran out of wipes. After I realized there weren't any, I never went down there again."

She stepped forward, and I cupped my hands on her hips. Soft amusement flashed in her eyes. "Hmm. No wipes down there. What did you see?"

"I saw one of the cells was occupied. I didn't talk to him though, even when he tried to yell at me." Tried, because his voice was reed thin from either overuse or dehydration. Maybe both. He, like the basement, wasn't any of my business. If he was down there, then he must have done something very bad. Vienna didn't hurt innocents. She kept them safe from the monsters.

"He never said," she mused, then shook her head. "It doesn't matter now. He's no longer down there."

"Do you want me to take this person down? I'm happy to. Then you can relax and enjoy dinner. I've got chocolate chip cookies in the oven too." Luckily, I'd just put them in. We had time for me to drop him downstairs.

Pulling her hand from the trunk, she slid it up my chest to rest on the side of my neck. "You're so sweet, Rick. I'm glad you came into my life." She glanced down where the offender waited and sighed. "We better get this done. If Fletcher makes it down before we get him secured, he might lose it again."

"Again?" I hid the bit of glee that roused in my chest. Not that I wanted him sick, per se. I did have some guilt from when I'd gotten him drunk. But if he couldn't handle her work, then maybe she'd take me next time.

She shook her head and motioned me to step away from the trunk. "It was a very intense situation. I'll tell you about it later, but I'm proud of him. He surprised me, but more than that, I think he surprised himself. We still have this problem to take care of." She motioned to the hidden person. "I need Fletcher to do some research before I figure out how we're going to handle him."

With a press of the key fob, the trunk popped open. Inside, a large man was crammed in the small space, his legs tied to one wrist. He must have worked one hand out because that arm wasn't tied to anything. His pale eyes nearly glowed in the shadows as he glared at us.

That wouldn't do at all. He needed to be fully restrained.

Moving Vienna back gently with a hand to her stomach, I cocked back and then slammed my fist into his face. I watched for a few seconds to make sure he was truly knocked out, then I unknotted the rope connecting his hand to his ankles. I tied his free hand up again. Just in case he was pretending to be knocked out, I didn't want to inadvertently give him any advantages.

From the looks of it, he was similar in height to me, if not a little taller, but I had more weight on him. I grunted as I pulled him out and threw him over my shoulder. He was silent during the whole thing. Good. He really was unconscious. Otherwise, he would have grunted or made some noise from the force of his stomach hitting my shoulder.

"I'll grab the door," Vienna said as she closed the trunk, then moved around me. We'd need to vacuum out the trunk, but I could do that after dinner. I didn't want Vienna to have to worry about anything else tonight.

Following behind her, I made sure to keep a firm hold on this guy.

I didn't ask her any questions because I trusted her completely. But he didn't seem like her usual target. There wasn't anything physical that I could place my finger on. He was dressed in slacks and a button down, which was on par with many of the men Vienna had me watching.

He just seemed different. I shrugged. It didn't matter.

She went ahead of me and opened the second cell door. It was different from the first time I'd been down here. It smelled clean, like she'd soaked the entire room from the ceiling down in bleach. Maybe she had, because the man who had been in the other cell before was now gone. Beyond the cot, the cell also had a toilet and sink. The bare minimums. A thin plastic mat covered the cot. There were no sheets or blankets. I glanced at it but decided against laying him on it. Instead, I dropped him to the concrete floor. If Vienna wanted him in this cell, he deserved no kindness from me.

"Do you want me to undo the ropes?" I turned to Vienna as the man groaned at my feet. He wouldn't be out for very much longer.

Tough bastard.

Granted, he couldn't have been comfortable in the trunk. The red marks on his wrists suggested he'd been working to get himself free for a while.

Behind me, Vienna sighed. With the guy stirring, I didn't dare turn, but I wished I hadn't asked her the question. It meant she had to consider the options. I'd rather send her upstairs to relax. Today had apparently been far more difficult than she expected.

"Untie him," she said with a kind of finality. "He might be down here for a while."

Fine by me. I undid the knots, aware of him the whole time. There was the faintest stain of pink against the concrete beneath his head when I shifted him. If he made even a hint of a move, I was going to make sure he had a concussion. Done, I backed out of the cell and closed the bars before I closed the door.

I wound up the rope and hung it on a hook before I

glanced at Vienna. She watched me with the softest smile. Unlike the garage, the lighting down here showed me everything *including* the dark, if faint, smudges beneath her eyes.

That decided me. "Let's get you upstairs, I'll deal with him tonight if necessary." I could make him a meal and bring him water. Whatever she needed.

"I don't know what I did to deserve you," she said on an exhale, and I grinned. "But I am glad you're here."

"Me too," I assured her. "This is where I need to be." Protecting her was what I'd *needed* my whole life, and I was exactly where I should be. To my immense satisfaction, she let me usher her upstairs. When she would have gone to the garage, I said, "I'll take care of the car after dinner, if you need anything brought in and anything cleaned out."

"Rick…"

"I'd like to do it," I continued, and her swift smile and little huff made me grin wider. "Especially since I wasn't with you, this is the least I can do." The oven timer went off and I turned smoothly to slot on an oven mitt and pull out the cookies. The sweet scent of chocolate chips filled the air. Perfect. They were exactly the right darkness to be done and chewy without being too hard.

"You're going to spoil me," she said as if that were a bad thing. When she touched my arm then kissed my cheek, I went absolutely still. "Do I have time to shower? I don't want any of your meal to go to waste."

"You have all the time you need," I promised. I'd remake it from scratch if I had to. "Get comfortable. Do you want a glass of wine to take up with you?"

"That would be lovely." She was also eyeing my cookies, so I set the tray down then lifted one right off with a spatula and set it on a plate before handing it to her and going to pour the wine. Her soft laugh was all the reward I needed. Wine glass and cookie in hand, she headed up the stairs.

I tracked her path and met Fletcher's gaze as he shifted to

the side to let her pass. Only she didn't, she paused to speak to him. The softness of her voice didn't carry, but Fletcher ran a hand down her arm. It was a brief touch, but a little too proprietary for my tastes.

After she ascended the steps, Fletcher turned and seemed to square his shoulders before he crossed the living room to the kitchen, where I waited. He'd showered and changed into a t-shirt and sweats.

Irritation rifled through me, then her words from earlier tickled the back of my brain.

"I'm proud of him."

"Well?" Fletcher asked when I said nothing. "Go ahead, let me have it."

Cocking my head to the side, I raised my brows. "We're not eating until she comes back down, but I can get you a drink if you want."

He blinked slowly. "That's it?"

"What else would you like?" Vienna was the only one getting a cookie before dinner. She got anything she wanted. Fletcher could fucking wait.

The other man opened his mouth, then closed it again. A deeply puzzled look on his face. "This is not going how I thought it would."

"He surprised me, but more than that, I think he surprised himself."

"You did good." Huh. It didn't kill me to say it. Nice to know.

Fletcher gaped at me.

"Take a seat, relax, I'll get you a beer. Only one. Vienna mentioned you might need to do some research tonight."

He was still staring when I went to the fridge to get it for him. It wasn't until I actually handed him the ice cold bottle I'd just opened that he seemed to react at all. "Thank you."

"You're welcome." When I cut my gaze to the chairs at the bar, he moved to take a seat. Hey, look at that. Even Fletcher the flirt could be trained. Vienna was proud of him and he'd behaved, so… "Would you like some cheese and crackers while we wait?"

Being nice to him was almost as much fun as punching him.

Almost.

CASH

GOD DAMN. This night didn't go as I had planned. At fucking all.

My head was killing me, both where I'd been hit in the back, and my face where I'd taken that punch. That guy had a hell of an arm. Shit, my entire body was sore, but it didn't detract from the excitement from my break in the case.

I'd started the night off giddy that I'd finally solved half of the puzzle that had plagued me nearly all my life, then somehow, I ended up in a cell. A very used cell.

If the overpowering smell of the last cleaning didn't still hang in the air, the state of the concrete would be a dead giveaway. There were no stains, no water spots, not even any mildew collecting in the corners of this damp space.

Torn between irritation I'd gotten caught, and excitement to be experiencing life as one of the Judge's victims, I paced the small space. At least they'd let me keep my shoes, although all of my weapons and personal belongings had been stripped.

That gorgeous woman could be deciding all the best ways to torture me right now. Nah, she wouldn't do that. Their victims had a very clear MO, even if the media never picked up on all the kills. They were despicable people who did nothing but hurt the innocents of society. She'd have seen my badge and had to know I was an officer of the law.

All it would take was a little bit of elbow grease in the tech department to pull up as much of my history as publicly possible. Granted, there wasn't much. Being in service to the FBI meant I needed to stay out of the public eye, but there were some things printed about me. She'd also be able to pull my credit, my schooling.

Nothing that would trigger her happy little hands to want to hurt me.

Now, kill me because I threatened exposure for her and her partner? Yes, that might be a possibility, but I was prepared to use all my skills to manipulate her. Maybe we could even make a deal.

I'd been too cocky at the warehouse, sloppy. That had been a rookie mistake. One I wouldn't make again.

But damn, the thought of getting to spend time with her, pick her brain on their trade secrets and motivation. How they discovered their next target. I was getting a hard-on just thinking about all the things I could learn.

That might be worth the death she'd attempt to deliver.

I snorted, dying wasn't in my plans.

After what seemed like hours of pacing, I sat down on the cot, leaning my back against the cool stone of the wall. The real question I needed to ask was, who hit me in the warehouse? She was good, I'd give her that. Her gaze had never strayed from my own.

Of course, I'd been completely captivated, so I had admittedly been more than a little distracted. The woman was something to behold and I couldn't be held accountable for that. Well, I glanced around at my surroundings. I could be held accountable for my actions because they'd landed me here.

The partner must have been the one to sneak up behind

me. I should have searched the place before approaching her, but logic had completely left me at that point.

Repetitive noises reached me through the door of the cell. Footsteps. Someone was coming down to visit me. I sat forward, hoping it was the woman, but equally as curious to meet the other half of the Judge. Pops would have shit himself to have finally met the killer he'd chased his entire career.

The person stopped on the other side of the door, and it slid open with very little noise. They definitely took care of the slides and hinges.

They'd so kindly left the fluorescent light on in the cell, which highlighted the man's features as soon as he stepped up to the bars. Disappointment settled on my shoulders when I realized he was the only visitor. The man who fucking punched me.

He was...exactly what I would have expected of a serial killer. Although younger than I'd have hoped, he was large, beefed out, with a severe expression on his face. His eyes also held a note that was slightly off. Not like the woman. I could have passed her on the street and never realized who she was, or even suspected she was anything other than a beautiful woman.

A section of the bars opened to reveal a slot, and he stuck a tray through. The food on the plate looked gourmet, and there was even a fancy little napkin in the corner with two fresh cookies. Their sweet aroma almost overpowered the savory scents of the dinner.

I grinned. What kind of cruel and unusual punishment was this? I couldn't imagine this was how the Judge treated their guests.

The smell of the food added a far more pleasant aroma to the bleach-soaked room, with its hidden promises of painful and bloody deaths. Both made my dick hard. Meeting my keeper's steady gaze, I raised my eyebrows. Even if my grin relaxed to a smirk, it didn't go away.

I was *dying* to know what would happen next. If they offered up some aspirin or something, I wouldn't mind that. Probably wouldn't *take* it. Hell, I probably wouldn't eat that food immediately. As lovely as it looked and smelled, eating it would be a stupid move.

Pity. But I'd already made a couple of rookie mistakes. Not planning to compound them further.

He stared at me for the space of several heartbeats. I didn't say a word, just studied him unflinchingly. Interrogations always began by establishing dominance. I didn't stand up and I didn't speak. The food suggested one form of care that was in total contrast to the room I was in.

"Do you need ice for that?" While it wasn't quite breaking first, it would do.

"If I do," I said, shifting my weight to stop leaning on my forearms on my knees and then spreading my hands. "Are you going to bring it to me?"

My captor eyed me for another long moment. "Eat. It's better when it's not cold." He withdrew from the bars and reached for the door. "Or don't." It was all the same to him.

Message sent.

I snorted as the door closed with a kind of finality that made me chuckle. Point to both of us, it would seem. Yeah. He was *not* what I expected of the Judge partnership. Leaning back against the wall, I kept my eyes half-closed. The light didn't dim or go off. The food cooled while I considered the next steps.

While the aroma definitely tempted my stomach, I refrained. The ability to sleep anywhere at any time had never been so useful. The release of the tumbling locks on the outer door roused me, but I didn't open my eyes more than a bare sliver.

It wasn't the brute from earlier. The brightness in the cell impaired my view of the shadowy outline of the woman standing just beyond the bars. She didn't step closer, but it was her. My pulse picked up and the urge to sit forward was a violent, visceral impulse.

One I resisted. Like with my earlier visitor, I forced myself to be silent. If she wanted to talk to me, she would have to make the first move.

Please, fuck, want to talk to me.

If nothing else, I wanted to hear her voice. I needed to catalog it and add it to the rest of the facts I'd already collected.

She was beautiful.

Really fucking beautiful.

Her eyes were going to haunt me.

The regal way she'd stood over that corpse—well he hadn't *been* a corpse just yet but it was also inevitable—had been the spring on the trap slamming down on me. Or maybe that was whatever had struck me in the head.

Didn't matter, it counted.

I needed to hear her voice.

A scrape of a chair filled the quiet, but she didn't come closer. If anything, she disappeared into the shadows beyond the light in here. Was she sitting down to watch me? Was she waiting?

The food had long since cooled and the absence of the rich aroma, or maybe I'd just gotten used to it, made it easier for me to catch the hints of a far sweeter, and intoxicating scent. Roses? Not quite. It held floral elements, but there was something impossible to describe about it. The scent and the mystery of it was heady and exhilarating.

Another layer to be peeled away. Along with her clothes. I could see her in my mind. The delicate nature of her features, the lean build, the way her dark clothes did nothing to hide the sweet curves and gentle slope of her breasts down to her hips.

My cock stiffened to the point of pain. It was almost enough to compete with the dull thud of my headache. In order, I wanted to hear her voice, strip away her clothes so I could see her and explore the texture of her skin, and, fuck me, I wanted to taste her.

Those had nothing to do with my investigation and everything to do with the fascination that bordered damn near on obsession. The Judge had been my father's Moby Dick. His white whale. Maybe her male partner was still that.

But she was the enchantress who'd tormented and haunted me for years, long before I'd ever seen her. If I believed in the bullshit about fated mates or love at first sight —that would be exactly what she was.

My mate.

I almost snorted at the description.

Then again, if anyone got between us, I'd remove them. Hunting her had become my occupation. Now that I was here?

Nothing would stop me.

Nothing and no one.

Come on, my dark saint, come into the light and talk to me.

Yes, dark saint fit her. I'd carry her talisman and offer up prayers to her.

An hour, maybe more, passed. But she didn't come into the light and she didn't say a damn word.

When she did move, she closed the door. The food was still there, cold and unappealing. Particularly now that my hunger for her outweighed everything else.

The light in the cell went out and I had to strain to even catch the faintest hush of her steps. Stairs. There were stairs. Then another door closed.

And I was alone in the dark cell with a hard dick, cold food, and a desperation for answers.

Or was that just a wild, violent desire for her?

Fuck.

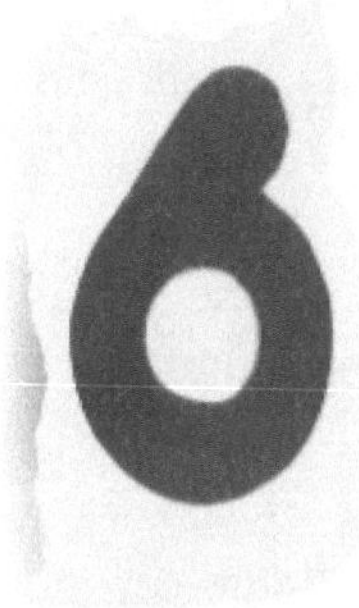

FLETCHER

THE QUIET OF the house was slightly alarming in the early morning hours. But that was coming from the night owl. Most days when I woke up, Drew was already up and moving softly around the house, like a sensual wraith. Rick would be puttering around the kitchen, either making a sweet spread for breakfast or cleaning up afterward, depending on the hour I rolled out of bed.

The Fed was also quiet in the basement. I glanced down, as if I could see through the floor like Superman and find him in some closed off cell. For a second, curiosity plagued me, then I shook my head.

I didn't need to know what the basement looked like. And I sure as hell didn't need to see the Fed in that type of habitat. One evening of puking up my guts from a weak stomach was enough, thank you.

Really, the lack of sound from the basement shouldn't have shocked me. Knowing Drew, it was probably sound proofed to the nth degree.

Stumbling down the stairs with all the grace of a drunk flamingo, I yawned and rubbed the sandy sleep from my eyes.

Was it really that early?

Once I hit the kitchen, I checked the clock. Barely after eight, so *way* fucking early for me, but where were Rick and Drew? It was like I hit the Twilight Zone to be down here by myself.

Caffeine. I needed caffeine to jump start my brain. I started a cup, then loafed around in the cabinet looking for something to munch on.

Bingo. A Ziploc bag of cookies was front and center. They'd go nicely with a large cup of bitter coffee. When I pulled out the bag, I frowned. Why was there a slice of bread in the bag? I poked it, expecting my finger to sink through it but it was hard and stale.

Delicious chocolate perfumed the air as I opened the bag. I went ahead and grabbed three as my stomach rumbled. Damn, so good. They were nearly as fresh as they'd been last night after dinner. The bread must be the key here.

Whatever. I didn't care what sorcery Rick had found to keep cookies fresh, as long as I was able to benefit from it. The day Drew asked me to leave would be hell. They'd have to pry me out of here with crowbars…for an array of reasons, with Rick's culinary skills at the very bottom.

The stairs creaked. Someone was on their way to join me. I fixed my coffee as Rick appeared in the doorway, pausing when he saw me.

"About time you got up. It's not like you to be lazy, man." I shook my head at him and sipped my coffee as if I had any room to give him shit. I practically lived here, though after the stunt he pulled that one night, I actually did.

And it felt good. But I wouldn't be too hard on him. After all, Drew had promised me that I could watch if Rick gave the okay. I squinted at him. He didn't behave even close to bi, so I doubted hitting on him would work.

"Vienna was up late last night, so I'm letting her sleep in. She set her alarm for nine-thirty and I didn't want her breakfast to be cold." He shrugged, moving to the fridge to start taking out ingredients.

Probably a good thing he was unfazed by my razzing. It would suck if I pissed him off before I could butter him up.

"You did an amazing job on the cookies," I said, holding one up for emphasis. "What's with the bread? Is that why they're still so soft this morning?" When all else failed, flattery was the path with the greatest results.

A smirk hinted at the corners of his mouth before he turned back to the fridge and pulled out even more. Eggs, milk, bacon, buttermilk, chives, and so much more lined the counters by the time he was done.

"Yes, it's a trick I learned from my mother actually." Our conversation died again. I partly blamed it on the fog still attached to my brain.

He went about chopping and prepping while I leaned against the counter and finished off my coffee. Then I made a second cup, because why the hell not?

Although, when Rick's gaze darted to the fresh brew with more than a little disapproval, I had to hide my smile. He really didn't like me all caffeinated up and ready to go.

An idea popped in my head and I didn't realize why I hadn't thought of it last night. The way to Rick's heart was through cleaning. I bent down to grab wipes under the sink and busied myself with cleaning off the knobs and anything else that could hold our fingerprints.

His confusion as he watched me spin around the kitchen was mildly gratifying. *See there, Rickster, I can connect with you on your level.* First, we start a true friendship, then, I'd get to watch you rail Drew like your life depended on it. They just seemed like they had all-consuming, wild sex.

Well, actually, maybe Drew was the dominant one. Shit, I was getting hard. I'd just have to see for myself once I was on Rick's good side.

And I couldn't wait.

First step, watching.

Second step? Participation, baby. But right, first, first step —making Rick like me enough to say yes. Once I finished wiping things down, I made sure to dispose of the wipe then *washed* my hands before I finished my coffee. In my efforts, I even poured the son of a bitch a cup *before* I poured myself a third cup.

At the faint narrowing of his eyes, I flashed him a grin. "Don't worry, I'm getting a fresh pot all ready to go so that we can hit brew five minutes before her alarm goes off."

That would mean it would be hot and fresh for the lady of the house. Since her pleasure and needs came before all else, I was kind of hoping Rick would just go with it. He was in the process of cracking eggs into a bowl one-handed with a kind of smooth precision.

I swore he seemed to be taking my weight and measure. Then he nodded toward his coffee mug. "Thank you."

"You're welcome, man." I took my life in my hands and clapped him on the shoulder. After all, I was the badass who took down the Fed, carried the bastard out *and* dumped him in the trunk of the car. Patting her Pitbull-like psycho puppy on the shoulder should be in my wheelhouse.

The look he fixed on me when I gripped him had me more than a little grateful I didn't pull back a bloody stump. Right. No touching. Got it.

"Can I help?"

"You can go sit down," he said. The mild tone was total deception though. Rick didn't yell. He didn't shout. He got even.

Fast. And brutal.

Course, he did get me drunk. But—bygones were bygones, so I'd go sit down. "Actually," I said as I circled around the bar to get out of his territory. "I'm going to grab my laptop and do some work. Maybe I can have some answers for her before she gets down here."

"Thirty minutes," Rick called after me and I chuckled as I walked toward my "office" with my coffee mug in hand.

I'd actually wanted to do it the night before. Drew had vetoed the idea, instead she'd given Rick a thumbnail sketch of our day, skating over several items including the profound disappointment she'd experienced at the storage facility. She didn't mention our kiss either, but that was her call. When it came to the Fed, she'd told Rick he'd come across her while she was dealing with another problem and that I'd prevented him from interfering.

Like I said, thumbnail sketch. I didn't contradict her or offer up any other explanations. After dinner, she asked Rick about his day, then we all settled into the living room for a movie. She seemed to need "normalcy." No lie, I'd enjoyed it myself. It was—ridiculously peaceful to just sprawl and watch whatever was on. Rick made popcorn, she drank wine while Rick had a beer, I stuck to water.

It was either hydrate or get blind drunk. I wasn't in the mood for her to have to scrape my drunk ass off the floor again, so we kept it casual. It wasn't until she nudged me awake and guided me upstairs that I'd even realized I'd fallen asleep. After I'd brushed my teeth, I came back into the bedroom to find her waiting for me.

"Are you alright?"

The question had surprised me at the time. Then again, my angel of death was a source of constant, and at times, delightful surprises. "I'm alright," I'd said. "Are you?"

Puzzlement flickered across her face. I knew damn well Rick checked on her regularly, so she couldn't be unused to people asking. Then again, I tended to be allergic to shows of affection that didn't involve swallowing my cock or letting me fuck them into a mattress, so what did I know?

Instead of blowing off the question though, she seemed to think about it. "I don't know yet," she finally admitted and real concern flooded me. "I'll let you know, okay?" Before I could say anything though, she brushed the lightest of kisses to my lips. "Thank you for today, my little pincushion. Thank you for coming in after me."

Yeah, my brain pretty much epically failed at that point. I managed all of an, "I'm glad I was there." Then she was gone and the door whispered closed behind her.

Sleep proved elusive, thanks to the fact that not only was I hard as a stone, but also worried. Rick would look after her though. Right? I had no idea when I finally fell sleep. My dreams were active. Too active. I woke, only to realize all the work I'd done had been in a dream and not real. Dammit. I wanted some answers for her. So I hauled my ass downstairs to get to work for real.

Thankfully, between the sugar rush from the cookies and my first two cups of coffee, my brain seemed ready to start firing the cylinders.

I left the big machines alone and went for the laptop right now. First level digging would go a lot faster, then I'd know what searches to set up while we had breakfast.

Drew needed answers and I would damn well get them for her. I needed her to know she was all right too.

By the time Drew popped her head in the study, an hour had passed, and I'd just completed my high-level search on our new friend. The lack of information made me both excited that he seemed like a boring, harmless man on paper, or wary because ain't no way there wasn't more to that story.

Growing up the way I did taught me the most crucial facts were never on paper.

"Hey," Drew greeted as she leaned a shoulder against the doorjamb. "I didn't believe Rick when he said you were up before him."

I grinned as my gaze trailed down her delicious body. Today must be an off day as she was dressed in a workout tank and running shorts. Her face had an almost elfin air to it, with her hair pulled up into a high ponytail. I mean, if elves were temptresses. She really had a great body. When I was allowed to participate, I'd tell her as often as possible.

Drew didn't need validation that she was a sexy, beautiful woman. Honestly, I wasn't sure she even put much stock in appearance like that. She was all about skills, and stealth, and moral high ground, even when it was a bit murky. But women deserved to be praised and I wanted her to know just how attractive she was to me.

"He's right. So much happened last night, I had a hard time sleeping and once I woke up with the light in my eyes," I shrugged, "I just couldn't go back to sleep. I'd like to mark this down in the books though. I doubt there'll be very many days I'm up before either of you."

She sobered as she stepped farther into the room. "Was this a residual effect of a stressful day, or you were processing what happened with Channing Morgan?"

I gave her one wry shake of my head. "I was processing, but not in a bad way. I'm good now. In light of a new day, I already feel like last night is miles in the past." It also gave me a little confidence boost that I'd pulled through when she needed me. I had zero fighting instincts, so to know that I could actually do something to keep Drew safe…

Let's just say, I added a new piece to my self-worth puzzle.

I'd try not to let it go to my head too much.

"Great. Breakfast is ready. Are you coming to eat with us?" She was already on her way out, but she paused to glance over her shoulder.

"Yup. I'll join you in just a few minutes."

She waved and disappeared as I set up the more complex searches on my system and logged off my laptop. Most people left their machines on, but I took better care of my babies than that. In the random, and very unlikely event, someone snatched my laptop and broke into it, as if my fail safes wouldn't wipe the machine—like I said, very unlikely—

there would be no history or open tabs to share what I'd been doing.

"Aw, you waited for me." I smiled extra big to show Rick how much I appreciated the plate he'd already made up for me. Then I pulled out my chair and opened the napkin in my lap.

Instead of going for the pot of coffee, I filled a glass with orange juice. Glancing at Rick out of the corner of my eye, I pursed my lips. He was staring incredulously at me and I almost broke out in a giggle.

"Have you started looking into the Fed?" Drew asked as she slathered orange marmalade over a stack of crepes.

"I have. I'll most likely know more this afternoon, but I've done the prelims." I cut my omelet into bite size pieces and took my first bite. Oh damn, I didn't know eggs could taste like this. Every day that fucker got better and better in the kitchen. "Channing Cash Morgan. Single white male. Thirty-two. Career FBI Agent. About two thousand in credit card debt but it's paid off regularly. Public schooling. Bachelor's in criminal forensics from Purdue. Never been married. No kids..."

"All of that is good, right?" Rick leaned forward. "Or do we wish we could find evidence of criminal activity?"

Drew glanced at him but didn't answer right away. She would absolutely kill the Fed because he threatened her and us, I had no doubts about that. But it would weigh on her conscience if he was innocent.

The guy came in clapping like a lunatic when he found her. How innocent could he be?

That wasn't what concerned me though.

"It's more about what I haven't found. Everyone has a few skeletons in their closet, Rick." Sad fucking truth right there. The bones rattling in mine still gave me nightmares. That said... "I can't tell you if this is good or not until we know his."

The sword of Damocles hanging over her head was the very last thing Drew needed. If there was dirt on this guy, I'd find it.

Then we'd know what kind of shit storm we just found ourselves in.

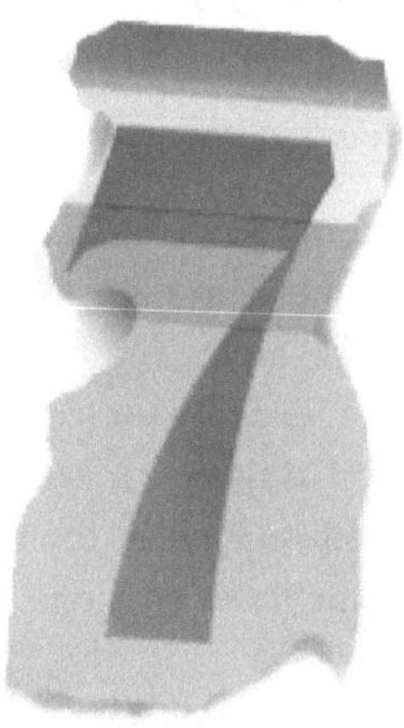

VIENNA

SLEEP DID nothing for my exhaustion. I couldn't quite put my finger on what made me so weary. It could have been that I got *nothing* out of Bailey before he bled out. Stubborn old man. He refused to admit to anything—verbally. His reactions to my questions had told me a great deal more, but then he shut down.

Shut down because he was more afraid of what would happen to him if he spoke. Nothing I did broke the grip fear had on him. Would I cry over his death? Certainly not. The world would be better without him in it. But if I had learned anything the last few months, for every void I created— someone else was more than willing to descend to the depths of depravity to fill it.

It wasn't a matter of if someone would take over his business, only a matter of when. Fletcher destroying his server would make it more difficult, but not impossible. The smartest among us kept backups of backups. Strip me of everything I had, the house and the accounts in the name of those who owned this property—hell, take my fucking car—I'd be setup elsewhere within a week, and back to work in a month.

Maybe sooner.

"Vienna," Rick said my name in such a soft voice, so filled with concern, it took me a minute to process that he was sitting to my right at the table. The plate in front of me was empty and he'd just refilled my coffee. Fletcher wasn't even sitting there anymore. "Maybe you want to take a nap? We have time. I already fed our guest, though he didn't eat last night's meal. I doubt he'll eat this one. But I took it down anyway."

A sigh escaped me. When Fletcher asked me how I was the night before, I didn't have an answer for him. I still didn't. Reaching over, I closed my hand over Rick's and he turned his hand beneath my palm to return the grip. "Thank you. You don't have to look after him. I should be doing that."

He was my prisoner after all.

"I told you," Rick said, the chastising note matching the firm look he gave me. "I'll take care of it. I'll take care of anything you need taken care of."

Another sigh escaped me. Twisting in the seat, I lifted my other hand to cup his face. Clean-shaven and smooth, I enjoyed the strength in his jaw. More, I loved how his eyes warmed as he looked at me. No secrets lived behind the beautiful cobalt shade. I traced my thumb over his cheekbone.

"I don't know what I'm going to do about him yet," I admitted. Something I'd been avoiding saying even to myself. If the man really was an FBI agent, it was a whole different kind of problem. Fletcher was so certain he could find something on him. The determination radiating off him helped, but the question of what if he couldn't, chased circles in my head.

"You don't have to decide anything," Rick assured me. "Not yet."

Perhaps not, but this was just another complication we didn't need.

"What do you need?" The question was another in a string from both him and Fletcher that never failed to catch me off guard. I was capable of taking care of myself. More than capable. Even this wrinkle with the agent. I would sort it out. That wasn't the question.

The unease in my gut though, the ache of missing Daddy, the frustration of finding no answers at the storage locker, followed swiftly by the annoyance of not being able to get what I needed out of Bailey, it was all balling up inside of me like twine made out of lightning.

"Kiss me." Need unfurled as I split my focus between his lips and his eyes. The faint dilation of his pupils promised he was just as affected as I was. Or maybe his desire had been burning there all along and that was the light that kept the shadows from his eyes.

Poetry was not my thing.

Wrapping my hand around his nape, I tugged his head down and his mouth crashed into mine. This was what I needed. Him. The contact. The fierce heat of his lips as they massaged mine. Our tongues dueled and stroked each other's in equal measure. Drowning out the voices in my head, I drank in his kiss like water.

The rumble of his groan was my only warning before he hauled me out of the chair and into his lap. When I'd gotten dressed, I'd planned a workout. This was better. The tank top and shorts were hardly barriers to the heat scorching the air around him.

As he stood, he tilted his head, breaking our kiss only to surge against me and reclaim my lips again. The rub of his erection was there, but frustratingly elusive thanks to our clothes. Impatience sizzled through me. Why had we bothered to get dressed?

More, why hadn't I woken before he left the bed?

Balancing myself with my thighs, I ground against him as I found the edge of his shirt and pushed it upward. He kept a hand clamped against my ass, keeping me pressed against him as I fought to strip him down.

The next time he lifted his head was to let me pull the shirt up and over, then it vanished as he traced his fingers against my face before cupping it and then dipping his head for another kiss. He made it another two steps, the bump of his cock a fucking tease that would make me wild if we kept this up.

I dragged my lips from his, checked our position, then twisted my whole upper body and pulled him with me. I took his balance and we rolled over the sofa. He caught himself, and me, pushing a hand out to shove the coffee table away as he landed on his back with my full weight pressing down on him.

Sex in this house had already been a first. My room. The gym next door. Now the sofa. In some ways, each time I claimed a piece of this, a piece of him, I carved away my past. It hurt. The pain stole my breath even as Rick gave it back to me.

The glide of his skin beneath my hands pulled my focus to the present. His eyes were on me as I rose up, the pressure of resting against his still clothed dick aggravated me even as I rolled my hips. The sensual tease only heightened my need for him.

Fuck. I swooped down and sealed my lips to his. His kiss demanded and gave in equal measure. He slid a hand up my back and pushed the tank top with it. I didn't waste time as I sat up and ripped it and the sports bra off and dropped them before I dipped back down to kiss him.

"I need you," I told him between kisses. A shudder went through him as he groaned, the vibrations were another tease against my senses. Hungry for every reaction, I dug my fingers into his shoulders. But it was his turn to flip us over and I was on my back against the sofa as he lifted his head.

Drunk on him. I was completely drunk for him. Nothing else existed. His eyes were heavy-lidded as he raked that hot gaze all over me like a caress. The caress of his hands followed across my chest as he cupped each breast and then flicked my nipples. My cunt tightened and flexed. We needed to be more naked.

Before I could say anything though, he lowered his head to capture one nipple against his teeth and I arched upward. He twisted the other with his thumb and forefinger. The pain sparked against the pleasure. With a gasp, I sucked in oxygen even as he laved his tongue over my nipple, then sucked it with such ferocity I could feel the pull in my cunt.

One arm around me, he lifted me as he moved upward, transferring his attention to my neglected nipple. It ached in anticipation, even as the other throbbed. At the scrape of his teeth, I fisted his hair.

"Yes," I hissed. Every harsh suck pulled my pleasure upward like it would geyser through me. I fumbled for his jeans and he knocked my suddenly clumsy fingers away and undid the snap. The zipper was loud against the silence punctuated only by our harsh breaths.

Leaving my breasts, he settled me back on the sofa before he straightened. It was the perfect view to see his cock thump against his belly as he stripped off his jeans. Training had begun to add definition to his body. The dip of his Adonis belt was a work of art. The muscles in his thighs rippled with every motion. He gripped my shorts and ripped them downward.

It was speed, not a lack of gentleness that ripped them and the tearing sound split the silence even more than his zipper. Rick paused, pulling the shorts free from my legs and staring at them.

"I have plenty more," I assured him, heat suffusing my

chest and even my neck. Hell, my ears got hot. Then Rick stared at me with a kind of predatory hunger that had me curling my toes even as I spread my legs. "See something you like?"

The corner of his mouth kicked up. Whether it was my question or my attempt at a sultry tone, I had no idea because he dropped down, catching his own weight before he settled between my thighs. "I see some*one* I adore," Rick murmured in between light, nipping kisses. "Someone I need."

Need.

That goddamn word again.

Yet, my whole body flushed at his admission.

"I don't know if I could handle it if something took you away," he confessed.

"No one is taking me," I said flatly. "No one is going to take you. I'll kill them. I'll kill anyone who tries." Without hesitation or mercy.

Rick paused at my words, a hint of vulnerability peeking out at me. "Fletcher wants to take you."

"No, sweet man," I whispered, wrapping my hand around his nape again. "Fletcher wants to watch us. He wants to flirt. He may even want to join us. But he doesn't want to take me from you. Share me, maybe. Not that I know what to do with that at the moment."

Fletcher was definitely a temptation. One that ignited something within me I didn't quite understand. It was different from what Rick gave me. I wanted to protect them both. I would protect them.

But in Rick's arms, I found a peace I had never known, and in Fletcher's? I found a promise for more. Maybe I was a greedy bitch for wanting it all.

"Right now, this isn't about him," I continued. "It's you and it's me." Arching my hips, I stroked the length of his cock where it rested against my cunt. The glide back and forth teased my clit, but it lacked any kind of real friction. With one hand, I skated it down his back to his ass. The muscles clenched beneath my fingers, but Rick's gaze held me riveted. I never looked away.

Not when he cupped my breast or teased the aching nipple. Not when he ground against me and gave me that friction I wanted. Not when he dipped his head closer until only a breath separated our lips.

I lifted my hips, then dragged my hand between us so I could wrap it around his cock. He hissed out a breath and when his lips parted, I swooped up to kiss him as I drove myself mad stroking his tip against my labia, then my clit.

Wet and aching, I sucked against his tongue. When he clasped my face and deepened the kiss, I angled him so I could surge up as he sank down. With one powerful thrust, he filled me and our groans echoed off each other. The thickness of him stretching and filling me was an ecstasy all its own.

Wrapping my legs around him, I dragged him closer as we rocked together. With every surge upward, I swiveled my hips and with his every thrust, he began to hit that spot that made my vision go white.

The pace we set was brutal. He answered my kisses with a growl and a bite that stung my lip, even as he thrust relentlessly, driving me higher. I writhed with every stroke, the scrape of his teeth sent tingles radiating over my skin. He abandoned my lips to kiss down my throat and the warmth of his breath just added another layer of pleasure to my already drunken senses.

The languid heat unfolding within me eddied me higher and higher, but the coil of tension was so tight, it had me clinging to him.

Right... there. The white edging my vision went blinding as my orgasm detonated, the snap of the tension flooded me with heat and I scrambled against him, clenching my thighs, dragging him deeper. He continued thrusting, pushing me over the edge into another orgasm before he came. The hot pulse of him filling me sent another flame to burn.

He felt so damn good. Together, we collapsed. The weight of him covered me, and I reveled in the contact as my soul gradually drifted back to my body. Slowly, I began to stroke my fingers through his hair. We were both panting, the air was warm and almost humid. The scent of Rick and sex were both intoxicating. The press of his lips to the corner of my mouth made me smile. Then one to my cheek, then the corner of one eye and finally the other before he lifted his head.

The relaxed expression, the fat pupils, the slow smile—we could just be drunk on each other.

The semi-hard thickness of his cock still rested inside of me. At my involuntary clenching as my muscles spasmed, his dick twitched and hardened gradually. We could afford to catch our breath. Then... "Round two?"

There were so many things we hadn't done together.

He didn't answer me immediately, just studied me with those drunken eyes but the hint of sobriety made me wary.

"Rick..."

"I can share," he said finally.

Shock fluttered in my chest.

He nodded as if he'd come to a decision, then he smiled at me. "I can share." The repeated phrase still stunned me. "As long as he behaves."

The last set a very real bubble of laughter free and I chuckled. "It might be a moot point," I reminded him.

"I know, I just want you to be happy."

The words echoed something in my soul. "I want you to be happy too."

"As long as I have you, I am happy. As for Fletcher..." He made a face. "He's not so bad."

It almost sounded like that pained him to say. Chuckling, I pulled his face back to mine. "Your secret is safe with me."

When he kissed me this time, he rolled his hips and his

cock thickened a bit more. Oh, we weren't going anywhere for a while.

"You said round two," he murmured against my lips and I let out a groan as he rocked himself.

"Yes," I exhaled. "Please."

It didn't take him long to get that second wind, but when he dragged us up and bent me over the sofa, fucking me hard and fast from behind, what few other issues I had with the world crumbled away.

Eventually, we even made it upstairs for round three—and a nap.

Round four was when I woke him up from our nap by half-swallowing his cock. Just us, no worries behind these doors. No one else here except someone we'd both grown fonder of.

Rick definitely made my world better.

He was also right, Fletcher wasn't so bad, at all.

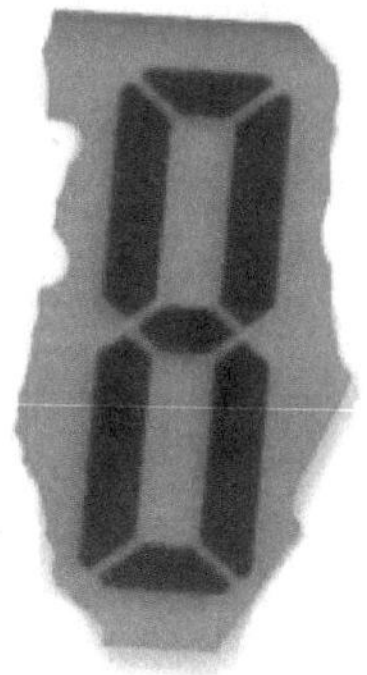

I SCANNED the work Rick had been doing for me over the last few days. He'd collected and cataloged data on each of the proposed targets, linking two together from a recent article of their businesses merging.

Interesting. I hadn't even realized they knew each other. Their proclivities weren't even close to similar, but something must have drawn them together.

"How did I do?" Rick carried a glass of tea and a few cookies on a tray as he joined me in my bedroom. I didn't always do this type of research up here, but with people in the house, even if it was only Rick and Fletcher, my instinct was to stay tucked away while I was on the dark web.

"You've exceeded my expectations, Rick." I smiled as I grabbed a cookie off the platter. "How many of these did you make? I feel like we've been eating them for days."

He preened under my obvious appreciation. "Those are the last ones. I made a second batch after dinner that night." Settling on the pillows next to me, he wrapped a hand over the top of one of my feet where it stuck out from under my thigh.

As the days wore on, Rick became more and more affectionate. At first, he'd only touched me when he'd had clear permission with verbal or physical cues. Now, he was more comfortable around the house, and around me. He often found little ways to touch me. Nothing overpowering, or even exceedingly possessive.

They were touches that seemed to reassure him. I was also coming to enjoy the connection it brought.

"Is this okay?" Rick started to lift his hand, but I stopped him by placing my own over his.

"Sorry, I was thinking." I bent forward to place the rest of my uneaten cookie on the tray and turned back to the screen. "This is really impressive. I can't believe how much you've collected on the list in just a few days."

"When I'm not prepping food or cleaning, I'm working on this. I like that I can be useful." Not the way he wanted to be useful, if the slight downturn to his mouth was any indication. My sweet Rick. He'd be plastered to my hip all the time if he could.

I wouldn't object, except that it was no way for him to live, and I would rather not have a target on his back for being seen with me too often. Daddy and I, we had our fair share of enemies, but most would never dare strike out at *us*.

Except...I swallowed hard. Someone had. And the storage unit hadn't been helpful. What had Daddy been thinking?

With everything going on, as well as holding the Fed in the basement, I hadn't had time to look through the boxes we'd brought back. I'd stuffed them in my hidden closet and started working on other things. Tonight, after dinner, I'd sort through the files. Frustration welled up inside me knowing everything was blank, but I needed to double check to make sure I hadn't missed any clues.

The phone buzzed on the bed next to me.

Uncle David.

I hit the green button and placed it up to my ear. "Uncle David," I greeted.

"Ladybug. I wish I wasn't always calling you with these types of messages," he said with barely any inflection at all. Even when I'd been a little girl, he'd kept his emotions locked down. He'd smiled only three times in my presence that I could recall.

I didn't say anything, and he didn't expect me to. Pandering to each other's feelings and engaging in small talk never was the relationship we had.

"Another link has been eliminated. Bailey. I don't know how closely you worked with him, but it's probable he could have been the source of the leak."

Doubtful, but I didn't interject.

"What jobs are you working now?"

"None at the moment. There's too much unknown." Meaning I wouldn't make a move until I had all relevant facts, and Uncle David knew that.

"Good. I wanted to make sure you were safe. If you need to do another job soon, contact me and I'll arrange anything you need within the network. I'd like to keep you separate from them for the time being."

"I don't think I'll be taking any jobs in the near future, but I'll keep that in mind."

Rick took the laptop from my lap and started surfing the web, hunting down information he might not have found yet to tag it in with the appropriate name. I wish Daddy could have met him. He'd have loved Rick's devotion and attention to detail.

Now Fletcher...I smiled. They might have clashed, or Fletcher would have erupted into a giggle fit and gotten sick when Daddy wasn't looking.

"It's your turn to call next time, Vienna. We'll grab lunch."

"Of course," I murmured and touched the end button.

"Family?" Rick asked.

"Of a sort. He–" I paused as loud barreling footsteps approached my room. Fletcher slid by on sock-covered feet before popping into my room.

Out of breath, he wheezed, "I found something you're going to want to see."

Finally.

Two days. Two days having the agent in the basement. He still wasn't eating. He had, however, finally taken a still sealed bottle of water that Rick left for him. After that, Rick took a whole case of them down there. Of all the actions he'd taken—or hadn't, as the case might be—the aversion to eating the food, no matter how gourmet it was, and his suspicion about all the drinks resonated with me.

If I were locked in a cell, I would die of thirst before I took what they offered—unless I could be as certain as possible that no one had tampered with the water—hence the sealed case of water bottles. But I'd only fight like that if I had a *reason* to fight. Survival only mattered, in as much as my work depended on me.

Daddy had. But Daddy wasn't here anymore.

I *hated* how thoughts ghosted out of the ether to remind me of the loss. As if, somehow, I was doomed to forget.

Fletcher's eagerness, however, had me closing my laptop and securing it before Rick and I followed Fletcher out of the bedroom and down the stairs. Excitement practically charged the air around him. In his office—because he'd really taken over in here—he pulled out the chair he usually occupied with a grand gesture for me to sit.

His hand trembled. I hadn't missed that. His eyes were over-bright. When I caught his fingers before he could tap the keyboard, he gave a little startled jerk. "What?" He snapped the word out. No sooner had the word left his lips than he let out a little shudder, then shook his head. "Sorry, Drew, you did not deserve that."

"You're exhausted." It wasn't news to him. "You haven't been sleeping."

"I've had a lot of work to do, you know." It was damn near defensive. "You should appreciate the greatness that is me because I found—"

"Fletcher."

His mouth closed with a little click of his teeth. While he'd been avoiding my gaze, he finally looked at me. He had one hand braced on the chair and the other I held.

Now that I had his attention, I laid it out for him. "After you show us what you found and I've made all the appropriate noises of appreciation, you're going to do three things."

"I am?"

Behind me, Rick let out a little grunt. "You are."

"Love you too, Big Guy," Fletcher tossed off easily, but he didn't look away from me and I waited for the smirk on his face to fade. "I'm listening, Drew."

"Good. First, you're going to leave this room and stay out of it for at least eight hours and one full meal."

Mutiny filled his expression. "But I—"

"I'm not done talking."

He shut up.

"Second, you're going to upstairs and showering. You definitely need to change your clothes. We'll wash these clothes..." I flicked my gaze over the coffee and food stains on his shirt.

If I didn't know how meticulous he was about his equipment, I'd have expected the room to be a disaster area. Instead, it was Fletcher who was a wreck from his disheveled hair to his bloodshot eyes to the stained clothing. The fact his nipple rings were visible through the dirty white shirt had nothing to do with my desire to get him clean.

"No, we're burning these. They look like they could stand up on their own."

There was enough light in the room to make out his flush. Now he glanced to the side and down, before giving his armpit a surreptitious sniff. Considering he had his arm braced on the chair and right over me, I couldn't miss it. Luckily for him, I was quite well acquainted with the smell of hard work.

"Fair," he admitted. "Third thing?"

"You're going to have a meal and spend some time with us. If you're having trouble sleeping, we need to talk about that." Since Rick had moved into my bed, I'd slept better than I had in years. I'd never thought of myself as having sleep problems, but if I was *this* rested with Rick in my bed compared to before?

Yeah, I wasn't trading that. Maybe I needed to invite Fletcher to sleep with us. The idea had some merit. I'd discuss it with Rick when Fletcher showered. My bed was more than big enough to accommodate all three of us.

A lick of heat curled through me at the idea. Tempting. Too tempting. Running my tongue over my lower lip, I doused the need I'd aroused all on my own with a little pragmatism. "Deal?"

Fletcher hadn't answered me immediately. The unfocused nature of his eyes and the fact he had to give himself a little shake would have convinced me he needed this if I hadn't already decided.

"Deal," he said with a sigh. "Sorry, I guess I got caught up in the hunt." Then he shot me a grin, all cocky again. "Can I now dazzle you with my excellence and show you what I found? You're going to want to congratulate me. I'd say it was almost worthy of a blowjob, but we're not there yet. So maybe you could spot me a quick squeeze and maybe a little feel?" There was literally nothing subtle about how Fletcher cut his gaze up and past me.

He was totally trying to yank Rick's chain. The only thing my sweet man did was let out a long, if aggrieved, sigh.

Biting back a laugh, I let go of Fletcher and leaned back in the chair. Steepling my fingers together, I said, "Please continue, I am eager to be astonished and amazed."

"Me too," Rick tacked on and I just grinned. Fletcher though, his grin grew even more daring. Yes, he was enjoying this.

Good. The man needed sleep. The moment he tapped the space bar, my humor swirled away, draining as I read the report Fletcher had left on the screen.

Channing Cash Morgan.

FBI Agent.

Previously attached to the BAU.

His father's name, a list of credentials, also with the BAU.

But it was the red line below all that I focused on.

Terminated. Removed from position by consensus when risk-taking behavior exceeded all Bureau mandates and regulations.

Our guest *had* been an FBI agent.

"He's not a Fed," Fletcher said with profound relief. The man he'd knocked out wasn't actually an active agent. It was still assault, but it wasn't the instant felony attacking an officer or federal agent would normally be. "And…"

He moused over the report, then pulled a screen out from behind it. Accounts. Withdrawals. Credit card receipts. Hotel reservations. Everywhere Mr. Morgan had been prior to arriving at the warehouse on the docks.

"The blue lines are his movements, the black are places he's been back to at least three or more times in the last three months." He tapped one last button. "Those red dots are unsolved deaths—some murders, still open, all committed within hours of his arriving. Sometimes before. Sometimes after."

Silence unfolded between all of us. I studied the information, then switched back to the report. It was heavily redacted, and it looked very official. "Fletcher?"

"They never saw me. There's a trapdoor you can get

through when filing a public request for access. Once I was on the server, I just had to find his file. I limited the intrusion, because I'm really fucking good at what I do, and I did a batch grab. This file was in it. I can go back in for the full file, now that I know what I'm looking for—"

"No, this is good."

It was better than good.

Our mute, stubborn prisoner had some explaining to do. Fletcher's giddiness wasn't quite contagious, but a wave of relief hit me too. Killing an agent had not been high on my list of desirable tasks. Fletcher had done more than astonish and amaze me. He'd given me a gift and the freedom to deal with another possible killer.

The former Fed wouldn't be the first serial I put in the ground. Some of those "deaths" were mine, but most were listed as "undetermined" or "accidental." Fletcher eyed me with a worried look. That wouldn't do. He had *nothing* to be worried about. Even if I found his shirt distasteful, I gripped it and rose up on my toes. The kiss I planted on his lips was not perfunctory but it was also not passionate.

It was a fleeting moment of intimacy and a thank you, for now. At least until I could reward him properly. "Now, go shower, my little pincushion, and you will take better care of yourself or we will do it for you."

"Agreed," Rick added, much to my relief. I should probably not have included him in the sweeping gesture without talking to him first. Thankfully, he was on board. "What do you need to do to secure your machines?"

Gratitude swelled in me as Rick took charge of Fletcher. The computers were locked down and put to sleep and he bullied Fletcher right out the door and up the stairs. I picked up the remnants of an energy drink can and what looked like a couple of empty bags of chips. After depositing that into the can, I considered the stairs where Rick and Fletcher had vanished.

Instead of following them, I checked the clock over the stove. We had at least two hours before dinner. I scrawled out a quick note and left it in the middle of the counter next to my coffee cup. Rick would find it.

Blowing out a breath, I glanced down at myself. Loose pajama bottoms, in soft gray, and a tank top. My feet were bare and my hair was loose. Absolutely nothing about me was a threat. Playing up that vulnerability allowed me to get close to my targets. Closer than they'd ever dreamed was possible.

I had a new target.

I went through the laundry room and opened the secret door.

Time to wake up former Agent Morgan. You and I need to have a conversation.

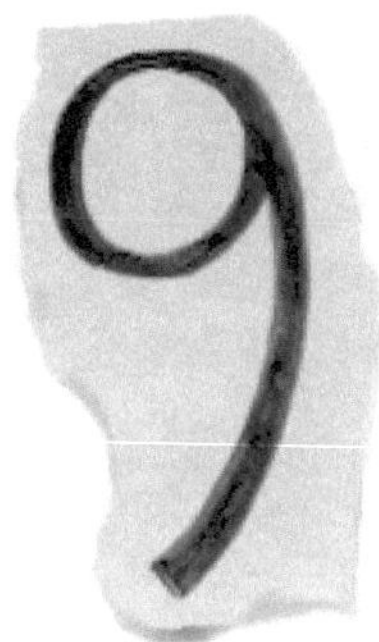

UNLIKE THE FIRST NIGHT, I turned on the lights as I reached the basement. Then I unfolded the metal chair I had leaning against the wall, placing it directly in front of the sliding door. The last couple days I'd been debating what to do with Channing Morgan, not quite willing to kill an innocent man, which left the question, what were we supposed to do with him?

But now that we knew he wasn't an active Fed, it was like the murky waters I'd been treading through suddenly became crystalline clear. That small piece of knowledge made it easy for me to see the path forward. Oh, there were still uncertainties that were based on so many questions.

Why had he been suspended?

What led to his termination?

Why was he at Bailey's warehouse?

How had he known who I was?

The only way to find that out would be to go straight to the source, assuming he would divulge the answers easily. Up until this point, I hadn't wanted to subject him to the same torture I'd used on targets such as Doctor Salinas.

Now that we knew he wasn't necessarily the upstanding citizen we were led to believe...our treatment of him moving forward depended on this conversation.

I slid the door open and flipped the dial to turn the florescent lights up in his cell. Then I took a seat and crossed my feet at the ankles, resting my clasped hands in my lap. The pose was all unassuming softness.

The case of water Rick had brought down was half empty by the wall and our guest was sprawled on the cot with his arm thrown over his face. At least he wasn't going to die of dehydration.

At the sound of the door, he twisted his head to peek at who he thought was most likely Rick. Outside of that first night when I watched him through the shadows, Rick had been his only visitor, taking care of him the way only Rick enjoyed. Well, his instincts were probably not as strong with Channing, but he took it upon himself to feed him without prompting.

He must have also persuaded the man to pass his untouched plates back through the cell door because there were none stacked up against the walls, except for one from the last meal. The smell of days old food would have been too strong to miss. A ghost of a smile touched my lips. It would have driven Rick crazy to leave dirty dishes with the food in there, cell and prisoner or not.

It seemed to take a solid ten seconds before our guest realized who had come to visit him. Most likely his mind was sluggish from lack of food, and there was a chance he had been sleeping. But the moment it dawned on him, he jerked up to a sitting position, gripping the metal frame of the cot on either side of his legs.

After starving himself for two days, he still looked just as alert and fierce as he had in the warehouse, only a little tired. And unkempt. His sandy blond hair was disheveled, the longer top pieces sticking out at different angles. The darker scruff on his face was on its way to a full beard. The fluorescent lights washed out some of the warm tan from his skin. Even in this state, he was classically handsome, the kind of man women and men alike would both stop and stare at on the streets.

But his pale eyes, almost a light turquoise, burned with intensity.

I had absolutely no doubt this was a dangerous man. He exuded too much confidence and not enough fear, given his current predicament. There wasn't a trace of irritation, fury, or any of the emotions my other guests had exhibited.

No, if it wasn't for the fact I knew he wasn't eating, I'd think he was content to be here. I'd asked Rick about his behavior when he'd come down, and Rick had said he was quiet. They didn't chat, which didn't surprise me, knowing Rick. Channing Morgan didn't argue, scream, plead, or rage at the bars. Which was very, very intriguing.

Neither of us spoke, not for a long time.

Channing Morgan was perfectly happy to trace every visible inch of my face with his gaze, as if he were memorizing every minute detail. I warmed under his attention, but I didn't look away. I couldn't. The snap of sexual awareness wasn't surprising in itself, but the strength of it...

It momentarily paralyzed my mind, and my mouth.

So, we continued to watch each other, as if in a battle for dominance we weren't in a rush to end.

He had the look of a man who'd found a cool spring after spending months in a roasting, wind-crazed desert. It unsettled me. Was this his game? Or did he feel it too?

At the warehouse, he had said he knew I was one half of the Judge. He'd clearly done his research. Based on his reaction, I had a gut feeling I was either dealing with a man obsessed with a case like a starving dog with a bone, or a morbid super fan.

Given his background and that he'd been terminated from the FBI, it could really go either way.

I was the first to break our staring contest, glancing at the wall clock to check the time. My skin suddenly tingled as if all of my limbs had fallen asleep. I wanted to rub feeling back into my arms, but I easily resisted showing such weakness.

Fifteen minutes I'd been in this chair. If I was going to get answers, I needed to start my interrogation. I just hadn't expected that kind of reaction.

"Channing Cash Morgan," I said when I turned back.

Never moving his gaze from mine, his mouth slowly curled up at the edges in a devastating smile. "I'm not surprised you know my name. You did take my wallet after all." Even though his voice was scratchy after lack of use, it was still a deep sensual rumble, causing goosebumps to raise along my arms.

Nodding, I crossed my legs, bouncing one foot. He might believe I was nervous. On occasion, when men felt empowered, for whatever reason, their lips were a little looser. We'd see about Mr. Morgan. "I did. Why were you there that night?"

"I told you, I was looking for you. Not that I knew you'd be there, I was really only following a lead." He hitched one shoulder up in a shrug, then grinned. "Enough about me. If I'm right, you've already investigated me thoroughly and found out where I went to school, my credit rating, my marital status, maybe even what I had for lunch the day I found you. I'm more interested in learning about you."

He had said he'd been looking for the Judge his entire career...

"You never said why you thought I was one half of the Judge."

"You're right, I didn't." He smirked, standing from the cot to walk over to the bars.

I didn't move, waiting to see what he would do. Slowly,

he lowered to crouch until he was eye level with me. His eyes were even more spectacular from this distance, reminding me of the clear Caribbean waters under the noon sun.

My chair was just out of touching range if he tried to attack me. Although, that didn't seem to be his intent at all. Up close, his gaze became even heavier.

"Care to share?"

"How about a trade of information? I'll share a piece of my truth if you share a piece of yours." He gripped the bars with large hands. They would fit a blue collar man more than an ex-Fed who most likely never did manual labor.

"You believe you have any bargaining power?"

"I must, or else you wouldn't be here."

Touché, Channing Morgan.

"Maybe I prefer to know who I let in my house." I didn't need to point out that he was a prisoner, he was well aware of the fact, even if he had received the royal treatment.

"Then all the more reason. But I'll go first, in good faith…" he paused, as if he was considering what would draw me in the most. The man most likely assumed his truth would have to be good in order to get me to play. Silly of him really, if he truly believed me to be the Judge. Then he'd know I'd have no problem getting messy.

Our initial meeting had been proof of that.

"My entire life, I've been obsessed with serial killers. One in particular, actually. I'd already told you hunting the Judge was a family tradition, but it's more than that. I wanted to know the mind of the man or woman—or partnership—who took vigilante justice into their own hands. I can admit the justice system is flawed, especially for key, affluent members of society. Color me intrigued from an early age. Your turn."

I studied him even as he studied me. Keeping my expression neutral wasn't difficult. Even as I bounced my foot. His gaze didn't leave mine. If I were to "judge" his choice at the moment, he refused to be distracted by anything. Interesting.

Moreover, even though he'd said "your turn," he didn't press me to respond. No, he waited to see *if* I would. "I've never been obsessed with serial killers."

The corner of his mouth kicked up, giving him a faintly crooked, if amused, grin. "Touché." The echo of my own thought amused me. Tipping his chin up, he rested a hand on the bars. "My turn then?"

I just raised my eyebrows.

He smiled, a real one. "All right. We'll play it your way."

The technique intrigued me. He wanted to establish rapport, not dominance. Sometimes, you just had to wait and let them tell you all the things they had no intention of telling you. Men liked an audience, they loved to show off.

The confidence and self-possession displayed by former Agent Morgan hadn't even taken a dent with my exploitation of a loophole in his game.

"Second truth," he said, pursing his lips. The crouch kept him at my eye level, but it couldn't be comfortable for him. Not long term. Still, he didn't shift his position. The lack of tension around his eyes and forehead, along with the focus in his pupils, seemed a decent indicator of how his concussion was going.

The bruise on his face, however, was technicolor. But it didn't even seem to affect him.

That… fascinated me.

"You already know I was an FBI agent."

Since I already knew that, it was clearly not a truth he planned on sharing, just something to lay the groundwork.

"They suspended me for reckless behavior." A shrug. "Was it reckless if it got the job done?"

"Reckless like approaching a stranger, applauding for their skill, and being less than cautious about the threat they presented?"

Another shrug. "When you've hunted for someone all

your life, you don't run away from the opportunity to meet them."

Some of my skepticism must have shown, because he rocked back a little on his heels and released a sigh.

"That said, I could possibly have chosen a better approach. Live and learn, right?" Self-deprecating didn't fit him, the fact he flashed an amused grin confirmed the move for what it was. A move. "Honestly?"

I waited.

"Damn, you are a hard lady to read," he exhaled the words, but they weren't an insult. If anything, the flare to his nostrils, the faint dilation to his pupils, even the way his breathing deepened spoke volumes for how much he *liked* how hard I was to read.

Good to know.

The aggravated exhalation of air was every bit the move his self-deprecation had been. He wasn't annoyed. If anything, he was having fun. Not exactly what I expected either. Nor was the fact I took some pleasure in his enjoyment. The distraction, however, I couldn't afford. Not with so many unanswered questions between us.

Especially not when I had two men upstairs who needed my protection, and a mission that had already encountered numerous delays.

The living first, I reminded myself. Daddy would understand. Across from me, Morgan's expression changed. It was a minute shift, but clearly something in my own expression concerned him.

With that in mind, I stood. No one could afford for me to slip. Standing put my head above his and gave me a moment to compartmentalize the concerns. I could have them, but I wasn't allowed to show them.

A breath escaped Morgan as he stood. There was the barest flicker of relief as though easing discomfort. No mistaking the faint pop of his knees though. He'd been too still in that cell. A fact that was just now registering with him.

"I had no idea you would be there," he said finally, dropping his hands to rest on his hips then seeming to think better of that before he let them hang loose. "Bailey was an informant. He—had upon occasion exchanged information for reduced charges or to have charges disappear."

Well, good to know I hadn't been remotely wrong about him.

Nor had Daddy.

Still, something didn't add up… "Then why did you think I was 'The Judge'?"

His expression relaxed and a slow smile curled his lips. "I'd tell you, but it's not my turn. It's yours."

I didn't roll my eyes.

Tempting as it was, I didn't.

"Bailey was in charge of a transportation chain." Not that this information caused me any issues to share it. It was no longer relevant. "Whatever a person needed, wherever they needed it. Drugs. Money. Liquor. People." Information.

Morgan didn't seem the type to need me to draw him a map.

"That fits." Nodding, he paced away from the bars and back. As subtle as he tried to make it, he moved slowly and deliberately. Working out cramps in his muscles and legs. Lack of food wore at him, even if he managed to stay hydrated. "Smuggling," he said as he faced me again, "we knew about that. Human trafficking? Not so much."

I shrugged. "Someone knew."

Because someone had cleaned up after him. A lot.

Had he turned Daddy over to the Feds?

That didn't fit.

Or did it?

"Probably." Morgan grunted, then rubbed the back of his neck. "Greasing the wheels was a way for some agents to pay bills. For others?" He shrugged. "I never looked that closely at my colleagues. I prefer to not be disappointed."

"Willful blindness assumes responsibility and complicity."

"Agree to disagree," he retorted. "That said, sometimes you have to be willing to get dirty to get the job done."

Since he opened the door…

"And you?" I asked. "How dirty have you gotten to get the 'job' done?"

CASH

THE WAY this woman verbally sparred with me...

I hadn't expected this at all, or how much fun it would be.

This push and pull, what I was willing to share, what she was trying to uncover, it was better than the best sex I'd had in the last few years. It could have had something to do with the fire in her personality that attracted me so much.

Just the sharp look in her eyes was enough to reel me in like a moth to an open flame. She was intelligent, with a strong moral code it was clear she lived and died by. And she was passionate.

Don't ask me how I knew that. At this point, it was more like an intuition I'd honed after years working in the field. Even so, there was this tendril of it shining through in the way we lobbed our truths back and forth, shallow as they may be.

I'd thought she would have been surprised to find out Bailey was an informant, but she'd shown no reaction at all. Had she suspected?

Probably.

I *had* found her standing over his gutted body.

"And you? How dirty have you gotten to get the 'job' done?" She taunted, maybe even teased. I couldn't hide the grin that curved one side of my mouth. This was blatant flirting, although I wasn't sure she realized that.

Then again, her eyes sparked, so maybe she did.

My stomach chose that moment to rumble loudly in the quiet. Weaving on my feet, I fought the fatigue suddenly plaguing me. I hadn't noticed it while sitting down, but standing close to her, my heart pumping hard in my chest, it was like my body was warning me that I'd gone way too long without food.

"You haven't been eating." A statement. A thread of concern floated through her words, and I'd bet my childhood home she hated that her emotions had betrayed her.

She was the ultimate puzzle, and I couldn't wait to peel back more of her layers, figure out the cogs of her personality and how they all fit together to make up this complex woman standing in front of me.

I shrugged, gripping the bars to hold myself up. "How do I know you're not trying to poison me?"

"If I wanted to kill you, there are a thousand different ways to do that without stepping foot in that cell. I also don't make a habit of feeding such nice meals to our guests." Her tone was matter of fact.

"True," I agreed. I didn't doubt her words, but she was trying to make me feel like I was different, when at the end of the day my presence here threatened her entire way of life. In her position, I'd also attempt to set my prisoner at ease. Seduce the information I wanted, then cut my losses. "But maybe your goal isn't death. Maybe there's something else you want..."

"Yes, well starving you to death isn't in my plans either. I hate to disappoint you."

"What is your plan where I'm concerned?" I wanted to ask her name, but she wouldn't give it to me. Or at least her real name. Unfortunately, I'd have to settle for our tantalizing banter for now.

One feminine brow arched. "That Mr. Morgan, depends entirely on you."

Hopefully, she wasn't expecting fear from her mild threat. That was the last thing I was feeling as her golden gaze ensnared me. I'd never seen eyes that color before, not without contacts. If she were smart, she covered them up when out in public. I couldn't imagine such memorable eyes would go unnoticed.

Any other day, I'd be sporting a massive erection from the intensity of our exchange, but the lack of food must have been messing with my body's responses. As it was, I had one hell of a twitch game going on.

"How so?" I crooned, resting the side of my face against one of the bars.

"Are you enjoying our conversation?" she queried, tilting her head as she looked up at me. This woman was sensuality incarnate. From the footage, I'd expected her to be beautiful in a refined sort of way. But up close, from the arch of her brows, the fullness of her bottom lip, to the beauty mark over the left side of her mouth, she was a wet dream. Add in her skill with a knife, and she was the perfect weapon for many of her victims.

"Two days without much human contact? You know I am," I lowered my voice as if the context of this conversation was entirely something different. The guy who brought my meals hadn't been big on the small talk. Or talk of any kind.

"Then here's my deal. I'll stay here a little longer, we can continue our chat, while you eat the food on the tray. Even cold, that will be one of the best meals you've ever had." She nodded toward the tray a few feet away from me.

I glanced at the food, then back to her. It could be poisoned. What would be her motive? She was absolutely correct; she could kill me very easily without tampering with my meal.

When I didn't immediately answer, she reached for the

sliding door that served as a barrier between the bars and the rest of the basement. All my senses said this was a basement.

She would leave, she wasn't bluffing. There wasn't a twitch of her nose, a tick, or anything to suggest she wanted to stay. But I didn't want her to go. Not when I felt this connection with her.

"Wait," I croaked, reaching a hand through the bars to stop her. I didn't touch her. She wouldn't have taken kindly to that when she didn't trust me, but the motion was enough to halt her progress.

"You'll eat?"

Damn, this dark saint played a tough game. I believed she'd actually follow through. Who knew when I'd see her again if she climbed those stairs.

Walking the few steps to the tray, I picked it up, raising it toward her in a smartass move to show her I was following her request. Then I went to my cot and balanced the food over my lap.

Tonight, the plate was filled with roasted chicken and some type of grits smothered in a red sauce. A fruit sauce from the smell of it. Cherry, I confirmed when I dipped my head to inhale.

"Good. Now, back to my original question, how dirty have you gotten to get the job done?" she asked as she sat back down and crossed her legs. The metal chair creaked with her weight as she made herself comfortable.

I smirked. Part of me was thrilled she hadn't been successfully snowed by my deflection. Her adeptness was intriguing. However, in the end, she would get me to eat, but I was getting her to stay.

I was the clear winner. Especially after talking with her, I knew she hadn't poisoned my food.

Now…How did I want to answer that delicate question?

I debated that while I eyed the food. Yes, it was cold, but it had done nothing to diminish the sweet scents of it. Despite her assurance, I allowed myself only one cautious bite. She waited with a kind of patient stillness that proved just how much her bouncing foot had been lying earlier.

As far as descriptions went, passionate fit her. It *more* than fit her. But this stillness, this perfect patience—it also fit her. Artful, beautiful, clever, and *dangerous* all played into the enigma of her. The chicken remained tender and full of flavor, it gave me something else to focus on and helped me organize my thoughts.

Lightheaded didn't make for swift comebacks or snappy retorts. Two bites into the chicken and my stomach rumbled loud enough that she twitched an eyebrow upward. The fact she didn't hurry me along gave me another reason to *like* her.

Huh.

That gave me pause. It also had me focusing on her bare feet. For all her innate elegance and beauty, she sat there comfortably in loose pants, a tank top, and bare feet—just like we were hanging out. Her toenails were also a pale pink color, utterly feminine, and they suited her.

I'd finished most of the plate before I finally formulated a response. "I've probably gotten a fair share of muck on me over the years—not from dirty dealing, but from violating the rules." That admission, honest as it was, didn't cost as much as it might have were I someone else. "Like I said earlier, the system is flawed. I believed in it, I believed in justice. But I'm also a realist, the system gets twisted. People who can afford better attorneys and to grease the wheels are more likely to get off than someone who can't."

After eating nothing for a couple of days, my stomach ached from eating almost too quickly but I was also full. Hopefully, that pleasant feeling wouldn't grow to be something more uncomfortable later. Setting the tray down, I twisted and reached for another bottle of water. I held one up as if to offer it to her.

The corners of her lips curved but she shook her head.

Well, it couldn't hurt to offer. I twisted off the cap and took a drink.

"That said, I've tried to never let my pursuit of a conviction or a case, compromise my judgment."

"Until it did." That wasn't a question and as much as I'd like to deny it, she wasn't wrong. I tipped my bottle of water toward her in a salute.

"Until it did."

At the confirmation, she nodded but didn't ask me to explain. That seemed odd, but I leaned forward, elbows on my knees and met her gaze. Fuck, what I wouldn't give to be able to read her, or at least decipher what was going on behind those eyes.

"I have broken laws." The ease of her admission didn't rob it of any weight. "At least the laws as they are currently written." A careless shrug that somehow managed to be anything but. "A necessary evil to accomplish the job."

The last thing I'd expected was a confession of any kind. "But sometimes," I said slowly, testing each word before giving it voice. "Sometimes you have to do a little bad to deliver justice and to make sure the right people pay for what they did."

Chin dipping, she appeared thoughtful. It was the first time she didn't keep her gaze on me, watchful and wary. The lack of it left me naked and almost chilled. Then she raised her eyelashes and we locked eyes again.

Better.

"Yes." One word. A very simple one and wholly evocative of so much more. The rapport on this single subject was hardly enough of a basis to build trust on.

"What are you going to do with me?" So maybe I should have waited to ask the question. As entertaining as this chess match between us was, and how provocative I found her, we needed to know where this was going.

And if I needed to persuade her otherwise.

"I haven't decided yet."

Well, not the worst answer. "Care to hear my thoughts on the subject?"

An actual smile curved that luscious mouth, adding a depth to her beauty that was absolutely breathtaking. "Maybe, not just yet."

Maybe. I could work with a maybe. "Worried about bias?"

That actually earned me a chuckle. Well. Goddamn. Go me. Because my dick twitched at that rich, sultry sound.

"That hadn't actually occurred to me," she admitted, amusement evident. "Still… why are you hunting the Judge even if you're no longer with the FBI?"

And just like that, we circled back to the beginning of this conversation and why we were *here*. Rubbing the back of my neck, I tried to ease some of the tension and the low-level headache I'd had since I first woke up in the cell.

I'd survive it, but the flashes of pain and discomfort, not to mention the tender spots on my skull and face, served as a constant reminder of my own reckless choices. Look at that, maybe I could learn from them.

Doubtful, but maybe.

"I wasn't kidding earlier when I said I've had a lifelong obsession with serial killers and that hunting the Judge was a family tradition." Pops would probably shit himself if he was right here, getting to meet one half of the pair. If he could wrap his head around the fact this beautiful creature was in fact one half of the serial killer he'd hunted for decades.

That was a big ask.

"The FBI wasn't taking that away from me." I shrugged. "Badge or no badge, tracking you down is something I was born to do."

It was the first time I'd ever admitted it aloud. The hunt for the Judge ended Pops' marriage to Mom. It had long since left a fractured chasm in my relationship with her. I loved her, but she didn't understand me. Didn't understand us.

"And you have the resources to conduct such a hunt even without the FBI?" Skeptical? Or impressed? Hard to tell.

"I have connections. I'd tell you more but…"

"Professional confidentiality."

Exactly. Sounded better coming from her.

She nodded, then glanced at the clock on the wall.

An hour.

She'd been down here for only an hour and already she was going to leave. It seemed forever and nowhere near long enough.

Rising, she moved the chair back to its spot on the wall. I wanted to ask her to stay. That would tip my hand, give her leverage.

Like she didn't already have it. I ignored the snotty mental voice and focused on her. Even as she approached the bars, I stayed where I was on the bed.

"Slide the tray out?"

I considered it, but keeping it and refusing that ask would be akin to pettiness. After sealing the cap on the water bottle, I picked up the tray and carried it back over. I had to kneel to slide the tray through, but she was nowhere close enough for me to reach even if I had wanted to try and grab her through the bars.

The pale pink of her toenails held me riveted for a moment. I lifted my gaze as she gripped the edge of the tray with her toes and pulled it free of the door. She was closing it.

"Don't suppose I could bother you for something to read, or a television?" I rose and she hesitated with the door open just a crack. "I'd take a magazine if that was an option. Just something to do."

If they brought me more food, I'd eat it.

Then I'd start stretching. Sitting still was a good way to lose muscle mass and agility. That was a sure path to getting dead.

I had a lot to continue to exist for—like getting to know her better.

"I'll think about it."

Then the door closed with a definitive clank as the locks tumbled into place. I didn't move as the soft, hushed sound of her steps retreated from the cell and then up the stairs. This had to be in a basement. Best retrofitted basement ever.

But I was hidden away somewhere she felt secure.

That meant there really was only one way I was getting out of here alive.

My dark saint would have to let me out.

RICK

"WHAT ARE YOU DOING?" Fletcher asked as he grabbed an apple out of the fruit bowl.

I was glad to see he was eating something that was actually good for him. If left to his own devices, he'd try to survive off of caffeine, and processed fast food. Honestly, I wasn't sure how he remained so skinny. Probably because he had long periods where he forgot to eat when he was working.

"Getting stuff ready to take down to our guest." We'd all taken to calling the ex-Fed our guest over the last few days. Prisoner seemed too harsh when Vienna wasn't quite sure what to do with him.

Not that she openly showed that. But I knew her, and I could see the indecision stamped all over her actions when it came to this man.

Case in point, when I asked if I could take him some supplies to clean up with, she readily agreed. For me, it was so I didn't have to smell his stink when I went down to his cell. For her, I believed it was a consolation for keeping him down there even though he was the unknown.

"Hmm," Fletcher hummed as he moved closer, picking a

few things up to read the label before setting them back down. "I didn't realize he deserved a spa day."

"Spa day?" I looked down at the wicker basket with a variety of hygiene items such as soap, shampoo, and a toothbrush.

"Why else would you be taking him a gift basket?"

"It's not a gift basket. It's easier for me to carry everything down in this. I also like the way this looks over putting the stuff in plastic grocery bags." Not that we really saved them the way I used to. They collected DNA and we weren't in the habit of leaving anything around that could give us away.

"You're right. It does look very nice. Say, is that a smudge on the cabinet?" Fletcher pointed behind me, then grabbed the wipes from under the sink. With slow, deliberate strokes, he cleaned the face of the cabinet and paid extra attention to the handle. Before he stepped away, he glanced over his shoulder as if to make sure I was watching.

I was.

"I'm glad you're taking this seriously. Vienna likes it when the house is clean." I thought about buying that clutter free best-selling book for Fletcher to read, but maybe it wasn't necessary.

"Of course, of course." Fletcher nodded. He was acting over the top suspicious lately. I didn't like it.

Narrowing my gaze on his face, he shuffled from foot to foot. "Well, I probably need to get back to work. Outside of a few things I'm working for Drew, I actually have other clients I owe work to." He hooked his thumb over his shoulder.

"Wait. Since you're here, you can help me." I lifted the five-gallon bucket of hot water from the floor. "Can you carry this down?"

"Oh, yeah. Sure." He picked it up, but eyed the basket.

I smirked when I turned away. I could have carried both, but if he wanted to be helpful, I'd find little jobs for him to do. The sour expression on his face said he knew exactly what I was doing as I grabbed the handle for the basket and headed toward the trap door.

"So, what do you think of this guy?" Fletcher asked, his voice strained. I really needed to take him over to the gym if a bucket of water was a struggle for him. Vienna was pleased with how he reacted the other day, but I was still unconvinced he was an asset in high-intensity situations.

I shrugged. I didn't have an opinion, nor did I try to get to know him. That was for Vienna to decide.

"Yeah, I can see that this wouldn't be an optimal opportunity to see into someone's character," Fletcher continued the conversation by himself as he followed behind me.

At the bottom of the stairs, I flicked on the lights and opened the door. Channing Morgan laid back on the cot with his hands threaded over his stomach. For someone stuck in a cell, I was impressed with his lack of animosity.

Who knew, maybe this was a nice break from the responsibilities of the real world. My rehab programs always offered a similar reprieve and I had enjoyed them. Needed them even.

He watched us curiously, his gaze straying to Fletcher more than he watched me. That made sense. I was the one who visited him the most. Actually, depending on the way Fletcher knocked him out, he might not have seen him at all.

"Set the bucket down right there." I nodded to the front of the bars as I pulled out a keyring. The slot for food at the bottom wouldn't be big enough to slide the bucket and basket through.

It would be too dangerous to open the door, but the slot did slide up to create a bigger opening with the key.

Before I unlocked it, I grabbed the taser gun out of my back pocket. I handed it to Fletcher, meeting his stare so he'd understand this was important.

"If he comes close to the door, hit him with this." I placed the gun in Fletcher's hand. "And don't touch the bars."

He recoiled as if it was coated in acid. If I hadn't still been holding onto it, he would have dropped it on the floor. I grunted in frustration.

"Here."

"Nuh-uh. No. Sorry. I'd wield a crowbar or a bat happily for you. I'm not touching that thing."

"It's not a real gun." I frowned. "It's a taser. And it's a precaution in case he tries to do anything he shouldn't."

"What are you going to do?" His gaze flicked to the side where the cleaning supplies and hot water sat. "How are you getting those things in there?"

"Through the slot." I held up the key.

"Why not taser him now, then you slide the stuff through. See, easy peasy solution." He clapped me on the shoulder and turned as if to head back upstairs.

"Do you really want to hurt him when he's being amenable?" I pitched my voice low so the guest wouldn't hear us.

"Not my problem. He shouldn't have acted like a wacko and got caught in the first place."

"Fine. I'll hold the taser, but you slide the stuff through. Deal?" I doubted the man would try anything. From watching him during the times I'd come down, he didn't seem at all violent. The taser truly was a precaution.

I could also do these things on my own, but watching Fletcher squirm was almost as much fun as being nice to him. If nothing else, Fletcher offered up an array of entertaining responses. Maybe that was what Vienna liked about him.

The happy hacker sighed like the world was letting him down. "Okay. The things I do for you. You should appreciate me more."

"I'll take it under advisement."

Our guest sat up as Fletcher got the slot unlocked, then lifted it so he could push the basket through. Then he grunted as he moved the water over. He managed to shove that through with only a little sloshing.

Puffing like he'd just carried that bucket up several flights of stairs instead of down one, Fletcher glanced at me. "That it, Boss?"

Boss.

I smirked.

"Or do you have something else for me to do?"

"Yeah," I told him, amused as he narrowed his eyes a fraction. Yep, he wanted my attention. Well, he had it. "Lock the slot back down for the tray."

"Oh. Shit." Fletcher scowled then pivoted only noticing then that our guest had crossed over from the bed to stand almost directly on the other side of the bars. He let out a squawk of sound and jerked back a step. "Holy shit, asshole. Don't do that!"

For his part, our guest just raised his eyebrows. "I didn't do anything."

"You're being all creepy and shit. Now, back up before the boss tases you."

Right. I didn't say anything, just kept a dispassionate eye on our guest while Fletcher glared at him. The man raised his hands in a show of submission that I wasn't remotely buying. He was far too watchful, tracking every move Fletcher made. Just like he'd known that Fletcher hadn't locked the slot back down.

No, our guest may still be a guest in a locked room, but that didn't mean he didn't pose a threat. As long as he stayed on that side of the bars, I would make accommodations for him. But if he got out, that was a threat to Vienna.

I wouldn't allow that.

Ever.

Only after he retreated a couple of steps did Fletcher kneel again and lock the slot down.

"I know you," our guest said, his gaze still on Fletcher.

"No, you don't," Fletcher said easily as he stood and backed off from the bars. He passed me the keys. Everything about his posture, his tone, and the way he cut his gaze toward the stairs said that he was done with being down here.

Course, I didn't think he'd been down here before, either. He came willingly though.

"You're Jason Reed's son," our guest continued, taking another step up to the bars. "You were reported missing a few days ago and there was a fire at your place."

"Never heard of him and clearly," Fletcher said, his expression morphing from panic to something far smoother. "I'm not missing. So—wrong guy. I'd say it's been great chatting with you, but it hasn't. C'est la vie."

With a half-salute, he turned on his heel and headed for the stairs. I filed away the names he mentioned. Despite the change in his expression, Fletcher didn't waste time in fleeing the conversation.

"Right," our guest called, "I know what you can do, Fletcher Reed."

Fletcher stopped dead.

"I know what you did too."

From this angle, I could only make out Fletcher's profile. I'd seen a lot of expressions on that guy's cocky face, from flirtatious to furious. But this one? This one looked sick to his stomach and terrified.

He didn't respond, just took off up the stairs and the door would probably have slammed if it hadn't been weighted.

Only after we were alone did our guest look at me. He frowned as he studied me, then he glanced down at the supplies I'd brought. "This is for?"

"Cleaning up," I told him. "You're starting to smell. There's a change of clothes in the bottom of the basket too."

At least he ate the food instead of wasting it, but there was a distinctly sour odor of sweat down here now. This cell had a sink to go with the toilet. Nothing else. It was more than the other cell had.

They hadn't been designed for long-term incarceration. Or maybe they had been and comfort wasn't high on the list. I could appreciate that. Still…

"The water is hot, or it was," I continued as the man studied the supplies. "You will not find anything sharp or penetrating. All of the soaps are organic, there is a week's worth of clean underwear." We weren't savages after all. "When you've washed up and changed, empty the bucket in the sink and put everything back by the slot. I'll remove it when I bring dinner."

"Is that it?" The man seemed amused. "Not going to stand there and watch me bathe?"

"No," I answered him. "Not a sight I need to see. Oh, before I forget, there is a toothbrush. If you turn it into a shiv, I'll take it away from you after I beat you unconscious. Understand?"

Surprise—and maybe a little respect?— filled the man's eyes. "And if I just refuse… Boss?"

I nodded, then walked over to the far wall where I patted the hose that was coiled up there. "You can take a nice warm sponge bath like a reasonable person, or we can do it the hard way." I shrugged. "Your choice."

The guy chuckled. Actually fucking chuckled. "Well, at least you're direct." He crouched to look in the basket, grimacing at the move and I narrowed my eyes. Faking an injury or actually bothered by something?

He emptied out the basket, setting the items out one at a time on the floor. When he got to the clothes, he seemed almost surprised again. When he reached the bottom of the basket, he grunted.

"Problem?"

"Was really hoping she'd let me have a book. No offense, but you and Reed are the most entertainment I've had in a couple of days and it's boring as fuck in this cell."

He was stripping off his clothes.

"I'll take it under advisement." I went to close the door and the guy paused.

"You're really not staying?"

"Do you really need me to hold your hand?" Or was he that desperate for company?

Our guest said nothing, just resumed stripping off his clothes.

That was what I thought.

"One last thing," I said as the door was almost closed. "Go after Fletcher again for any reason, and I will taze you until you drool into the concrete. Clear?"

That got his attention. "Clear."

"Good."

Shutting the door, I left the lights on. He'd need them to bathe. I checked my watch. Plenty of time to set up bread to rise before I baked it for dinner. I was already doing a mental inventory of the kitchen on my way up to make sure I had what I needed. First though, I would check on Fletcher.

Then dinner.

VIENNA

THE DRIVE to the meet up spot with Uncle David was long. We'd decided on a town a couple hours away, partly because he wasn't close to our current residence, and partly because he didn't know where I was currently living. Regardless of his history with us, that was always something we'd kept to ourselves, even when we needed his expertise.

I'd never really enjoyed driving, but knowing Fletcher and Rick were at the house, especially with our guest, I wished I could have put this off for another day.

At least until we knew what to do with Morgan.

But it had been too long since I'd seen Uncle David. He was the one link to my childhood that still existed. If I wanted to reminisce about Daddy with anyone, Uncle David was really my only option. Daddy just hadn't been the kind of man to make friends. Our mission was too important, and trust was too hard to give.

That was the thing about trust once given, if it was broken, we'd be the ones to pay for it.

Daddy had been a hell of a judge of character though. If he hadn't liked someone, or kept them at arm's length, there was a good reason.

Besides, I needed to know the most recent news traveling through the Network. The Network wasn't what anyone would call a close group of friends. More like, we each had a skill set that complimented other skill sets, but when it came to relationships…

There was barely any depth to the friendliest connections.

The sun was high in the sky by the time I pulled into the diner off the highway. Uncle David preferred to meet in lowbrow locations, with minimal security and camera equipment that hadn't worked in a decade, if they even had it.

Mimi's, the truck stop, was the perfect place. The highway was a fairly busy supply route for both legitimate and illegal businesses. I considered this a "two birds with one stone kind of trip," just in case anything caught my eye.

I'd never forgotten when Daddy and I visited that truck stop when I was a teenager. The man had taken too long a look at me, said one thing wrong, and Daddy took offense. Monsters, he'd told me once, couldn't help themselves.

I parked off to the side of the parking lot, right in the cluster of cars. Only people who wanted to be noticed parked at the very edge by themselves. Being separated like that, it made people pay attention.

Turning the car off, I pocketed the keys in my sweatshirt, and turned my frayed ball cap backwards. Of all the disguises I'd worn over the years, this kind of casual was my favorite. Not the most practical in a lot of cases, but for meeting here, it worked.

When I was within feet of the entrance, Uncle David popped up next to me and opened the door. I grinned. He always dressed the part too.

Most people wouldn't believe this towering older man's chameleon-like talents let him merge with the upper echelon of society just as easily as he could with drunkards on a mission to destroy their livers.

In a lot of ways, he was responsible for teaching me how to best read a crowd and blend in. Sometimes, blending wasn't an option so removing anything that would make you exceptionally memorable was the next best thing.

"Hi there, little lady. Lunch?" He tipped his head toward me. The couple days of scruff and lack of a haircut complimented the grimy vibe of his stained and wrinkled T-shirt.

"I'd love some food." I passed through the doors and headed left, leaving the gas station for the diner.

We grabbed a booth in the corner, far away from the other tables, but not so far we stood out for wanting to get away. The waitress took our drink and food orders, then we were left alone.

Sighing, I slouched back against the hard plastic of the seat. "It's good to see you."

"It's good to see you too, Ladybug," he murmured as he rested his elbows on the table. "How have you been since…"

I couldn't hold his gaze any longer as a sharp pain speared my chest. "I've been doing okay. Staying afloat and doing what Daddy taught me to do."

"I miss him, kiddo. In a world where there is so much evil, I knew he was a good one." He tapped his fingers on the table. He was a cold man normally, and that he would share such warm words was out of character for him. I was shocked.

Unable to find my voice, I nodded.

All these months, I'd been able to hide behind my work. But sitting here with the one person who knew Daddy, it was like the grief I'd pushed to the edges of my mind wouldn't be smothered any longer.

A thick knot clogged my throat and I coughed to clear out the emotion. Daddy wouldn't be happy if he knew I was getting choked up over him. "What's been going on? Any other word on what's been happening?"

He leaned back in his seat as the waitress dropped our drinks. Once she was gone, he opened his straw and stirred up the ice. "Nothing since I spoke to you last. But everyone has been on high alert. It's not the safest time to be carrying out jobs, not when everyone is an unknown."

"Do you have any theories on what's going on?"

Shaking his head, he rearranged the salt and pepper. To an outsider, he was a nervous truck driver sitting with a young, pretty girl, something that blended in more than I'd care to think about.

"I'm concerned someone feels like they've been slighted. Two members to go down in this short of time…It's unheard of. I'm trying to make the right connections to see how their work has overlapped recently, but it's taking more time than I had hoped."

Yes, it would take time when their servers were stolen. Dion and Bailey were also notorious loners. I bet that made it very difficult to gain any answers.

"I can't say I'm sad to hear about either."

Uncle David gave me a rueful smile. "Me neither. They weren't the best of us, that's for sure. I'm more concerned for you though. The rest of them can fuck off."

We enjoyed a short laugh before he sobered. "Listen, there was another reason I wanted to catch up with you. Have you been watching the news at all?"

"No," I said, furrowing my brow. "Not particularly. Only what's required for my work, and I'm in between jobs right now."

Truckers a few tables over started yelling at each other in a friendly argument, drawing the attention of the dining room. Uncle David bent forward, taking advantage of the distraction. "There's a hotshot journalist making waves, and I don't have a good feeling about her."

"Let me guess, she's an investigative journalist?" I asked drily.

He hummed his agreement. "She's got a hard on for making a name for herself, and she thinks solving some old cases is the way to go."

"She wouldn't be the first to think so, and she definitely won't be the last." Daddy's mission spanned decades. I'd seen countless documentaries of people trying to solve the identity of the Judge. But Daddy was too good at what he did to leave any damning clues around for them to find.

"There's something different about this girl, and she's got something the others didn't have." His mouth was set into a hard line, like he didn't want to deliver the next piece of information.

The fact he called the reporter a *girl* was a distinct hint. Uncle David wasn't a misogynist, not totally, but he was old-fashioned. Opening doors for ladies, pulling out their chairs, and taking charge of carrying anything, from supplies to bodies, seemed engraved into his DNA. Every once in a while, a hint of deep southern drawl trickled into his voice.

Daddy always said people didn't change that much, no matter how hard they tried. Who Uncle David was—well, that was just him. Take it or leave it. If he wanted to carry the bodies for me when I was done, I wouldn't stop him. Some bodies were damn heavy. That said…

The argument escalated as a couple of other truckers joined in. They seemed distinctly less friendly than the first group. The waitress hesitated, clearly unwilling to come out from behind the counter while this was going on, so we had a little more time.

"What's so special about her?" I cut a look back to Uncle David as he restacked the sugar, and lined up the condiments. He didn't bother looking at the dispute. It was behind him and I'd warn him if anything came at us.

"She's got files, Ladybug."

Files?

Before I could ask more, the fight tumbled out into the lot —taking a lot of the noise with them. That worked. Crazy men.

"What kind of files?" He finally spared his attention from reorganizing the condiments to look at me. His hazel eyes were a little bloodshot. Though hazel was generous, they were paling each year it seemed. The shadows beneath his eyes fit with the two days of scruff.

"Files that civilians shouldn't have," he said finally, as if that actually pained him to admit. "I caught part of her series a couple of days ago. She's talking about the Weston cases from thirty years ago."

Weston cases. I only knew a little about those. They were well before my time. Like six or seven years before my time. Daddy kept most of the details in his head. Writing shit down was stupid. Something I appreciated. So, what I knew about those days were only from his stories and those only had to do with the list of targets.

The Boys of Weston Prep. Eight "fine young men" who made a couple of "bad choices" while drinking. In a time before DNA evidence had been routine and where victim-blaming involved everything from a girl's sexual history, to her choice in clothing, to why was she even somewhere she could have run into these men. After all the press, really, should they have to suffer for the rest of their lives for a few bad choices?

Daddy had vibrated with a kind of barely suppressed rage any time that story had come up. It had taken him three years to track down and deal with each "fine young man." He'd visited the horror on them, one at a time, they'd have died screaming. It would have taken a long time too. But he hadn't stopped there.

The judge. The prosecutor. The investigators. Every single person involved in the cover up of the crime and the persecution that drove a girl to suicide. After the boys had been sentenced to time served and for a far lesser crime of assault in the third degree—a Class A misdemeanor that carried a maximum penalty of a year in jail, she'd fled the courtroom.

Those assholes barely spent twenty-four hours before they were released on bail with ankle monitors. The judge had actually apologized to them at the sentencing. I hadn't even been alive when this went down and it pissed me off. Daddy even dealt with the school officials and the fathers of two of the boys. He'd told me once that he'd been a little dramatic back then. But something about that girl's death haunted him.

"You know it?" Uncle David confirmed as the noise level increased. The fight was apparently over. The waitress swung by with our meals and glanced at our drinks. When we both put our hands over the open mouths of the cups, she just nodded and hurried off. She had plenty to keep her busy.

"I do. What could she possibly have in files that old?" And where would she have gotten them?

"That's a damn good question, Ladybug. She's a threat though. One we should probably deal with."

She was a reporter. That wasn't a crime. "The cases are old. Whatever she might have would be what law enforcement had." And they had nothing.

"They have evidence," he reminded me. "And far better techniques now than they did then."

I picked up a french fry off the plate and contemplated it. She wasn't doing harm to anyone, if anything, most documentarians and journalists who dug deep in these cases reveled in the dirt they could spill out on the actual criminals. We liked it when that happened.

It had even led to an arrest or two that I could recall.

"It's a thread no one needs to pull. We don't know what else she might have." The last sentence seemed tacked on, like he reconsidered what he was saying. However, he was right.

If she had access to those files, then there was a chance she had more. Also, investigations didn't happen in a vacuum. I highly doubted someone just mailed her a package and said, "here is everything you need to know."

"What if she has access to journals? Or investigation books? A lot of agents keep their information compartmentalized and they can only put actionable intel into their files. Not their speculation. Or guesswork." He hadn't touched his food, other than to unwrap the silverware and cut the burger into precise halves.

Still, if anyone had something like that on Daddy, I didn't think law enforcement would have sat on it. Morgan's confession about being obsessed with serial killers flickered through my mind. Then again...

"Maybe this is asking a lot of you right now," he said finally. "I'll take care of her."

"It's fine." I shook my head. "I can deal with it. You have enough to take care of."

His smile seemed a little less warm. "I do, but I don't want to burden you."

"No burden." I forced lightness into my tone and smiled at him. "What's her name? I'll need to do some research."

"Sandra Jane."

I nodded. "I'll let you know what I find."

"Are you sure?" He put his hand on mine, a brief touch. "I mean it, Ladybug, I can handle it."

"I'm sure," I told him, summoning a smile I didn't feel. There was every chance I'd have to end Sandra Jane, but I'd do it for the right reasons and not for expediency. "I'll take care of it."

"You do your father proud." He went back to eating his burger.

Yeah, well... I wasn't so sure about that. Not to say we never took care of a problem when it could ruin everything we'd worked hard to achieve. If we were taken out of commission, monsters who would otherwise run free would continue to hurt those weaker than them.

Until the system took care of such people without overlooking their crimes in deference to their fame and wealth, we were needed. *I* was needed.

But Daddy always warned about killing innocents. It muddied the mission and what started as good intentions could easily become monstrous in its actions. Which was why we never took that particular act lightly.

I wanted to laugh at myself. That was exactly why I'd found myself in such a predicament with Mr. Morgan. Although after our conversation, I was perhaps even more confused with what to do with him.

He wasn't anything like I'd expected. Although his comment about being obsessed with serial killers had to have been said to shock me, I didn't get the impression he was the rabid fan his words might otherwise suggest.

There was something steady about him. Maybe it was his conviction when he spoke about the broken system, although that could have been another attempt to bond with me. As an ex-agent, finding common ground would have been part of his training. With his knowledge of the Judge, it wasn't a stretch for him to figure out why we targeted the people we did.

"Thanks," I finished off the last of my food and pushed my plate back. I reached for cash in my pocket but Uncle David waved me away.

"I'll take care of this. You'll let me know as soon as you've taken care of the problem?"

Nodding, I said, "I'll be in touch." I left my answer vague. How I handled Sandra Jane all depended entirely on what I was able to glean about the evidence in her possession and who she was as a person.

We parted ways, me heading out to my car as he putzed around in the gas station. I'd barely had time to strap on my seatbelt when my phone rang.

The phone connected to the Network.

"Hello," I answered as I started up the car. Lingering was also something I never allowed myself to do, no matter how distracted I was.

"Hi Dollbaby. It's Mart." Her strong southern drawl flowed

through the speakers. Speaking to Mart was always pleasant. She was the only person I'd ever met who had a voice as smooth as warm honey, reminding me of a true southern belle. For a minute, I had thought something might come of her attraction to Daddy, but he was too focused on his work to entertain anyone. At least as far as I saw. That hadn't meant he didn't find his time to have fun when I was out on a job of my own.

I grinned. Mart was a small package of sugar and spice. Out of all the connections I'd made in the Network, her work was the most closely aligned with mine.

She'd been severely beaten and abused by a wealthy husband. Using a friend she'd met at some point in her career as a trophy wife, she'd fleeced him for all he was worth and arranged for him to find an unfortunate demise.

Which was how I'd met her a decade earlier.

Once she was free, she had enjoyed getting her revenge so much, she started working cons on other wealthy men. Although she didn't care if they were good men or not. To her, men in that social circle were all disgusting pigs who deserved what they got.

"Mart," I returned. "It's been a while. Is there another job you need assistance with?"

She'd call us for help from time to time, but she'd learned extremely early we had a moral code we didn't deviate from. Ever.

So, if she was calling with a potential request for help, she must believe the person deserved it.

"Yes. I'm in need of transportation. Don't worry, honey. He meets all your criteria in more than one way. He also has a basement full of smuggled art I'd really like to divest him of."

"And what's to be done with the goods?" I glanced at the bars on the burner. Now that I was on the highway, I had about ten minutes before I lost service. But we should be done with our conversation well before then.

"You know me. I'm a sucker for culture. There are a

couple pieces I'd like to keep for myself, but the majority will be donated to the right museums and charities. The rest will be sold on the black market. I haven't decided what to do with the funds yet."

Which meant, she'd most likely use it to fund her own organization that helped battered women find homes and jobs so they could escape their husbands. She didn't know we knew that little fact about her business, but we made it a point to know as much as possible about our connections.

As far as the Network went, she was probably the one with the purest intentions, even if her view of the world was a little skewed. A shame Daddy never gave her a chance.

"You know the drill. Send everything over and after I've had time to review it, I'll let you know if this is a job I'll take."

"Sure. You'll have it within the hour." The line met dead air.

Fletcher was already working a number of things for me, and Rick was monitoring the list. Those took precedence over Mart's job, but I also needed to make sure our funds stayed over a certain level. Investments didn't always provide the security we needed to maintain our properties and resources. Untraceable funds I didn't have to scrub to pay taxes were also nice.

By the time I reached the house, I had several thoughts fighting for dominance in my brain. First and foremost, we needed to look for the next link in the chain. Sandra Jane was also a priority. I'd rather not have Uncle David go after an innocent woman. His methods weren't always kosher. Then finally, Mart's request. She paid well, and if the job ran smoothly, we could be set for another three to six months.

Despite all that, as soon as I pulled into the garage, Mr. Morgan also popped into my head. I never did take him a book…

FLETCHER

SANDRA JANE WAS A BORING TARGET. Deep diving her online profile was a fucking snore. It also seemed like a waste of my skills. Nothing about her social media accounts was blocked or private. They were also carefully curated to demonstrate a very active life. Rick could pull everything interesting about her all by himself. Except, Drew asked me to find out everything I could about her.

Everything.

So, time to look where no one else would look. After all, no one had a good day every single day. Leaning back in the chair, I had every one of her profiles open and spread out over the three large screens. The more work I did here, the more I settled my equipment in. When a fifty-inch monitor arrived the day before, I hadn't even questioned it.

Rick carried it in here, then waited patiently to lift and shift as I set it up. There was also a new side table added. A place for my drinks and food *away* from my machines. So, I could take a meal break and not leave the equipment unattended. A fact Rick made abundantly clear when he said either I ate and then went and took a shower, or he'd drag me bodily out of here and lock the doors.

Right, so I ate when he brought the food and when the alarm went off that he set, I went and took a shower. Well, usually after a couple three snoozes. Drew had been absent a lot the last four days.

Four days since the former Fed showed up at the dockside warehouse. Four days? No, five. Five days. In that time, Drew had made three trips without either of us. The first time, she'd only been gone for a few hours. Rick had cleaned *everything*. The second time, she was gone for more than a day and not only had Rick cleaned, he'd dragged me to the gym.

I swore my muscle soreness had muscle soreness. The man was a machine. But he was also tense and on edge the whole time she was gone. The two days in between when she didn't leave had been almost blissful.

The house smelled like a cross between a gourmet restaurant and the finest bakery. He was positively indulgent—except about the gym, he made me go running with him every day. I kind of hated that about him. If I was in Drew's bed, I would not be getting up early to run.

Drew's bed. I hadn't even finagled my invitation to watch yet. So, I had to keep buttering Rick up. It seemed to be working. We'd transitioned from grunts and glares to monosyllabic answers and pointed looks.

At this rate, we'd be besties in no time. Best friends shared, right? Rubbing my gritty eyes, I ignored the crick in my neck. The sandpits were on fire and the muscle ache stretched from my shoulders all the way to my ass.

Too long in this chair. Maybe I needed a break. I'd go run, not that I was a fitness nut or anything, but running helped clear my head. I didn't want to give Rick any ideas. He'd decide we needed to work out more than once a day and I already thought that was an aggressive schedule.

Something had to give though, the low-level headache behind my eyes nagged at me and split my focus. Pushing the chair back, I stood and stretched. Two of the vertebrae in my back gave a crack and it loosened some of the tension.

No one was this squeaky clean and open. No one. Even

the nicest people tended to be somewhat guarded about their public profiles. Arms folded, I studied the screens, reading each one as though by standing I could change my perspective. Weirdly though, it worked. Her profiles on each platform offered a similar window into her life.

She had to use a coordinating tool to update and project the image of calm, cool, sophisticated, and tenacious reporter. Investigative reporter. Only, she *wasn't* exactly an investigative reporter yet.

Midday news correspondent, out of the Carolinas. Born in Charleston to Renee and Mike Jane. The youngest of four children. Three older brothers. Father was an attorney, he died fifteen years earlier. Cause of death—I dropped back into the chair and I moved to the screen and tabbed over to a new terminal window to run a background on him.

Died in a car accident. News indicated he'd fallen asleep behind the wheel of the car on a late-night drive home from the office. Car went off the road, he died in the vehicle—oh that sucked. He was likely alive down there for a couple of days before he died.

Sandra Jane was in junior high when that happened.

I tabbed back over to her profiles, then went on a hunt for as many of her news segments as I could find. Most of them weren't going to be anything, but we had to start somewhere. My coffee mug was empty. Did I dare brave the kitchen and possible scolding by Rick?

Pushing the chair back, I scouted the hall then turned to push the door closed slightly and opened the cabinet behind it. The cooler was tucked away neatly and I pulled it out. The energy drinks were nice and cold. I popped one open, carefully. It hadn't escaped me that all the energy drinks in the house had vanished and the only coffee I could find to brew was decaf. If I wanted leaded, I had to go to Rick.

Filling my mug with the drink, I grinned then downed the remnants so I could slot the empty can back into the cooler, then I tucked the cooler away. Contraband was good for the soul. The drinks were better for my brain.

Rolling back over to the screen, I stared at the list of video clips. Kill me. I hit play on the first one. I was fifteen in, wading past dog show reports, local sports hero interviews, and restaurant owners participating in a culinary fair, before the breaking news video opened on Sandra Jane standing outside what looked like a school building.

Active shooter flashed on the screen and a rush of white noise drowned out the words. Kids hurried out of the building. People yelling. Somewhere, the crack of gunfire. Thump. Thump. Thump.

Screams.

Running feet.

Lockdown.

Shelter-in-place.

Mousy Mary was trying to give Johnny Blowhard a handy in the back row during this ridiculous show and Mrs. Berkshire didn't even care. The lights weren't even dimmed. Johnny was the son of the school's most esteemed donor. She probably feared for her job if she called a halt to his fun. He was bastard enough that he'd get her in trouble.

The Reeds were only second best because Johnny's daddy just paid for the new sports complex in the name of the founder no one cared about or even remembered.

I rolled my eyes.

This place was a joke. Spitting out the most influential members of society because our mommies and daddies shelled out the big bucks. Please. I almost made the hand motion of a handy before I caught myself. I was at the front where everyone would see me.

And out of context, I'd look like a pervert. Not that I cared, but I tried not to make things unnecessarily hard on myself.

Distant rat-a-tat-tat sounds echoed through the room and everyone stiffened. It was a surreal moment where we all heard it, but no one wanted to acknowledge what we thought it was. It could have been part of the show. We were watching Downton Abbey as part of some shitty historical lesson.

Except the scene playing was of the servants bickering over preparing dinner. Not anything that sounded remotely like what we just heard.

I tipped my head, straining to hear it again, to confirm this wasn't what I fucking thought it was...

Then reality snapped tight around us as the sound picked up again, but closer this time. My heart did a great job of trying to escape my chest as screams of students came from all directions and feet pounded down the hallway.

This was absolute pandemonium like I'd never heard.

The door flew open and several kids pushed in, crying or eyes wide in shock.

Mrs. Berkshire was the first of us to react, jumping up and pulling the cord out of the wall to shut the movie off. With quick, deliberate steps, she closed the classroom door and locked it with a trembling hand. Phones were whipped out as kids called their parents, screaming and crying.

"No!" Amanda screamed. She was the school's sweetheart. If people could win awards for caring, she'd have gotten every one, because in this cesspit of entitled assholes, I was pretty sure she was the only one who had the capacity to see anything past the end of her own nose. "You can't lock the door. Other students might need help." She rounded the desk to usher the kids who'd burst into the back of the classroom.

"Shut up, Manda." Johnny zipped up, turning his reddened face toward the teacher. "Keep it locked."

As if she were a puppet, Mrs. Berkshire nodded and walked back to her desk on stiff legs.

The alert sounded. Every single phone in the room buzzed with a message. The principal came over the speaker.

"Students. Please lock your doors and shelter in place. There is an active shooter on the premises. This is not a drill. Shelter in place until we've secured the school. Do not, under any circumstances,

engage the shooter. I repeat, do not engage." The intercom crackled before the white noise from the speakers clicked off.

Hell, I was surprised I understood what the principal said through my pulse pounding erratically in my ears.

"You heard Principal Martin. Get to the back of the classroom. Stay quiet." Mrs. Berkshire's voice was shrill as she waved her hands around, motioning for us to move.

What the fuck was that supposed to do? This wasn't some B-rated monster movie where the shooters would move on if we weren't at our desks, too stupid to see us all huddled at the back. Even making no noise, there were students in nearly every classroom. If anyone came through that door, they'd see every single one of us in less than two seconds. We'd be sitting ducks.

I was unable to speak.

Unable to move.

I watched everyone around me as they followed Mrs. Berkshire's instructions while she squeezed herself under her desk that had full side coverage. What a waste of space.

Only Amanda had any brain cells, as she convinced a few kids to shift the couch forward a few feet and hide behind that.

What did I do?

Nothing. Fucking nothing, while screams continued and the shots grew louder. More students tried to push their way in, banging on the door when they realized it was locked.

"Let me in! Please, Mrs. Berkshire!" A girl called, terror stripping her voice to a reed thin scream. The door shook with each hit, the top of her face visible through the window.

Shit, I couldn't watch her out there. I'd never seen actual fear like that on anyone's face and I couldn't take it. It twisted my heart until the acute pain started to radiate through the rest of my body. I couldn't even hold her gaze because it felt wrong to see her that way. That raw.

Another student appeared next to the girl, this one a young guy. Both of them were probably freshmen. He was crying. Shouting. Jumping as he glanced over his shoulder.

The shooting got closer.

Like I was released from whatever stasis had glued me to my seat, I hopped up to let them in. We couldn't let them die. Not when we could do something about it.

"Don't you fucking dare open that door, Fletcher Reed!" Johnny shouted from under his desk. The shithead was bawling.

He didn't deserve a response. Coward.

If I thought Mrs. Berkshire would stop me, or help me, I would have been disappointed. She whimpered as my feet plodded across the floor.

Why wasn't I running? I tried, but I couldn't. The slow walk was the best my body could do, but I was going. That was the important part. I was making my way to the door.

Both kids started screaming, slamming their palms against the glass.

Finally, I started to run.

But I halted when the gunfire was close. Too close. The girl grunted and fell to the ground.

Another shot.

Blood spattered.

The boy disappeared from sight.

Andrew Maynurd's face appeared on the other side of the glass, solemn as he looked at his feet. Something scraped across the floor. I started to gag. He was moving them. The lunatic was moving them so he could come in.

My useless ass continued to stand in the middle of the room watching him through the glass.

When he glanced up, he smiled.

I shivered.

Andrew turned his head, stuck his fingers in his mouth and whistled. I don't know how I heard it over the deafening silence and the hammer of my heart, but I did.

The door rattled as he tried the handle. When it didn't open, he shrugged and shot the lock.

Around me, underneath the fear, was an overwhelming amount of soft sniffles and whispered prayers. Muffled, scared voices asked what was happening from the phones. No one answered.

Andrew stepped in, a handgun in one hand, and in the other...a machine gun?

Where the hell had he gotten his hands on something like that? His mom was part of the Peace Corps...

Ben Shrowder stepped in after him, he only had two handguns. When he looked at me, his expression was blank, like there was no one home.

And I still fucking stood there.

They moved through the room and I jumped with each shot. There were so many.

But there were no screams. No pleas. Like my classmates knew it was pointless. The only sounds they made now were from the pain of the initial wound. If they made any at all.

I'd squeezed my eyes shut at some point, I didn't even know when. Probably when I saw the first splatter of blood. With every death, the silence in the room got louder and the cloying scent of iron grew stronger. Their slow footsteps echoed eerily through the room as they approached Mrs. Berkshire.

Her guttural sobs broke free, as if she couldn't hold them any longer, but they stopped as abruptly as they had started when the gun went off.

Ben and Andrew got closer. I couldn't do it anymore. If I was going to die, I needed to see their faces. Right? I should see their faces?

My mind warred with itself as they stopped in front of me. One clapped me on the back, and the other nodded. Heart hammering, I finally opened my eyes as they walked away.

Then they left the classroom. They didn't go very far. Their elbows were in my line of sight as they raised the guns. Two more shots fired, and they collapsed. The soft thumps were so muted, considering all the chaos that had just rained down through the halls of Cresthill Academy. A weird whisper against the symphony of silence they'd left in their wake.

This entire day. All these deaths.
They were my fault.
And I still just stood there.

A knock at the door jerked me around like someone yanked every string I possessed. I half-expected to see the blood-spattered window and pale, blond wooden door. Instead, Rick stood in the opening of the door wearing a frown.

His lips moved but it took a moment for the sound to rush in. "It's time for lunch," he said. "We need to feed our guest, then Vienna wants to brief us on some things."

Lunch.

I might vomit.

Our guest.

Fuck him.

Drew?

Yeah, I could go for seeing Drew. Maybe I wouldn't vomit.

Rick's food was good. "Yeah," I said, finally. "Coming."

I did *not* look back at the screen. Nope. I kept my eyes on the whackjob. I'd never been so fucking happy to see him. Downing the rest of the energy drink in one long swallow, I tried to shake off the ghosts. But I could still feel him patting my fucking back.

Striding forward, I threw an arm around Rick's shoulder. "Big guy, have I ever told you how fucking beautiful you are?" Then I smacked a kiss on his cheek for good measure. Without preamble, he shook me off and cut me a look. But he didn't punch me. So—win?

Yeah. Win.

Not waiting, I strode ahead of him and rubbed a hand over my face. If only I could put more distance between me and my fucking past.

VIENNA

IN THE FOUR days since I met with Uncle David, I'd accomplished very little. Well, that wasn't entirely true. I'd gone through Daddy's boxes from the storage place. The files didn't fill in a lot of blanks, only illustrated that Daddy had his own suspicions. Suspicions he hadn't shared with me. The war between being hurt by his exclusion, and concerned by why he saw the need, played out all the way through lunch.

Though I'd planned to brief them on the job I had to do for Mart, I let them drive the discussion. Rick kept shooting me concerned looks and Fletcher seemed torn between antagonizing Rick and getting lost in his own head. If anything, the lunch clearly illustrated some of the fractures in the current status quo.

"Vienna," Rick prompted me gently, eyeing my plate. I'd barely touched my food. Honestly, I wasn't hungry. Probably not fair to the meals he prepared. No probably about it.

"I'm afraid I'm not very hungry," I said by way of apology. "I think I need a workout." Or a long run. But I didn't want to roam too far right now. I was waiting on too many pieces. I needed confirmation on my target. I needed to figure out what to do with our guest. I needed Fletcher to finish running down Sandra Jane.

The list.

I needed to work on the list.

The irritation rifling under my skin was like an allergic reaction that I couldn't seem to shake. A hard workout could help. Rick cut his gaze over to Fletcher and I followed his concerned look. He wasn't following our conversation either. It was enough to worry Rick and that decided me.

"Pincushion, go get changed, loose clothes."

"What?" He blinked, raking his hair back from his face as he glanced from me to Rick and then back. "Why do I need to change?" He actually tugged at his shirt to sniff it. Since the day I'd burned his clothes, we'd kept him from letting himself spiral that far again. "I showered this morning—wait—" He frowned. "I showered yesterday afternoon. Yeah, not even twenty-four hours ago."

"It's not about showering," I told him. At least, not yet. Rising, I picked up my plate and stopped Rick with a look when he would have taken it. "I'm going to cover these up so we can eat them after. No way I'm letting this beautiful meal go to waste." His quick smile of pleasure speared through me. I needed to remember to acknowledge both of them more. The last few days had been hard on all of us.

"Do you want me to get changed as well?" Rick asked.

"Yes, please. Make sure Fletcher does?" He did love a good task, and his grin widened. "I'll meet you both in the gym."

Rick was the only one of us who'd actually eaten. I took care to store my plate and Fletcher's under sealed lids in the microwave, then I cleared away the rest of the plates and set them in the sink to soak. A part of me wanted to take back the kitchen, wash the dishes and set everything to rights. As it was, I still wiped down the counters and all the handles as well as the tables and chairs.

Old habits and all that...

I made myself stop there and diverted to the laundry

room. I was already dressed for a workout. Upstairs, Rick barked something at Fletcher but there was humor in the command that Fletcher responded to with a laugh. So, while I couldn't make out the words, the attitude told me a lot.

Pausing in the laundry room, I eyed the bag I'd hung there when I returned the day before. I'd picked up three books for our guest. Most of what I read these days I kept on an e-reader. Easier for me to transport and if I was forced to leave it behind, I could wipe it remotely and reclaim my books with a new device.

If I went down to drop off his books, I'd be tempted to stay and talk to him. Better to not do it in my current mood. For now, I headed to the gym. The boys would be there shortly, and I needed to take the edge off before we "trained." My goal wasn't to hurt either of them.

By the time the boys made it over to the gym, I'd had a solid fifteen minutes to myself, maybe a little more based on the clock. I'd needed it. The gym was equipped with every type of equipment, but my favorite pieces were various boxing stands.

The one I used the most had a few stationary pads for hitting, as well as a few that spun around the stand at different speeds depending on the strength of the hit. It was a great tool to not only increase the accuracy of your punches and kicks, but it also helped increase reflex times.

I did a combination of hits and kicks, ducking, more hits, then sliding back to avoid one of the pads skimming my stomach. Sweat dampened my skin; my thin workout tank clung to my torso. For that fifteen minutes, I gave it every-thing I had. Using all my strength was invigorating, providing a satisfying outlet I'd only ever been able to obtain from fighting or quick and dirty one night stands.

In the past, I'd have taken a good workout any day, unless my craving for human connection became too much. But now, after meeting Rick, my opinion was changing faster than I'd thought possible. Especially because there wasn't anything dirty or quick about being with Rick.

Delivering two punches against the shoulder height pads, I ducked as they flew over my head from the momentum, then hugged the stand and kneed the groin pad. My breath hissed through my teeth as I controlled my breathing.

The door opened, and I shot a quick glance to the entrance just to make sure it was Rick and Fletcher, before going back to finish my solitary workout.

Daddy had always stressed how important it was to remain strong and maintain an impressive level of stamina. We never knew what kind of situation we'd find ourselves in, even when we'd put the most thought out plans in place. An extra minute or five of energy could make the difference between getting out alive and unseen, or even worse, getting caught.

Holding onto your mental faculties was just as important. At some point, I'd needed to start working with Fletcher and Rick on strengthening their mind while torturing their bodies. But only when they were ready. Rick would probably swear he could handle anything, even if he couldn't, because he'd want to do it for me. That meant limits were on me. Fletcher? I had no idea about Fletcher. I didn't think he'd handle torture well at all, then again, he hadn't told Dion shit.

Fletcher whistled long and low as I stepped back from the equipment. I grabbed my water bottle and towel from the floor to rehydrate and clean myself up, while Rick started guiding Fletcher through the warmup stretches.

"You have to take care of your body before you workout, otherwise you'll get injured." Rick shoved Fletcher's shoulder to get him to focus when he craned his neck to ogle me.

"I'm sorry, you expect me to touch my toes while Drew is over there looking like a wet dream?" Fletcher scoffed as if he were actually confused.

I laughed and set my stuff back on the edge of the mat, although I didn't try to rein him in. Rick would do that for me.

"Getting distracted will get you killed. If you were getting attacked in a strip club, you'd be useless, not only to yourself but to Vienna." Rick didn't hide the mixture of accusation and disgust from his voice. From the look in his eyes, I'd almost believe he was disappointed in Fletcher's reaction.

After Rick had lost his desire to constantly want to kill Fletcher, he'd come to terms with him being a part of our lives, at least for now. For him to be disappointed in Fletcher, that meant he had expectations. Rick was a fascinating man, and the only way he would have expectations of our little Pincushion was if he was starting to like him.

I kept my smile to myself as I walked over to the stereo to turn the music down enough I could instruct them. Rick had been alone so much of his life, I was glad to see him making a connection with Fletcher. And Fletcher...from what I had gathered, he had plenty of socialization and acquaintances, but he needed someone to actually care. With Rick's particular love language, they might be good for each other.

"Those strippers aren't a sweaty Drew," Fletcher argued.

"Doesn't matter, same concept applies," Rick growled and pushed his shoulders until he complied. While they finished their warmup, I did my own short routine just to keep my muscles warmed up. Already, I felt more like myself now that I'd taken the edge off.

"What are we working on today?" Fletcher asked as he climbed back onto his feet. Standing in gym shorts and a T-shirt, he seemed out of place. Where Rick had strength stamped all over his body from his bulky build to the visible definition every time he moved, Fletcher was slimmer, leaner. That could work to his advantage though. No one would expect him to be able to fight and he could capitalize on their assumptions.

"Quickly disabling an opponent," I said as I moved toward the center of the mats where we sparred. "You did a great job knocking out Mr. Morgan when his back was turned, but you won't always have surprise in your favor. There are some tricks to help you in any situation, although admittedly, every scenario could be vastly different."

Fletcher scrubbed his face. "I think I need more caffeine to comprehend the lesson you're trying to teach. It's too early to work my brain this hard."

I glanced at the clock. It was just after one in the afternoon. Rick shot me a look as if he had the same thought, but neither of us addressed that comment. Fletcher was a night owl no matter what time he woke up for the day.

"Rick, come here." I motioned for him to stand in front of me. As Rick took his place, Fletcher moved off to the side but chose to remain standing. That didn't surprise me. Unless he was working on his systems, he had extra energy to burn. That could be attributed to caffeine intake. That had dimmed slightly since Rick had made it his mission to control the coffee in the house. "Rush me," I ordered.

He didn't need to be told twice. I loved that about him. There was never a need to question what I was asking him to do, he simply trusted me.

Twisting his face into a fierce expression, he dipped his shoulders as if he were going to tackle me. I dropped to the mat, using my weight and momentum to flip him over my head by gripping his shoulders and using my feet on his stomach. He grunted as he landed on his back.

I didn't give him time to recover as I shot to my knees and restrained him with an arm bar. Rick was strong, much stronger than me, and I wouldn't want to give him the chance to throw me off. Instead, I used a move that caused just enough pain that he wouldn't risk it unless he wanted a broken arm.

The entire exercise only lasted seconds, but I'd effectively pinned him. When he tapped my leg with his free hand, I hopped to my feet and extended my hand to help him up.

"Your body weight is your leverage and an invaluable tool, especially when up against someone significantly larger than you." I looked over to Fletcher to make sure he was paying attention.

He was, but not with the right frame of mind. Raw desire clouded his gaze. And his shorts were tented.

A sigh escaped me. Fletcher flashed me a grin that was a little too brittle to be unabashed and a little too bright to be as carefree as he tried to project. Head cocked with a hand on my hip, I studied him.

Like I would a mark.

Twice I tried to catch his gaze, twice he let his slide away —at least until he could pull up that flirty smile that he struggled to hold onto. This wasn't him being cocky, arrogant, or overbearing. Rick's stillness next to me suggested a similar concern. Well, the stillness just said he wanted to wait and see what I was going to do. It was the absolute lack of aggression.

Pivoting, I faced Rick and gave Fletcher my back. Pitching my voice low and trusting Rick to listen, I said, "I need to bait him into fighting me and getting out of his head."

Rick nodded. Yeah, the worry was real when he didn't offer to do it for me.

"You may not like what I do to get him there."

Gaze sliding back to me, Rick raised a hand, pausing only until I nodded before he cupped my cheek. I leaned into the touch. Now that my nerves weren't quite so jagged, I could appreciate this again. Appreciate the trust in his eyes. The confidence.

"You're going to tempt him."

"Well, yes, offering him what he wants if he does what I ask—that's definitely a play." And was I curious about him? Yes. The kiss from the storage locker had replayed at the oddest times lately, but I remained steadfast on the fact that Rick had to agree to this.

"Don't let him hurt you," Rick said, a grin curving his lips because he'd said the same thing about himself. The private joke had depth and unmistakable meaning.

"Yo, guys? Not that it isn't sexy as fuck, watching Drew lean into the Jolly Cooking Giant, but what does a guy have to do to get in on some of the action?" Yes, deflect. Distract. When necessary, attack. The technique was a familiar one.

Rising up on my tiptoes, I brushed my lips to Rick's. It was a barely there kiss, a moment, but a steadying one. He nodded and stepped back even as I pivoted. I smiled slowly as I caught Fletcher's gaze sweeping up from my legs to my breasts then to my face. If he were genuinely that obsessed with my body, he'd be a lot dirtier in his attentions than his flirtier quips and behavior had been.

I enjoyed his flirtations. More, I enjoyed his quick wit and his sarcasm. That man was a delight, one who challenged me to stay on my toes but still played with a kind of sweetness to soften his more cynical side.

I'd grown very fond of *that* Fletcher.

This one was far more abrasive, with a hint of something cruel that only sharpened the edges of the barbed personality he shared. As I walked toward him, I added the faintest of sways to my hips. They drew him like a magnet.

He rubbed his palms together then scrubbed them over his face before he seemed to physically force his eyes upward. Yes, he watched *me* now, not my body. "Did you know that most men look at a woman and never see a threat?"

The sharp report of his laughter came out a little too forced and this close? Yeah, Fletcher was locked so deep in his head right now, he couldn't see a way out. I was surprised he wasn't trying to antagonize Rick. Then again, maybe he didn't want to get hurt so much as he wanted help.

"I'd never consider you anything less, Drew," Fletcher

remarked, his attempt at a smirk failing. "I mean, that'd be downright disrespectful, you know?"

And there was the unease.

"Maybe," I said as I circled him. This close, I was within arm's reach, but he only shifted his weight on his feet. He didn't try to retreat or give us distance. "It could also be a ploy." That was all the warning I would give him. He didn't pivot to follow my path as I moved around him. That put me in his blind spots. Twice.

"If you wanted me dead—well, I'd probably be dead, yeah?" The crack in his voice betrayed him. Something had really rattled my pincushion. I didn't like it.

No, I didn't like that at all.

Walking right up behind him, I paused and waited. Barely a breath separated us.

"Drew—" He pivoted sharply and jerked at how close I was. Paler beneath his tan, he froze in place. He hadn't even raised a hand to defend himself nor had he fallen in an effort to get away from me. "Fuck. I thought we were training, not traumatizing."

"Actually," I said, walking my fingers up his chest more to test how fast his heart raced than to tease him. Though the tent in his shorts had definitely added some definition to it. "We're going to play a game."

That seemed to be the very last thing he'd expected. Surprise flickered over his face as his pupils relaxed a fraction from their constricted state. His nostrils flared. Oh, there he was, emerging slowly as he sucked in a deep breath of air. "A game?"

"Hmm-hmm. You're going to do everything I ask you to do."

Fresh suspicion crept into his eyes. "How is that a game?"

"Because what I want you to do is attack me. I'm going to show you how holds work and grapples. You're leaner like me, but you have a longer reach. I'm going to show you how to protect yourself without a weapon." His pupils expanded more and his breathing deepened. "We're going to be wrestling all over this mat. You're going to have to pin me and I'm going to pin you."

He licked his lips and I got a flash of that piercing I was so curious about. Well, one of them anyway.

"Still not sure how this is a game…" But he was definitely interested. On the far side of the mat, Rick actually put a hand over his mouth to hide a smile. Not fast enough that I didn't catch it, but he was doing his best not to laugh.

"Well, the game is played by training. The score is kept in how many holds you master, how many you can break, and if you can disarm me."

"Okay." He elongated the word, searching for the trap. There was his brain. It had come out of whatever dark cave it had been lost in.

"The winner gets to do whatever they want with the loser."

"Anything?" His voice dipped and his pupils flared. Yes, I had him.

"Anything," I promised. Now I brushed my knuckles up along his neck as I pushed up on my tiptoes again. Only this time, my goal was not to kiss him, but to just barely brush my breasts to his chest. "Anything the winner wants."

He swallowed. "Fuck me."

I smiled. "If you wish…"

The weight of his hands landed on my hips.

"…but only after you win." Then I tumbled, legs twisting around him as I flipped him with me and he hit the mat landing flat on his back. I kept rolling until I was back on my feet.

Now was the real test.

Fletcher stared up at me and there was no denying the heat in his eyes and how they scorched me as he stared at me. The split-second pause seemed to last an eternity before he scrambled to his feet. Gone was the brittle expression and the jerky movements. He was still tense and hard—but for an entirely different reason.

"On the slim chance that I win, I promise to be a generous and giving lover." Grin firmly in place, he continued, "When you kick my ass—please want to use me. A lot."

FLETCHER

A TINY EROTIC smile tipped the corner of Drew's full pink lips and nearly made me lose my mind. As it was, I lost the grin. Although I could have blamed that on her tawny eyes glittering with just as much longing as with fiery determination.

Like shit… We danced around each other, and shared some epic kisses, but she'd never looked at me like *that*. What little bit of form my happy guy had lost, shot right back until my dick was bent at an odd angle against the soft mesh of the shorts.

When it first popped, I thought about covering it, but then decided against it. We were all friends here, and Drew would have told me to take a walk if it had bothered her. But she hadn't.

Suddenly, the weird disconnected haze I'd been in since that lovely little flashback earlier released its straggling hold on me, as my mind and dick were thinking on the same wavelength. It was like being shocked back into reality by plunging into frigid water.

But damn, how could I not appreciate how fucking lethal my death angel was. There were some guys who didn't have the balls to be with strong women, offended when she could kick their ass.

Me? Hell no. Clearly, from the state of my dick, that was not the case at all.

"Let's go over the holds, then we'll play." Her voice took on a husky quality, teasing me in all the best ways. I couldn't even remember why I'd been off just a few minutes ago as I tracked her while she circled me.

"Show me," I said through another flirty grin. Demonstrations meant full body contact, and I ached to have her touch me again. Just those little grazes from moments ago had my blood on fire.

"First lesson," she said seconds before she swept my feet from under me, grabbed my wrist, and locked it straight to her torso with her legs hooked up by my shoulder. She bent backward enough to strain my elbow in a way that shot pain down my arm. "The first lesson, is not to let yourself get into this position."

A garbled mess of sounds left my mouth as she hurt me just a little more. My happy man lost some of his enthusiasm, even as she understood what I was trying to ask.

"The way you avoid the arm bar is to keep your arm bent, because there is very little you can do once you get in this position that will save you. If the enemy is trying to lock you down, and they're not overly larger than you, you can also pick them up and slam them down. The goal is to dislodge their hold and quickly pull away." She released my arm and sat on her heels.

"Ouch." The ghostly whisper of pain remained in my elbow as I curled and straightened it to get the feeling back in it. Without warning, she dropped to sit behind me with her thighs on either side of my hips.

My mistake was thinking she'd explain the next hold as I glanced down at her legs cradling me. Shoot me, but I wanted to see that. Much like the other two times, Drew waited for no one, and had her arm around my neck in a tight grip while pushing my head forward. Air was a thing of the past as I rocked to try and get away while all the blood in my head revolted by throwing a nice little rave.

Hell, I felt like my head was going to pop off.

Drew relaxed her hold enough so I could suck in the smallest breath, then tightened her grip again. "This is the rear naked choke. Look in the mirror."

I did, and if I wasn't currently fighting for my life, I might have been self-conscious about the fire engine red color of my entire head. Even my ears were on fire. Then she relaxed her hold again. Longer this time.

She nuzzled the back of my head, and my cock twitched, the traitor. "This hold is dangerous, because if you don't stop it, or get out of it, you'll pass out. Or suffocate, depending on how long they held you. See how my hand is on my biceps? I'm also using my forearm to lock it into place, which allows me to use my free hand to push you further into the hold." She demonstrated, and it became harder to breathe.

Her arms dropped and I gulped air like the life currency it was. Instead of moving back, she braced her chin on my shoulder and ran her palms down my sides. My skin tingled in the wake of her movement.

"For this one, you'll want to tuck your chin to prevent my arm from sliding under your chin. If I'm over your face, you can still breathe." And my lethal ninja pushed my head forward and wrapped her arm around my chin. I could in fact still breathe. It wasn't comfortable, by any stretch, but it was better than strangulation. "You'll want to roll or turn toward me if possible. If you're able to do that, you might be able to breathe, if only for a short time. But that few seconds could keep you from passing out. Try it."

God damn it, Dave! She had me again. I tried to roll toward her, thinking I could lift her weight because she was so much smaller than me, but no. She locked her legs around my body just like she had with her arms around my neck.

"And this brings us to the body lock. What do you think you need to do, if you get stuck in this position?" She pulsed her arms and the edges of my vision darkened.

What kind of test was this? She hadn't given me the answer yet! But another few seconds and it would be lights out.

No, wait. I could do this. The hold was the same for the body as the neck. Roll, I needed to roll. I tried. I tried with all my strength, but it didn't work.

Drew loosened her arms just as I was about to kiss it. "What's your answer?"

"Roll…" I gasped, my voice a wraith of its former self.

Her appreciation poured off of her and if the circumstances were different, I might have preened. In the mirror, I could barely make out her wide smile through my still blurry vision, but I knew it was gorgeous.

I was one fucked up man. As she showed me these holds and how to get out of them, or prevent them, the feel of her toned yet soft body pressed against mine, the sweet smell of her skin, and the soft grazes she continued to rain down on me had my dick in a perpetual chubby state.

We went through the guillotine, heel hook, and the head and arm triangle. By the time she was done with her "demonstration" I was a puddle of sweat and muscle aches at her feet.

She stretched out her hand like she'd done with Rick. I glanced at it, then met her gaze. The beautiful woman was lightly flushed and slightly damp, perhaps more stunning than usual. Me on the other hand, if she wrung me out, I could fill up a small family swimming pool.

Lifting my arm took more effort than I had and I watched my hand sadly flop back to my stomach. Drew laughed, and reached down to grip my forearm, then hauled me to my feet. "Take a five-minute break. Then we play."

"What the hell?" I rasped. "You already kicked my ass. Can I just forfeit and you win?"

She tilted her head to study me, although I had no idea what she was looking for. Small baby hairs had escaped her ponytail to float in wet curls around her face, adding a cuteness to her appearance that she normally lacked. Drew was all woman, all sex appeal, all day long.

But this was… adorable.

I kept that to myself, otherwise she might kick my ass even harder. Or have Rick do it. From the *Garfield-eyeing-Odie* grin he was permanently wearing as he sat off to the side, he'd happily oblige.

"Let's do a few drills, just to see what you remember. First to three points wins." The she bent down for her water, putting her delicious round ass on display.

I wasn't even ashamed to admit I enjoyed the sight, and from the hunger on Rick's face as his gaze was glued to her backside, we were at least on the same page in this.

Sometime I'd have to tell him we apparently shared a brain cell when it came to Drew. Male bonding and all that. I huffed a laugh to myself. Nope, I wouldn't be following through with that bad idea.

The full water bottle felt like it had two sips in it after I'd drained it. I was still thirsty, but my legs had at least stopped shaking. There were two minutes left of my break. If I sat down, it might make it harder to get—

Drew attacked, grappling me to the ground and placing me in a choke hold. I attempted to get out. I really did, but I couldn't even muster a flop worthy of a dying fish. The noises coming out of my mouth from the effort weren't flattering in the least, but they seemed to make me feel like I could almost roll her. She loosened her grip just enough.

"No one will attack you on a schedule. You always have to be ready. How do you get out?"

"Roll," I wheezed.

"Good." She popped up and faced me, all business and none of that earlier heat. "I'll give you a point for that, but no more going easy on you."

Going easy? That was going easy?

By the time I climbed to my feet, she was already on the offensive again. I attempted to prevent the holds as much as I could, but in the end, Drew was the winner every time. She acquired three points in record time.

Thank God.

Somehow, during the drills I had forgotten our deal, but now that she won, she could do whatever she wanted. Hopefully to me. And I found I was catching my second wind from anticipation.

"Hydrate," she told me as she walked over to where Rick waited with water. The affection on his face in no way detracted from the possessiveness that flared in his eyes when he looked at her.

Totally understood the attraction, Big Guy. I wanted to possess her too, or let her possess me. I was pretty open on the subject. She was the magnetic field and we were the objects in her orbit. Well, he was more like the moon, locked on, I was like a satellite, high tech and maneuverable.

Kind of liked that comparison. No alpha male bullshit for me. I didn't need to thump my chest or roar.

I'd just hack their shit and fuck up their lives later from the comfort of my own home. Unscrewing the top of the thermos that Rick had apparently refilled for me, I chuckled.

Drew shifted her weight and glanced over her shoulder at me. All the blood that had been pounding to my face earlier fled southward. Yeah, Mr. Happy was back on board.

"You did good, Fletcher." The warmth in the statement robbed it of any insincerity. She wasn't just feeding me bullshit, except...

"I completely sucked," I pointed out, then raised my bottle to her. I probably needed to drink a few more of these. "I was barely an exertion for you."

That sounded way better in my head than it did coming out of my mouth.

It was Rick who chuckled this time. "You made it through the whole workout. You listened. You applied. You survived."

Huh. Big Guy definitely wouldn't shine me on.

Drew lifted her shoulders. "You'll get stronger, quicker, more practiced."

I frowned. That meant…

"We'll just adjust so that we can work out more regularly than we have been."

Yay?

Wait, it meant I got to put my hands all over her. "In the interests of clarity and expectations," and the aching pulse in my dick. "Does that mean we're betting on every day's practice?"

She blinked. It wasn't quite shock, but it was definitely a surprise. Pretty sure anyway. Getting a read on Drew was like trying to translate hieroglyphics with only a screenshot of a part of the Rosetta Stone. The side that had none of the letters on it.

"We can," she said slowly. "But let's see how you feel after today."

Oh. Did that mean I wouldn't like today?

Before I could actually verbalize the thought, she set aside her bottle of water and stripped off her shirt. Sure, it was a tank top and beneath it was a sports bra, but the ripple of muscle along her arms and her abdomen as she moved was the sexiest fucking thing I'd ever seen.

It wasn't until she shimmied her shorts down that it even registered she hadn't been wearing shoes the whole time. Athletic didn't begin to cover a description for her.

My sexy death angel was—incomparable. With her back still to me, she peeled the simple black panties down. The tautness of her physique extended to her ass.

Yeah, if I hadn't already been sporting a boner, I'd probably have passed out from how fucking hard I'd just gone.

All the moisture in my mouth fled as she gripped the sports bra and turned as she peeled it up and off.

Fuck.

Me.

Perfection.

She was—perfect.

Vocabulary failed me.

What other words would do her justice?

From the golden color of her eyes and the fall of her blonde hair to the ripped musculature that included defined abdominals, flexing thighs that definitely housed so much strength, to the most perfect breasts.

Yeah, I had to jerk my gaze back up from that bare pussy to the soft curves crowned by those tanned nipples, all peaked and hard. From the chill in the air? Maybe?

Or from us watching her.

Right. Wait. Us.

My brain liquified as I fought to hold onto my thoughts. I wasn't some punk ass fifteen-year-old about to blow my load, but fuck me it was tempting.

I tried to wet my lips, but the spit just wasn't there and then a pair of huge hands covered her breasts, hiding them from me.

Rick.

Right. The big guy was right behind her and she leaned back against him as he rubbed his hands over her chest, flicked her nipples and then sent one of his hands down to cup her pussy.

At the first glimpse of pink, I reached for my cock.

"Don't," Drew said. The husky syllable halting my hand before I could give myself any kind of relief.

"No?" Oh, that came out a whimper just as Rick pushed his fingers into her and I didn't know if they'd planned this, but she had her legs open, there was no mistaking what he was doing as he pressed kisses along her throat and she rolled her hips to ride his hand.

"No," Drew exhaled on a half-moan. "You can't touch yourself until I give you permission."

Welp. This was how I died.

What a way to go.

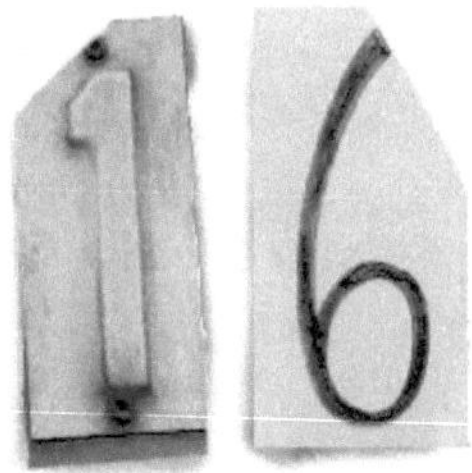

WHEN I TOLD Rick I planned to tempt Fletcher and tease him, he'd understood exactly what I meant. It also let me grant Fletcher one of his wishes. Fortunately, Rick and I had already discussed this beforehand.

I doubted I could have been anywhere near this cavalier otherwise. Fletcher was not someone for me to play with. Neither of them were. But this type of playing, when it was us together, knowing exactly what this was, it was intoxicating.

Rick's palm ground against my clit as his fingers speared inside me, rubbing against that delicious spot. Sparks lit up behind my eyelids as I let my eyes close. Just for a moment.

When I opened them, Fletcher's bright blue gaze locked with mine. His tongue darted out to lick his lips as he tracked every single place that Rick touched me. I'd never been watched before, and the heat washing over me was an aphro-disiac unlike any other I'd ever experienced.

With Rick, I was usually the one in charge, or at least it was mutual. He never did anything he thought I wouldn't like, and most of the time, if he wanted to do something new, his gaze would ask even if his mouth didn't.

But with Fletcher here, aching to be a part of what we

were doing, I wanted to give them both something they'd enjoy. I bit my lip to keep my smile from spreading too wide, enjoying every way Rick massaged and tweaked my needy body.

I loved his touch. He knew exactly what I liked. Still, there was something I'd never offered to him before.

"Rick," I murmured, my voice a breathy whisper.

"Hmm?" He ran his nose up the side of my head, breathing me in as he started to slowly fuck me with his fingers.

"I want you to take control."

His movements stopped, but his arm tightened across my breasts. "Control?"

"I'm the winner, and I want Fletcher to watch…and you to take control. Love me however you want. *Fuck me* however you want." I ran my thumb over the underside of my fingers as I let my hands hang by my body. I wouldn't touch him unless he asked me too.

Rick's guttural groan had my pussy pulsing around his fingers as he flexed his hips into my ass. His erection digging into me through the mesh of his shorts.

"Fuck yeah, Big Guy. Show me how much you love taking Drew. She feels good, right? Show me how hard she screams for you." Fletcher's voice deepened as he crossed his arms and braced his feet apart. The hard cock strained against his shorts, nearly touching the band.

I would have laughed at his commentary, but Rick pinched my nipple, eliciting a low moan from my throat. None of the flirty Fletcher was here right now. We had that darker version I'd seen hints of earlier, only this Fletcher was here with us, completely, and horny.

Oh yeah, this was turning Fletcher on. And Rick too, if the tension vibrating off him was any indication.

The hand at my breast slid up until he cupped my throat

with just enough grip to jerk me back into him. He used his foot to tap the inside of my calves, signaling to widen my stance. I obliged.

"Then I want you to come on my fingers, just like this," he whispered so softly against my hair, I wasn't sure Fletcher could hear him. The slow roll of his fingers as he fucked me picked up speed until the sounds of my desire filled the space between us.

"She loves that. Loves what you're doing to her. I wish you could see her face. Her eyes are half mast, clouded with lust. There's never been anything more beautiful…" Fletcher trailed off.

That satisfying euphoria that meant I was close wouldn't be held off as Rick repeatedly hit my G-spot with his blunt fingers. I didn't want to hold it off. My legs started to shake as wave after wave of toe curling bliss rolled over me. I gasped, pushing back against Rick.

I didn't have to worry about falling because Rick held me firm to him by my throat and pussy. I'd never felt as surrounded as I did now, and yet I didn't feel trapped.

His fingers slowed, until he only massaged that spongy place inside, prolonging the shivers that wracked my body. When the last tremor stopped, I registered his harsh breathing in my ear and the rhythmic press of his hips. He'd enjoyed that just as much as I had.

Pulling his fingers out, he brought them to his lips. I tracked the movement, needing to watch him taste me. His icy eyes sparked as he looked down at me, all of his desire and affection for me right there in his eyes for me to see.

"Shit, the way you're looking at her is fucking hot."

Rick didn't acknowledge Fletcher as he pressed his other hand on my shoulder. "Go down to your knees."

Unable to deny him, I floated down until I faced Fletcher. Rick's clothes rustled softly as he stripped down.

"Shit, Big Guy, you're packing. Not that I didn't think you were, but this gives a whole new meaning to calling you, Big Guy."

I choked out a laugh. His words were as hilarious as they were flattering, but the sexual tension was so thick in the room, the one orgasm did nothing to tamp down my rampant lust.

In the mirror Rick's long, tan body flashed in my periphery before he dropped down behind me.

"Fuck," Fletcher muttered and shook his head.

Using light pressure, Rick pushed me forward with a hand to my shoulder and small of my back. Once I braced my hands on the mat, he let up, but pulled the hair tie out of my hair and tossed it to the side. The damp waves fell around my face.

"You gonna pull her hair? Hold her to you as you pound into Drew?" Fletcher's voice lowered with each word.

One hand stayed on my shoulder as his other disappeared. Then the head of his cock rubbed against my lips, spreading the wetness over my clit.

"Mmm," I couldn't hold the sound in.

"We want your sounds, Drew. All your noises. Make me jealous that he's touching you and I'm not." Fletcher's gaze pinned me to the spot as Rick slowly slipped the head inside. His strong hands caressed my ass, before sliding up until he gripped both of my shoulders, using them as leverage he slammed into me.

My groan was answered by his grunt. Then he started to move in deep, hard thrusts.

"Arch her back more," Fletcher ordered and surprisingly, Rick pressed on my lower back. "That's it. Doesn't that feel better, Drew? Now grip her hair. The sensation adds to her pleasure."

Long fingers threaded through my hair close to the scalp.

They didn't pull so much as hold me with such enough pressure to make it ache. He never lost his pace and I had to lock my arms to stop myself from falling forward. Rick moved one hand to grip the cheek of my ass.

Oh damn. Everything Rick was doing to me while Fletcher watched was ten times more intense. It wouldn't be long, I could feel the next peak coming fast.

"Fletcher," I moaned. "Come kiss me."

"Fuck yes, I'd love too. Rick, man, you fuck like a beast, and Drew, you take it so good," Fletcher said as he dropped to his hands and knees in front of me.

Some of his hair fell forward as he dipped his head to meet mine. "You smell like sex and sin, Drew. I want to drown in it." The words, the tone, and the way his gaze held mine were hypnotic. The first brush of his lips ignited a fresh wave of heat that Rick's cock stoked higher. The tangle of his tongue lit me up, particularly when I stroked over the piercing.

How was that little piece of metal so damn erotic? I couldn't fathom it and even now, the tendrils of thought scattered nearly as soon as they were formed.

"I can feel Rick thrusting inside you. The rocking. Hell." The whisper of his breath carried the scent of coffee and hints of peppermint. Then that thought ignited as he tilted his head and I had to shift to chase after his tongue as he devoured my lips.

He deepened the kiss, his tongue mirroring the sensual strokes of Rick rocking into me. My thoughts came together and scattered again like a wild, violent pattern in a Kaleidoscope. I pulsed around Rick's cock, clamping down on him and holding tight. Fletcher swallowed every single one of my cries and all of my pleasure.

Behind me Rick growled, his hips pistoned erratically as he pursued his own pleasure and I was more than happy to rock with him, the angle of his strikes just sending up more sparks through my system. Fingers flexing on my ass, he gripped me so tight I swore there would be bruises as he released a long sound that stroked every one of my senses.

The liquid heat of his release filled me and I swore I shuddered. There was an intimacy in this, in Rick pleasuring us as I kissed Fletcher. Tasting one while the other filled me. Trembling assaulted me as Fletcher finally released me to breathe. Oxygen flooded my lungs.

That was…

Fletcher sat back slowly, his erection twitching in his shorts. The flush on his tanned cheeks darkened to ruddy, his pupils were so swollen and dark, I could barely make out the crystal of their blue. Raw. Torn open. Exposed

"Thank you, Drew. Rick. I hope we can do that again soon. Real soon. But right now, I have to go shower. A long, long shower," he rambled as he stood up, his voice damn near wrecked, broken. He stumbled as he turned, then half-ran for the door.

I could barely form words and I pushed upward, the trembling was a weakness I couldn't afford with Fletcher on the run. Rick wrapped his arms around me and lifted me to my feet. The powerful body that housed such strength was also capable of infinite gentleness.

Already, he slipped away from me and I half-turned to look up at him. "Rick…"

"I know," he said, understanding alive amongst the passion in his eyes. He kissed me soundly. "You need to go after him." He swept off his shirt and then pulled it over me. It hung down to my thighs.

Thighs that were still damp from the leg shaking pleasure we'd just shared.

"Go, Vienna." Another kiss and he snagged my shirt from somewhere, chasing the release escaping me before he nudged me toward the door. "I'll make sure you get over to the other house and then I'll clean up in here."

"Rick—"

"Go," he repeated, though with far more gentleness. "He needs you right now." Another kiss stole my breath. "I know I have you."

The encouragement and declaration soothed away any worries. If there was a problem, I'd deal with it after. Fletcher had been very involved but the intimacy—it had shaken me. I suspected it had shaken Rick.

It flat out terrified Fletcher.

Aware of Rick right behind me, I was up the stairs and then across the green separating the houses and into our garage. Habit had me scanning the area, even in the brightness of the day, we were alone out here. Nothing out of place.

Once I was inside, Rick slowed and let me head up the stairs on my own. Fletcher's bedroom door was closed, but not locked. I hesitated with my hand over the knob.

Fletcher wasn't Rick. He wasn't like anyone I'd known. He flirted like he needed to for oxygen. But he was also housing a lot of secrets and a lot of pain.

I didn't want to be the cause for more.

Curling my fingers into my palm, I knocked. Head tilted forward, I also listened. The water was running in the shower, but it was a clear sound. Nothing muffled it and nothing broke the sound of the water rushing.

He'd turned it on, but he wasn't in it.

I lifted my hand to knock again and the door opened. Fletcher stared at me, the rawness in his eyes was still there even as he tried to manufacture a smile. "Aww, Drew—you didn't have to chase me down."

What might have been playful banter any other time, came out almost hollow. He dragged a hand to the back of his neck as he cut his gaze away.

"May I come in?"

Surprise flickered across his expression as he glanced back at me. "Yeah, I just—yeah. Sure."

He tried to hide the pain lurking in his eyes, but I saw it, felt it. And his hurt kept dragging me closer. I didn't know what caused it, but I wanted to take it away. I wanted to end it.

Even when I rescued him from Dion, he'd not looked like this. Close—but not this.

Something cracked in my chest at that expression. Had I done that?

He retreated from the door and I followed him in, closing it slowly and then leaning back against it. Uncertainty wasn't an emotion I spent a lot of time with and I didn't care for it at the moment.

"I'm sorry," I told him in a solemn voice.

That pulled him around, his eyes widened and his mouth fell open. "What?" The syllable came out strangled and he shook his head. "Why?"

"Because you're in pain," I told him. Pushing away from the door, I took his wild eyes and confusion in as I narrowed the distance. But I kept my hands out, I didn't want him to see it as an attack or as cornering him.

"Well, this isn't the first boner I've had." He mustered more of a laugh to coat his words. "It's not even the first time I've gotten a major chubby over you. I mean you're—you."

That sounded more like him.

"Then why did you run?"

"Okay, so maybe we can call it a strategic exit, you know, rather than run? Running sounds like I took off like a little bitch."

I canted my head to the side. The pain in his eyes seemed to have retreated.

"Okay fine, I ran. But—that's more because I didn't want you to see me blow all over my shorts like some high school kid who'd never seen a breast before and you know, you said

I couldn't touch myself." The words spilled out of him in a rush.

I nodded slowly.

"And you only said kiss you, so I figured really touching you was off the table, so I double-timed it up here to get this in hand in the shower. But you didn't say that was okay yet so I was trying to figure out if you would be pissed if I did." He panted. "Are you mad?"

I shook my head. "Not at all."

"Cool—then do you mind if I go?" He mimed jerking off before pointing at the bathroom.

"Only if you don't want me to do it for you…"

"Great. I think it'll be better when I can get some blood flow back from happy land to my brain. You know—goddamn you're beautiful when you come." He was almost to the bathroom when he stopped like he'd run into a wall.

I waited.

Pivoting, he stared at me. "Say that again?"

"I don't mind, but only if you don't want some help, or me to join you." Then because he seemed struck mute—an impressive achievement—I tugged Rick's shirt up and off.

Fletcher raked his gaze over me and I swore it was like a tangible caress. He swallowed. "Just—to clarify—" He held up one finger. "My options are to jerk off in the shower by myself." Adding a second finger, he continued, "Or take a shower with you and…" He eyed me.

"And anything else you might feel the urge for—including touching me."

The man moved faster than I'd seen him at any point in our acquaintance. He hauled me up and, hands clamping on my ass as he dragged me to him. A split second before our mouths would have touched, he hesitated, "Anything?"

Thrill ignited in me and I cupped his face. "Anything for you, my little pincushion."

He closed his eyes. "Someone up there loves me. Or maybe down there."

Laughter burst out of me at the declaration. But when he opened his eyes again, they were blazing with pure heat. Gone was the uncertainty, the hesitation, and the pain.

"Shower," he whispered before he kissed me. "Because I have all kinds of things I've been dreaming about doing to you."

VIENNA

FLETCHER all but carried me into the shower, his mouth locked over mine and his hands tight on my ass. The tile was warm against my back as he pressed me up against it. Water slanted over us, plastering my hair and his. The slow grind of his hips pressed the full weight of his erection against my cunt.

Oh, that was a nice feeling, but it could be better. Fisting his soaked hair, I tugged. He sucked at my lower lip, nipping it with enough force to sting before he finally obeyed enough for me to catch a breath.

"This is not whatever I want," he grumbled, but his eyes were full of heat and mischief. "In fact, I have part of what I want right here..." He dipped his gaze to my chest where my nipples strained against him.

"Is that so?"

"Oh yeah." The vehement declaration caught me by surprise as he lifted me. I'd never considered Fletcher weak, not even when I'd found him bloodied and tied to a chair while Dion worked him over. While he didn't have Rick's muscle mass, he was all lean, corded muscle and there was strength in him.

Once he got my breasts to his head height, he locked his lips around one nipple. The suction was gorgeous, but that was just the beginning. When he began to roll that delicious tongue piercing all over the puckered flesh, everything inside of me clenched.

It didn't seem to matter that I'd just come only a short while before. The combination of warm metal, his tongue, and suction sent a bolt of lightning zinging through my system. Without any prompting, he moved to my other nipple and paid it similar affection.

Only training kept me from slamming my head back against the tile as I arched my hips. At this angle though, I couldn't feel his cock and my legs were hitched against his sides and not his hips.

And he still had his fucking clothes on.

"Fletcher…"

All at once, he lifted his head and looked up at me. "Holy shit, say that again."

"What?"

"My name—say it like that again."

Impatience vied with amusement, but both were losing the battle against need and want. "Fletcher…"

"Okay, not quite as sexy as the first time—let's try this."

I'd barely registered that his hand moved when he slid two fingers up against the inside of my thigh to trace against my clit.

Lower back arching, I ground against those two fingers even as he latched onto a nipple again. This time, I got his teeth, the steel piercing, and his tongue.

It shook a scream out of me even as I tried to repeat his name. The edge was right there, but just before I could tumble over it, he pulled back again.

Oh, I was going to kill him. No, not kill him. I liked him too much for that. But I might hurt him. A little. Even as that thought tried to take purchase, I banished it. I didn't want Fletcher hurting, even if I was a riotous mass of vibrating need at the moment.

"You are so fucking beautiful," he complimented me. I ran my tongue over my lower lip. "I just want to lick and kiss my way to every part of you."

Hips rolling, I shifted my weight to push him back from the tile wall. He didn't budge far, but it was enough for me to slide down his length to put my feet on the floor.

"Fletcher..."

"Yes, Drew?" The little shit wore the most wickedly mischievous smile. Terrible man. Absolutely adorably terrible.

I might just have to keep him, too.

"Are you done paying me back for *letting* you watch Rick and me?" Eyebrows raised, I dared him to deny it. Largely because the hot water wasn't infinite and it would chill sooner or later.

An unabashed grin lit him up. "It wasn't all about torturing you, I promise."

As ridiculous as it sounded, I laughed. My earlier irritation evaporated under the playfulness. Fisting his shirt, I dragged it upward. "Good to know."

He helped me peel the soaked cloth off of him. It was my first real up close look at the bars pierced through his nipples. Like the one in his tongue, these were silver, smooth, and inviting. His breath caught as I smoothed my hands down his chest, then up again. With care, I flicked the piercings, then studied him.

The slow grin stretching his lips beckoned me to explore. "I'm guessing we're done with my turn to do anything I want..." The droll comment deserved consideration, so I followed my thumbs with my tongue, tracing it in a light circle around one of his nipples.

Men didn't usually seem to have sensitive nipples. Maybe it was the piercings that did it or maybe I'd never known the right guys. Still, he sucked in a breath and gripped my hair, but he didn't jerk or pull.

"Fuck," he swore, and I could see his toes from this angle. They curled as his hips thrust forward. Oh, this was lovely. I traced a line of kisses across his chest to the other nipple, teasing the piercing there.

My little pincushion was full of surprises. A groan echoing the one I'd released earlier vibrated in his chest. I roamed my hands to his shorts and hooked my fingers in the sides of them before I went to my knees and pulled his shorts down.

The slam of his hands on the tile above made me grin, not that I took my eyes off the prize. The thick, curved length of his dick seemed to stretch out to me. The silver piercing differing from his others only in size.

It pierced vertically through the glans, from top to bottom. Like his cock, it curved, and there was very little space between the silver bobs at the ends and his cock.

"May I?" I asked, because yes, I had said he could do whatever he wanted, but I wanted to play too.

"I thought I was gonna die down there," he grunted and I lifted my gaze to meet his. "Not, die die—but yeah, die. You were so fucking beautiful and watching Rick rail you was probably one of the top five events in my life."

Holding his gaze, I ran my tongue over my lips. "Is that a yes?"

"Please," he whispered, his voice truly straining. "Yes, touch me anywhere you want."

Not looking away from him, I wrapped my hand around the base of his dick. It was like gripping fire. Pure heat under the satiny softness of his dick. He sucked in a breath as I stroked him, but I waited for him to look down at me again as I moved my hand up and down.

The slow pump and gentle friction weren't enough for him. He shook with the effort not to thrust against my hand. Only when he locked eyes with me again did I open my mouth and wrap it around his tip, tracing the piercing with the same thoroughness I had on his nipples.

"Holy shit," Fletcher exhaled even as he clenched his fists against the tile. A slight jerk of his hips escaped him, but I'd relaxed my jaw just in case. The fact his control frayed like mine was a pleasure all its own.

I could take him like this, swallow him until he came, but he didn't want that, or he wouldn't be fighting it so hard. Or maybe he just wanted me.

That thought ignited the coils of lust tightening in my core. I wanted him. Releasing him from my mouth with a pop, I pushed up to my feet, never totally easing up on my stroking. Shuddering, he stared at me in wonder.

"Will you rail me now?" I picked his term because his voice had dipped so beautifully when he said it earlier. "Please."

With a groan, he dipped his head and I met him halfway in a fierce kiss that demanded and gave in equal measure. The thrust of his tongue, an erotic tease all of its own. What would that piercing feel like on my clit?

Later. We were going to do a lot of things later. Including exploring all of his tattoos. I gave him a firm squeeze and he let out a growl that damn near echoed Rick's. With a bite at my lower lip, he gripped my arms and released my mouth.

Sensing what was next, reveling in it, I let go of his dick and he turned me around. His hands planted mine on the wall and then he dropped one palm down to grind against my clit.

I was so much closer than I realized because he nipped my throat just before he slammed into me. As slick as I was and as ready for the invasion, the first push had me rising up on my toes. The piercing was like nothing I'd ever experienced as it stroked along my walls.

Then he was pulling back and thrusting again. It took him almost no time to find his momentum and he cupped one of my breasts with his free hand as he flicked my clit. Warring sensations rioted through my system.

My vision whited out as I let out a soft keen, this was so fucking good. I spasmed around his cock, but he didn't slow down. He released a litany of chanted words that I could barely make out.

"Drew."

"Fuck."

"You feel so… fuck."

"Right there. Come…"

"Come Drew." The last was a demand, echoing clearly, and my body responded to both the command and the stroke of his cock as he struck deeper inside of me with every thrust. I came, shaking, and writhing as he kept me pinned to the wall.

I clamped down on him and he cursed again, as my orgasm triggered his own. He bit my shoulder. The fierce sharp pain of his teeth on my skin just heightened the pleasure and I swore I came harder.

We leaned there, against the tile wall of his shower, shaking and joined long enough for the water heater to finally give up and start hitting us with cold. My fingers were wrinkled and pruned. We were dripping wet and trembling, but I wasn't cold.

He whispered a kiss over the sting on my shoulder. Some distant part of my mind registered he'd actually left a mark. Next time, I promised myself, next time I'd leave one on him.

Reaching back, Fletcher turned off the water. Then he opened the shower door, and grabbed my hand to lead me out. I barely had my feet on the bath mat when he pulled a couple towels off of the shelf over the toilet. They were big, fluffy white towels and smelled like the clean fabric softener Rick preferred. All our linens were white. It just made for easier bleaching.

Fletcher set one on the counter and shook out the other. With quick movements, he squeezed the water out my hair. Then he wrapped it around my shoulders, tugging me closer as he briskly rubbed the material over my body. I grinned as he dropped down and dried my legs off. How very sweet of him.

When I brushed my fingers over his damp locks, he glanced up and shot me a boyish grin. His hair had half-dried in the time we took.

"I have to say, Fletcher, I didn't realize you were the caring type." We both knew that was Rick's department.

He shrugged. "I can't say this has ever been my thing before. With you…I just wanted to take care of you in some way," he finished as he looked down at my feet. Tapping my foot, he opened the towel to dry the bottoms of my feet.

The domesticity of the situation didn't escape me as I watched Fletcher kneel naked at my feet. His softening cock resting against his thigh, the silver metal of his piercing glinting under the bright light of the vanity.

With Rick, taking care of me was part of his personality. Just like he took care of the house, Fletcher, and our new house guest. It was practically ingrained into his DNA.

Fletcher was a different animal. He was hyper, somewhat goofy when he felt comfortable, and he lost himself so much we had to remind him to eat, shower, and sleep. For him to want to do this, seemed more intimate than maybe even what we did in the shower.

"All dry," he said, and I released his shoulder as he stood up. Tossing my towel in the hamper, he rubbed the other one over his body with quick efficiency.

"Not one for sharing towels?" My lips twitched.

Grimacing, he threw his in the hamper and picked up Rick's shirt. "Half the time I forget to change and it doesn't bother me. But there's something about drying off with a damp towel, it just weirds me out." He shook his head, then lifted the shirt to help me into it. "You don't have any clothes in here, obviously, and Rick didn't really work out. He would want you to wear this back to your room."

Our gazes met and held. I understood what he was saying without words. Rick was with us. He wasn't someone who was interchangeable or disposable, and neither was Fletcher. My little pincushion was letting me know he understood his place as well as Rick's in my life.

Leaning up on my toes, I brushed my lips against his, breathing him in. He fisted my shirt at the small of my back and molded me to his body as he pressed his mouth hard against mine. It was a quick, fierce kiss before he set me back away from him.

"We have to stop, Drew. If I don't, I won't have any control over what I do, and we wouldn't leave my room until way past dinner." His gaze smoldered before he abruptly spun on his heel and walked into his bedroom.

I laughed under my breath as he strutted his naked ass away from me.

"What are you working on today?" I followed, leaning against the door frame as he pulled on a pair of boxers.

"Well. I'll have more on our friend Sandra Jane this afternoon. There are just a few databases I want to check first. Then I have a couple long-term jobs I need to monitor. Just another day in the cave." He smirked as he walked over to the bed and dropped back against the pillows. "Sit with me for a minute before we have to go back into the real world?" He patted the space next to him.

There was so much to do with the list, Daddy's stuff, and Mr. Morgan in the basement, I didn't have a lot of time for luxury after spending the last few hours with them. But I could give Fletcher a few more minutes. Whatever had played on his mind earlier appeared to be gone, but I still worried about him.

Instead of crawling up beside him, I sat by his feet and stretched my legs so they touched his. This Fletcher was different still. He was relaxed, calm, and exuding a contentment I'd never seen on him before. It was a good look for him.

I debated asking about what had him so checked out earlier, but I decided against it. He'd talk to me if he wanted or needed to. And I didn't want to take the chance of sending him back into that space.

While I had been gathering my thoughts, there had apparently been something else on Fletcher's mind. "Rick was fine with me being there? And with you coming up here?" His brow pinched together as if he were truly concerned.

Rick had started to like Fletcher, but I hadn't realized that respect went both ways. Good. I was glad to see it. In my work, and especially with bringing Rick and Fletcher into it, we needed to be able to trust each other implicitly. And if friendship formed along the way, that was great.

Although, Daddy would disagree.

The pang in my chest that usually accompanied my thoughts of him wasn't as sharp. Maybe because he would have liked both Fletcher and Rick. He would have admired their moral compass. He might not have approved of me bringing them home—or taking them as lovers. Daddy had never usually liked men looking at me. Missing him ached. But I wasn't alone.

I squeezed Fletcher's calf. "He was fine. More than fine."

"Good," he breathed, resting his head back against the pillows, seemingly content just to have me in his space. "Tonight, would you..." Fletcher started, an uncertain note in his voice.

"Would I?"

He sat up so he could take my hand in his. "I know Rick sleeps with you, and I'm not trying to mess with that. Hell, I might like to join you two sometime, but for tonight...Would you sleep here with just me?"

A thought I'd already had, but I hadn't had time to talk to Rick about it. He wouldn't like it, but he wouldn't begrudge

Fletcher that time either. I tightened my fingers around his palm and changed my mind on my earlier decision.

"I would love to... Do you want to talk about what happened earlier to lock you in your head?" Yes, I hesitated to bring it up. But then he opened this door...

"What do you mean?" He wasn't defensive, but the quick cut of his gaze to the side told me he knew exactly what I was talking about.

"Rick and I have been with you almost nonstop for two weeks. We can tell when something is bothering you." I left it at that, not wanting to make him uncomfortable if he hadn't realized it was so easy to see.

Glancing down at our hands, he smoothed his thumb over my knuckles. "I've never had a great poker face. Well, around people I actually like, I've never had a great poker face." He paused, and I thought that might be his way to stop the conversation. Then he surprised me. "When I was working, I came across something that reminded me of my past. It's not often I get worked up like that over it, but something this morning hit me hard." He turned those beautiful, deep blue eyes on me. I was glad to see they were still free of his past demons. "I will talk to you about it. I mean, hell, you could probably find it in my background check if you dig deep enough, but not yet okay, Drew? I'm not ready to share anything about it yet."

I nodded. Asking him to talk had never been about me. It was to give him an outlet if he wanted it. Or to at least let him know the option was there. And I respected his decision.

"Okay." I glanced toward the door. Now that I'd lost that restless edge that had scratched at me earlier, I loathed the idea of returning to my work, but I needed to. I also needed to check on Rick. "Let's get our work done, and when we go to bed, I'll sleep with you tonight."

Rick could take my bed.

Fletcher rolled off the bed and helped me off, not that I

needed it. His tactile behavior surprised me, but it wasn't unwelcome. Since Rick, I'd learned the pleasure and draw of a simple lover's touch.

"I better squeegee the shower, get the wet clothes out, and clean the drain before going back to work. Now that I'm on Rick's good side, I don't want to give him any reason to kick me out of bed." He grinned.

On Rick's good side might be a little bold, but I'd let him work that out with him. The fact Rick looked after him said he'd have taken care of it anyway. But I liked the idea of them looking after each other. That was better.

"No caffeine today." I gave him a stern look. "I'm a light sleeper and I'd prefer you to actually sleep."

He waved my concerns away. "You underestimate my relationship with the good stuff. Anyway, if I can't sleep, you won't be sleeping either." He leered playfully.

I laughed and left his bedroom. If all went well, I'd at least make progress on one item by tonight.

TWO DAYS after Fletcher and Vienna shifted their relationship, we were leaving Fletcher to handle the house without us for twenty-four hours. Possibly longer, but we would cross that bridge when we came to it. When Vienna told me about the next job and how far we would have to go, I went to work preparing meals and a list of tasks for Fletcher.

Everything had been set up, all he had to do was follow warming instructions and he could feed himself and our guest. The guest was not something he really wanted to deal with. While he said nothing to Vienna, the objection reflected in his eyes. I waited until we had a moment before I suggested he put on headphones.

There was no reason for him to talk to our guest. He could deliver the meals and leave. I took care of his next washing, delivering bath water and clean clothes. It wasn't anything he would need to deal with. Something I assured him of.

"So you don't *have* to hurry back?" He'd tried not to look worried, but the way he rubbed the back of his neck and glanced at the laundry room like it might attack him said otherwise.

"No," I agreed. "We don't have to, but we will be back as soon as Vienna's work is done."

That was as much of a promise as I could make him. He'd

nodded, clearly distracted by the prospect. We left mid-morning, since Vienna preferred to drive to our destination. I didn't ask any questions beyond making sure I had a list of everything she needed.

"We'll be making a stop on the way with a supplier," she'd told me. "How much deniability do you want?"

That was the first time she'd ever asked me that. "None."

The warning look she wore made me smile. "Rick…"

"I don't need deniability. You will tell me what I need to know, but if I can do more, help more, tell me that too." The simple truth was often the best. When she told me about what Fletcher asked for, I'd considered it and I'd agreed. I'd even enjoyed how she teased and taught him in the gym.

Later, while I prepared their lunches for them to consume after they'd finally come downstairs, I searched for an element of jealousy. Fletcher's more irritating qualities—his flirtatiousness—was still in evidence, but calmer. Vienna also seemed far more relaxed than she had earlier.

This was a good thing. When she slept in his room, she told me I could still sleep in hers. I didn't care much for having her so far away. The second night, she'd slept in her bed with me, but Fletcher also didn't go to bed. Not as far as I could tell.

He was still asleep when we got ready to leave. When we got back, I would suggest he just sleep in Vienna's bed with us. Maybe not every night, but enough that he would actually sleep. One night with her had done him wonders, even the dark shadows beneath his eyes had improved.

"This is a two target job," Vienna told me. I had taken over the driving for the first leg, the idea had been to let her sleep, but she'd barely even dozed. "One of our targets is Corey Trebbler."

I knew that name. He was on the list of news articles I'd been pulling. "He enrolled at the university in Pointe Chase." The town, one I'd never heard of before, was located a state over and was actually a suburb of a much larger city.

"Yes." She didn't move or shift in her seat. "There's a party at his frat house tonight."

I cut a look at her profile. "You're going to have to go in alone for that." No one would ever mistake me for a college kid.

"Don't worry, you won't be far away."

I smiled.

"And our second target?"

"John Martin."

I didn't know his name. "Will he be at that party?"

"No, but we can drop in on him after we take care of Corey." She didn't offer anything more and the sun had begun to crest the horizon before she spoke again. "I have questions for Martin. So we'll need some time with him."

Don't kill him immediately.

"He might also have security," she continued after a breath. "I don't need them."

Them, I could kill.

Good to know.

———

Our first stop with the "supplier" turned out to be a huge flea market in Bannerston. I'd heard about these, but I'd never been to one. The partly cloudy weather let us enjoy some truly beautiful blue skies and Vienna seemed more like a golden goddess under the bright light of day.

She hid her perfect eyes behind a pair of sunglasses. We were dressed much like other couples and families shopping amidst the open stalls. It was more street fair than mall. We had to park a good half-mile away, but Vienna didn't seem to mind.

When she threaded her fingers with mine, I smiled and

gripped her gently. While we "wandered" along with so many others in the crowd, I had no doubt she led us on a direct path to the stall she wanted. Twice, she paused to look at items in one place or another, but they never held her attention for long.

Each time she paused, she scanned the area around us, often checking behind us via a mirror placed for customers to check out how they looked in something. When she paused to pick up a saucy red beret and put it on her head, she flashed me a grin.

I kind of liked it.

Digging a hand into my pocket, I pulled out some loose bills and she raised her eyebrows. Surprising her took some effort on my part, though I enjoyed doing it. The felt hat wasn't the best quality, but it was fun and it made her smile. Purchase made, we moved on.

"Oh," she said in a breathy voice, tugging my attention to another stall, this one was set back away from the "road," tucked behind some others. We had to walk across the beaten down dirt where grass probably didn't bother anymore but the occasional weed did. "Look at those bags."

Bags.

I studied the open-faced stall filled to the brim with all kinds of bags, purses, backpacks, duffels, suitcases, and even fanny packs of all things. Vienna practically bubbled to life as she made a beeline. It was funny and so dramatically out of character, but I kept my smile indulgent.

We'd seen lots of couples doing this over the last thirty minutes since we got here. In all likelihood, this was our destination. The supplier—in the middle of a flea market. Would her wonders never cease?

When we stepped inside, the shade offered seemed more intense than the others. Maybe because we really hadn't ventured deeply into any other stall. A man sat near the back corner, a pair of sunglasses on his wrinkly, careworn face.

With sparse salt and pepper hair crowning his otherwise bald pate, his skin seemed more like old leather after too much time out in the sun.

"Good afternoon, pretty girl," the man greeted us in a harsh rasp of a voice probably deepened by years of smoking. That actually clicked for me what the faint odor was there mingling with the leather and the dust. A half-smoked cigar sat on the top of an ashtray in front of him. "You brought someone new with you... does Daddy know what you're doing?"

The chastising note in his voice irritated me, but Vienna just squeezed my hand and sauntered forward. "Now Satchel, you know better than to ask about Daddy. He doesn't like it when we talk about him."

The old man laughed. "True enough, pretty girl. You shopping or just visiting an old friend?"

"If I said I was here to visit an old friend, you'd probably shoot me."

I frowned before I could smooth the expression away. Far from being remotely worried, Vienna walked over to lean against the counter.

"Nah," the old man said, his smile showed off shiny teeth only slightly yellowed from smoking. "I'd be flattered, then wonder if you were about to slit my throat." The musing comment made Vienna laugh. "Yeah, you laugh at me, pretty girl, but I've had a good run and there are worse ways to go out than having you be the one to say goodnight."

With ease, she hoisted herself up on the counter and leaned over to press a kiss to the old man's weathered cheek. He chuckled as she hopped back down.

"Now you're just teasing me."

"Maybe," she said, a genuine smile on her face as she glanced back at me and beckoned with a curl of her fingers. "Satchel, this is my friend."

"Big man," the guy greeted me. "Must be something

special if she calls you friend." He didn't offer a hand and so I kept mine to myself.

"He's mine, that's all that matters."

A burst of pride and warmth flooded my chest. Yes, I was absolutely hers.

"Good deal." The cheer on his face evaporated and his expression sobered. "What can I do for you, pretty girl and friend?"

"We need a couple of kits, probably an overnight bag, and one for hiking."

"Got time or need it today?"

"Today."

He chuckled. "It's a good thing I like you."

"It really is."

He tapped a hand against the counter, then rose. It was only then that I noticed the walking stick. Suddenly, so much of his odd mannerisms made sense. He was blind. Vienna made no move to assist him, so I stayed where I was as he tapped his way out from behind the counter.

She glanced up at me after he stepped out through a door in the back. The smile on her lips pulled one from me easily. "Satchel is good people."

If she said so.

Twenty-minutes later, I had a leather bag slung over one shoulder and Vienna had a brand new purse. Both were heavy and loaded. The leather work was of beautiful quality. She didn't check their contents before she paid using a code on her phone that she just tapped to his. Satchel waved us off and lit up his cigar.

The whole interaction had taken less time than we'd spent wandering. We were back at the car not long after. "We should grab some food," she said.

"Or you can eat what I packed in the back for you."

Fresh surprise flickered over her face, and I smiled as I settled the bags into the backseat rather than the trunk at her instruction. Her little pleased sigh added to my pleasure. I liked making her happy.

"We have time," I said after I got the car started again. "You can eat, then nap if you want."

Our next stop was still a couple of hours away. I liked taking care of her even more.

———

Despite my suggestion, she didn't sleep. Instead, she briefed me a little on Satchel. The codes she used and what types of supplies he provided. Her tone shifted though and she fell into a bout of quiet before she sighed. "I need to make provisions for you and Fletcher."

"We'll take care of it." Whatever she needed.

Despite the conversation, she seemed so far away at the moment, and I wasn't sure if it was the job or something else. I shifted my right hand toward her and turned it over, palm up. It wasn't so intrusive as to push at her but if she—

She covered my hand with hers and squeezed. Yes, if she wanted she could take it. "Did you have anything specific planned for either of them?" If the job troubled her, then maybe discussing it would help me see where I could be the most useful to her.

"For Corey, his uncle is a pharmacist and he has a history of drug abuse. A dangerous cocktail is the easy solution. Although how we decide to approach it will depend on where he's at and what he's doing in the frat house." She glanced at me, her head resting against the headrest and her light golden eyes reflecting in the passing street lights. I enjoyed her attention on me, even if she could barely see me in the darkness.

We were close to the frat house. Maybe about twenty minutes based on GPS.

She didn't volunteer any information on the second target,

and I didn't ask again, content to ride in peace as we crept along the residential streets. Like most fraternity and sorority houses, they were positioned close to the school, and this particular row of houses appeared to be on a street full of historical houses. We didn't drive down that street though.

If they used the surveillance doorbells, they might be able to catch a glimpse of our car. Although, I doubted very many of Vienna's jobs resulted in a murder investigation where the neighborhood was canvased, it was better to be cautious.

A busy strip mall came up on my left, and I turned in, intending to park on the last row. One, because it was away from the lights of the shops, but more importantly, this was the only row with any spaces left.

Vienna pulled her hair out of its messy bun as I turned off the car and fluffed her messy curls. My cock pressed against the zipper from the sultry picture she presented. Her curls were one of my favorite things about her.

She was so put together, so organized and purposeful. Then there was her hair. When she let it down, it was often a riotous mane rebelling against everything that was her.

I loved it. I wanted to sink my fingers into it, and when she was in the mood, I did. Which was often, even if just to massage her scalp after a long day.

The plaza was packed tonight, but with a tattoo parlor, liquor store, pizza shop, and comic store, that wasn't surprising. A pack of drunken college kids yelled to each other as they passed behind the car, barely able to walk a straight line, and it was barely after nine.

Unzipping her jacket, Vienna stuffed it in her bag at her feet. Underneath, she wore a silky green camisole that was almost a half shirt.

"It's chilly outside. You need a jacket." I frowned. The last thing I wanted was for Vienna to catch a cold.

"It's okay, Rick. We'll be outside thirty minutes at most. Look at those girls over there." She nodded to a group of about five girls walking down the sidewalk. I knew what she was going to say before she even said it. "Tiny tops and skin is what college girls wear when they're out partying on a Saturday night. The most important rule to my work is to blend in. Whether that's your outfit, accent, or body posture. People are predictable and for the most part self-absorbed. If you're part of the background, they won't remember you."

I reached out and touched my fingers to her cheek in a quick caress. "I don't think anyone could ever forget you."

She was stunning. Even her aura was proud and confident. She might get close to blending in, but I didn't think she ever could. Maybe I should do more of these jobs, so she'd stay out of harm's way and the public's eye.

She grinned. "You're sweet, Rick. But I know exactly how to cover the memorable details." As if to prove a point, she pulled a contact case out of the side pocket of her bag. With quick efficiency, she popped the contacts in and when she turned to me, her eyes were no longer the tawny brown I loved so much. They were a muted gray. Nothing memorable, like she said, and they were enough to hide her most recognizable feature.

I didn't feel the need to respond, and she didn't seem to need one. Vienna had picked out a pair of jeans and a long sleeve shirt for me. I was too mature for the college scene, but I was dressed like any of the workers from the plaza, maybe even one that was invited to the party. So, this worked.

As she tucked the bag under her seat, I opened my door and got out. The chilly night air smelled of pizza and smoke, as if the frat house was having a bonfire.

From the aerial map I'd looked at earlier, their house was maybe a five minute walk from here, and butted up against a public park, with a lake that almost touched the back of their yard. It would probably be best if we went to the house that way. Less lights. Less people to pass.

Although, watching the number of stumbling people

around us, it felt like we might have entered into a zombie apocalypse. If Fletcher were here, he'd probably make some kind of Walking Dead reference.

"What's that smile for?" Vienna looped her arm through mine and we started walking toward the sidewalk.

"I was thinking what Fletcher would say if he were here." I flicked my gaze to a group of guys heading toward the pizza place, slurring their words and zigzagging toward the doors. Then to another crowd on her side, who were playing that walk the plank game I'd seen others play as kids. If it were real, they would have died ten times over.

Vienna laughed and squeezed my arm. I knew she liked that we got along. And I supposed he wasn't that bad. He could use some improvement on his cleaning skills, but there was still hope.

"There's a park on the other side of this street," I told her, then realized she probably already knew. She had studied everything I'd unmasked on Corey Trebbler. I led her across the road while she weaved back and forth, giggling occasionally. I didn't giggle, but I did mimic her motions.

The farther we walked, the more the sounds from the plaza softened, but they were easily replaced by the thumping base of music from up ahead. High pitched shrieks accompanied low laughter and even some jeers.

Squeezing my arm, Vienna nodded to my left.

We stopped, standing in a grove of trees, too far from the houses to be seen. However, there were lights surrounding the lake, except the lamp that should have lit up the actual dock was out. A couple walked out onto it. No, not just walking. A man was forcing the woman in front of him. At least it appeared that way from here.

"Check it out?" I said under my breath.

She shook her head, then leaned closer. "You go check it out. I don't have a good feeling about that scene, but I need to go into the frat house. We're on a timetable and you can't go in there with me anyway."

Squeezing my forearm, she headed toward the back yard entrance, giggling at nothing. Vienna was right about how important it was to act and look like everyone else. A pack of people stumbled through the gate, and they didn't even give her two glances. To them, she was a drunken college girl there for the party.

Nothing special. Although, I knew that wasn't true.

Then there was me, standing like a midnight stalker amongst the trees. Shaking my head, I stuffed my hands in my pockets and walked toward the dock, doing my best to make myself appear smaller.

I was tall, muscled, and a little intimidating in the dark. I knew that. People had been afraid of me before when all I had wanted was to talk to them. Or get to know them. Vienna was the only one who seemed to see past that exterior shell that didn't matter all that much.

Except, she loved the way I looked. How she caressed my body and came alive for me during sex showed that. A shiver of pleasure tried to work its way up my spine, but I tamped down the desire threatening to distract me. Now wasn't the time for that.

People died when distracted, and I would never leave Vienna. Not willingly.

The group of people who had passed Vienna headed the direction we'd come from, likely going back to the plaza. The lake remained eerily quiet, with the exception of the couple. Their voices echoed off the water as I approached.

"I don't want to do this," the girl sobbed.

Stiffening, I glanced around, gauging my surroundings.

There was a dirt path around the lake that was lit up everywhere, except close to the dock. It went several feet out of the water, rocking gently as they got closer to the end. Vertical posts lined the sides but there was nothing in the way of a railing to keep people from falling in. Maybe the water wasn't very deep so no one had ever thought it would be needed.

Then there was a shack off to the side, right before the dock. The light from the closest working lamppost was just enough to see several fishing poles leaning against the building with a chest covered by an old net. The yellow glow and lapping water gave the scene an almost peaceful feel.

Except for the sobbing girl forced to her knees.

"Shut up, bitch. Your dad loves me. And your family is going bankrupt. Practically everyone knows by now," the guy slurred.

What a dick. This was exactly the type of person Vienna was trying to rid the world of. Entitled assholes who thought he could get away with anything.

"You should be lucky I'm giving you any time at all. In fact, you should be thanking me for letting you suck me off. Go ahead, say thank you." His zipper barely made any sound.

"No! Corey, I said no..." She tried to back up, but he fisted her hair to hold her in place. She whimpered.

That was our target... There could be tens of Coreys here, but I knew, especially given our target's history and this scene, he was the man we were looking for. He'd been a teenager when he'd gotten off of the charges. And he hadn't changed.

After what the judge did, he probably felt more empowered than ever. How many girls had he taken advantage of since then?

Anger seethed in my stomach as I narrowed my gaze and fisted my hands. I needed a solution fast, but without being seen. I would never hurt the girl, but I couldn't allow myself to be identified later. Vienna wouldn't like that.

The shack... Which was about twenty feet from me.

Whistling, I pulled out my keys, making as much noise as

I could, while keeping my face turned from the dock. I strolled like I had no idea they were there, approaching the door to the small building. Luckily, it was on the other side from where they were.

"Someone's there. Let me go." The girl whispered, her voice fierce even as it trembled.

"Fucking help. What are they doing out here this late at night?" Corey grumbled. He must have let her go, because within seconds, her feet pounded closer, then she was running up toward the house.

Perfect.

Pocketing my keys, I glanced back. No one was coming closer. I still didn't see anyone on the path. This would have to be quick and quiet, but I wanted to show Vienna I could do this. I would be a good partner to take on trips, then maybe I wouldn't have to stay behind so much.

I stepped from behind the shack and onto the beginning of the dock, just as Corey was closing in. Distracted from zipping up his pants, he didn't realize I was there until he was almost stepping on me. Which was hilarious. This guy was at least half a foot shorter than me.

"Whoa man. Why are you out here? The park staff stops their shifts at eight. Actually, never mind, I don't care. Just get the fuck out of my way."

Snapping my fingers, I grinned. "I know you. Corey, right? Corey…"

"Trebbler," he sneered. "I'm sure you do know me. My family practically owns this town." He tried to push past me but I stopped him with an arm across his chest. His arrogance confirmed my suspicions.

My grin spread.

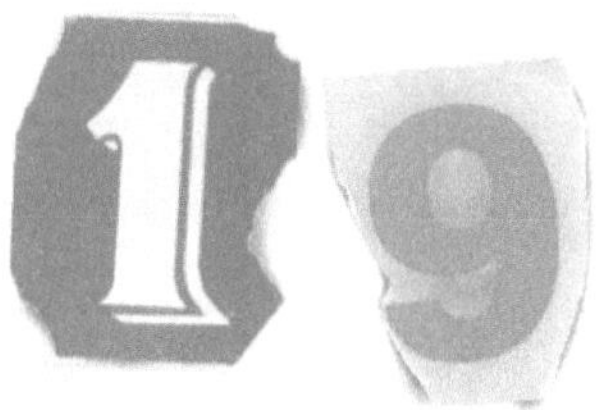

ONCE UPON A TIME, I'd talked to Daddy about going to college. He listened to all of my thoughts and ideas, then said he'd think about it. A few weeks later, he brought me to my first college campus. For the next two weeks, we visited colleges. Probably not the way other kids did, but Daddy understood something I had to learn.

College wasn't safe.

It was a predator's playground.

There was always a party, there was always a drunken idiot, there was always some kind of assault. It wasn't always sexual, but it didn't change the sad reality. After that, I told Daddy I still wanted to go to college, but I'd go our way.

A smile pulled at my lips as the memory of his firm nod and the faint curve of his mouth betrayed the soft smile he reserved only for me. I'd made him proud. That had reflected in his eyes, his smile, and his tone. A week later, I'd left to do my first solo job—on a college campus.

After all, I'd pointed out that college life was about learning independence. He followed me the first couple of times. I knew it. He knew that I knew it. I knew that he knew that I knew. But we allowed each other the deception because Daddy wanted me safe. I wanted to impress him and prove myself.

When I left for my fourth job and he went a different

direction to handle another on our list, I'd earned my spot as his partner for real. It had been the most amazing sensation. All of those memories cascaded through me as I weaved through the drunken crowd of dancing coeds.

They writhed together, some only half-dressed, others more naked than clothed. Apparently, this was a lingerie party, or turning into one. The alcohol flowed liberally. One girl actively mounted a guy at the end of a sofa and bounced on his dick while her breasts filled his face.

No one paid any attention to them. The throbbing music appealed to a more primitive part of the brain. It demanded motion, thrusting, even the rubbing and writhing a number of the party goers were engaged in.

One of the revelers, stripped down to his boxers, made a grab for my arm and I bent his thumb back, as I ground my foot against his and "stumbled" hard enough to knock him backwards. He crashed into other partygoers and they went down with a roar of laughter. Unfortunately, I couldn't linger to be identified later or I'd have given him a lesson in not grabbing people.

Sliding through the crowd, I made my way to the stairs and then up them. Corey Trebbler had a room on the second floor. He was a legacy in the fraternity and it was his second year. While he probably wasn't in his room, I wanted a good look at his potential stash.

The lock on the door was a joke, but I checked for cameras as soon as I was inside. There was one—pointed at his bed. Typical. It was deactivated. However, it was also digital. That gave me an idea.

I pulled out a thumb drive and inserted it into the camera. Fletcher had given me a couple of these, they had active programs on them that would image whatever they were plugged into, right down to the encryption.

I did the same with his laptop, letting it work while I did

my search. The boy lacked any creativity. His stash was located in his night table drawer, and on the desktop.

He was a coke head. Nothing injectable from the look of it. Pills. Lots of pills. Prescription oxy. Prescription uppers. Downers. And everything in between. The doctor's name was one I made a mental note of. No way he just prescribed all of this without cause or someone greasing his pocket.

I had the right combo, particularly because between the flow of alcohol downstairs and the sheer volume of his supplies up here—no way he wasn't already loaded.

Okay. Now, Mr. Trebbler. Where are you?

I left his room and headed downstairs. A couple groping each other passed me without ever looking at me. At the bottom of the stairs, a girl was crying in the arms of another. Her hiccuping sobs audible as I passed her.

"If that gardener hadn't shown up, he was going to make me suck him off…"

"I'm sure it wasn't that bad," the other girl said. "Corey has a reputation, but he's not so bad and he takes care of his friends. I know he's not the best, but there are worse things he could ask you to do."

Was that girl for real?

A part of me wanted to stay, to educate, and maybe to offer real comfort. But that wasn't the job. It was a distraction I couldn't afford. One I'd never dealt with before, either.

I made it three steps past them before it registered that the crying girl had been outside. She'd been the one on the dock. The one I'd let Rick go to check on the situation. I worked my way back through the writhing crowd. The girl still needed to find better friends, but she wouldn't have to worry about Corey again.

No one would.

Losing the dreamy smile as soon as I stepped through the back gate, I wasted no time walking to the dock. It wasn't easily visible from the frat house, and no one seemed to be venturing toward it. In fact, the few that were leaving through this exit were sticking close to the houses.

The park was public, but there was barely anyone around. It wouldn't surprise me if the frat had made it known this was their territory after hours. Wouldn't be the first time rich jackasses had taken possession of something that wasn't theirs.

Regardless, I was happy with the privacy.

Ah, there was Rick and our friend. They were on the edge of the dock having a conversation for all intents and purposes. Rick didn't even seem out of place from this distance, if you didn't count the fact that he was dressed much more casually than Corey Trebbler.

Just like the girl, anyone passing through would believe he was a gardener or some kind of park staff.

Rick glanced over his shoulder when my foot touched the dock. It dipped from my weight, alerting them to my presence. Whatever they were talking about, it must not have been very serious, because Corey leered salaciously at me over Rick's shoulder.

"Here's my girl now," Rick said, with a hint of a growl in his tone. He didn't like this man, but it seemed like Corey was too wasted to realize. Or his ego was so high in the clouds, from whatever combination of pills and alcohol he'd taken tonight, that he couldn't discern disdain if it slapped him in the face.

I'd let Rick know he'd have to check his facial expressions and emotions in the future, but it didn't matter right now.

"Hey, baby." Corey's words were barely recognizable as his smile drooped on one side. Yes, I'd chosen the correct method here, although if left to his own devices, he might have done the job for us. "Your boy here said you had the hookup."

"I do," I purred as I slinked up next to Rick. I slid my arm around his lower back and leaned my head on his shoulder. "What did you have in mind?"

"Oh, I love a good fuck up. I've already had some stuff, but I'm always down for more. If you're lucky, I'll even let you come back to my room with me after I check out the goods."

Rick grunted as Corey fell forward a step.

Pulling the baggie out of my pocket, I flashed the pills. My pills were much more potent than anything that he'd taken. It was the best way to fake an OD. Otherwise, I'd have to force them down his throat, and while I wasn't opposed, this was not the right environment for that.

"Damn, you didn't lie," Corey praised as his gaze flicked to Rick. "I'll give you two hundred for the bag."

"Hmm, that's a tough sell. But I have a customer satisfaction policy. I'll give you a taste now, and then if you like it, I'll sell you the bag for five." I waved the bag as if taunting him.

His head nodded so many times it was like he was a bobble head. "Yeah, that works. Totally works. Then my room after?" It was like Rick might as well have disappeared at this point.

I was so proud of him for holding his shit together. He was overly protective, and it was probably taking everything he had to allow scum like Corey Trebbler to talk to me this way. But he understood the plan and our goal. We were saving lives.

"If you can get it up, I'll follow you wherever you want to go," I winked and opened the baggie to get two pills. One would probably do it, but I took out two just to be safe.

He took them dry, then shook his head as if he could already feel them working. He couldn't, he probably just thought he did in his drugged up state.

"I've heard so much about you. Your family is legendary," I gushed.

Being out here on the dock under the cover of darkness

was perfect and I needed to keep him here. We couldn't have planned this any better ourselves.

"We practically founded this town. Granddad even funded the first library," he said as his chest puffed out.

"Hmm, right." I stepped away from Rick. There was probably about five, maybe ten minutes before we'd start to see the effects. When he did start to go down, I wanted to make sure both Rick and I had our hands free. "Your dad owns the golf club, doesn't he?" I tipped forward, grinning.

Corey tried to wipe the sweat off of his forehead, but he missed by a mile. "Yeah, it's been in the family for four generations. It's the most exclusive country club within a hundred mile radius."

All of his answers were on autopilot. He'd probably heard these exact lines recited since before he could walk. Too bad their country club was about to have a suicide scandal from their disgrace of a son.

"Why aren't there more people out here? It's a beautiful night," Rick chimed in, stepping forward as Corey seemed to be losing his battle with his balance. He must really be fucked up if the pills were already hitting him this hard.

"Oh, out here? This is our spot. No one comes out here unless they're legacy or if they have our permission."

That made me think…Was the light over the dock purposely not working?

We'd have to do something about that. Not tonight. We didn't have the time or the plan to shut down this playground for assault, but we would. The girls at this university had my promise on that.

"So Corey, what do you think your dad will say about your suicide?" I asked.

I wasn't normally one to taunt. It wasn't my style and Daddy wouldn't be pleased. We had a purpose and a role to fill, but that didn't mean we should be cruel as we carried out our work.

After seeing the girl crying inside, knowing Rick was the only thing that saved her from a sexual assault, I made an exception here.

My words took a long moment to register with Corey. When he finally spoke, his confusion colored his face just as much as his voice. "What do you mean?"

Almost too fast to track, Rick knocked him backward, but caught his foot so he didn't completely fall in the water.

Corey flailed a little as he dangled over the water. His head got wet, but Rick still held onto his shoe. It wasn't enough to let the frat boy pull himself up.

"Dude," Corey slurred the word so hard, it was barely understandable and foam bubbled at the corners of his mouth. Yeah, he was going quick. Too quick. "Pull me up man."

Rick said nothing, staring down at him dispassionately. I loved how well he handled that. Moving a little closer, I studied Corey's rolling eyes. His neck dropped back twice and his hair was soaked now. Muscle spasms would begin soon, if he didn't choke on his own vomit.

"I have a feeling your dad will pay a lot of money to hide how you died," I told him almost conversationally. He jerked his gaze to me, but his head fell back again and this time his shoulders went with him. His face was under the water.

He splashed and flailed, pulling himself up. It took some measure of understanding to use the leverage of Rick holding his shoe. Alas, Corey was losing that battle.

"But he'll do it, I'm sure they'll donate something in your expensive town and have it built in your name. Maybe a building at this school or a public toilet in the park. The toilet would seem appropriate." I gave a little sigh. "Then again, maybe they'll just forget about you. Your brother doesn't seem to have inherited your predilections."

"He…" The words trailed off into some kind of unintelligible slur of sounds without any clear consonants or vowels.

More foam bubbled at his lips and his right hand started twitching violently as the muscle contractures hit.

Yeah. He wasn't going to last long at all. Straightening, I scanned the area around the docks then back up toward the house. The thumping beat that had been almost soul invasive inside, carried like a distant drum.

No one was out here.

No one was coming.

"Take off his shoe," I said to Rick. It was the only thing on him Rick held. He nodded and pulled the shoe off him.

Corey's head and shoulders sunk into the water along with the rest of him, but his pants leg on his now shoeless foot caught on the wood of the dock and kind of hung there.

The dark water surged with more bubbles, then even those ceased. Goodbye, Corey Trebbler. Hopefully, he rotted in Hell. Those girls wouldn't have to think about him out in the world anymore and I could cross another name off the list. Facing Rick, I smiled up at him. He still held the shoe and he gave me a questioning look.

He was also wearing gloves. Pride and affection went to war as they swelled in my chest. He hadn't been wearing gloves when I joined him.

"Set it here," I said, nodding to the dock. He eyed Corey's still foot and then placed the shoe like it had come off while he struggled in the water. Then he rose and pulled off his gloves as he fell into step with me. "Thank you, Rick," I said as I wrapped my arms around his and leaned into him for real. "That was—more than I could have asked for."

"As soon as she said his name," Rick murmured. "I knew he was the one." The gloves had vanished, shoved into the pants of his jeans. We followed the path away from the frat house. The farther we got from it and its lake, the more students and kids appeared. They were all hurrying to and from their dorms or other parties.

I let myself notice the girls. None of them moved alone.

They were always in groups of two or more, unless they were with a male friend and even then, I saw only a couple of "couples." People knew when a predator was close, even if they didn't understand how they knew.

It would take time, but eventually some of them would relax. Not all the way, because there were always other monsters. "You did amazing," I told him as I glanced up. A smile flashed across his lips. "You did everything right, you thought on your feet, you got that girl away from him, kept him there until I came and then trusted me to deal with him."

He pressed a kiss to the top of my head. "The hardest part was not snapping his neck."

"I know," I told him. We were almost to the street and the sounds of traffic, music, and more people invaded the silent bubble we'd been moving in. "Look around though. Look at the women around us who are safer now."

Sliding my hand down his arm, I threaded my fingers with his as he guided us across the street. He walked me over to the passenger door as though he intended to open it for me and I twisted, facing him as I pressed my back to the door and I barely even had to lift my head before he swooped down to claim my lips in a breath-stealing, soul-burning kiss.

His hands clamped on my hips and he lifted me, still keeping me pressed to the door, but my ass was at the level with the window and he didn't have to bend quite so far to kiss me. He stroked his tongue against the seam of my lips like he was seeking the request of a genie to leave his lamp.

I opened to him and sighed as his tongue thrust against mine. All traces of hesitation left him as he sought out my tongue, then sucked it against. The pull went all the way to my cunt. Fuck, he tasted so damn good. Sinking my fingers into his hair, I clung to him as he devoured me with his kiss and the only air I needed was what little broke through the seal of our mouths.

Finally, though, he lifted his head and I could have

mewled a protest, only I didn't. I smiled at him, the pleasure unfurling in my chest at the savage satisfaction in his eyes and the hard bulge of his erection pressing against my stomach.

"Thank you," I whispered. "Thank you for helping me with another monster."

"My pleasure," he rumbled in a voice drenched in sex and promises.

"Oh, it most assuredly will be," I told him. Rick definitely deserved a reward. "Later."

He nodded, then grinned before he stole another kiss. This one was sweet, but firm. "Business first," he whispered before setting me gently onto my feet and then opening the door.

A little happy sigh escaped me as I settled into the passenger seat. I'd always enjoyed my work. Enjoyed meting out the justice so often denied. Too often denied to those who truly deserved it. I glanced at Rick as he settled in behind the wheel and started the car.

But this was different. It wasn't just the work that brought me joy. No, the work was done, but the joy? The joy was going with me.

CASH

IN MANY WAYS, what someone watches or reads can give insight into their psyche. What they believe, what they care about, what interests them. When I first went through training, we were taught that an invaluable amount of information could come from such inconsequential details.

But they weren't so inconsequential. They were tangible pieces of data that made up who that person was. When my dark saint agreed to bring me some entertainment, I nearly creamed myself at the rare look inside her head.

It took her a few days to actually *bring* me something. I was disheartened, slightly, but I knew she had a busy life, ridding the world of evil. Chuckling, I thought about what her life would actually entail.

Research. She probably spent tons of time on research.

Self-defense. I could tell right away she knew *exactly* what her body was capable of and how to use it.

Anatomy lessons. From the way she'd butchered Terrence, she knew her way around a knife.

I collected every little detail about her, filing it away to review later when I had a much larger picture. The one thing that confused me was who her partner was. The Judge had to be in his mid-fifties. At least. She also didn't give me copycat vibes, although it was a possibility.

During my time here, I'd seen two men. I thought maybe the first man, who had brought me food and cleaning supplies, was the one who knocked me out. Then Fletcher Reed strolled down the stairs.

Now *him*, I recognized. His family was well connected, with whispers of shady dealings, but nothing that would have drawn the connection to the Judge.

So where was the partner?

Hmm. A question for another day. Right now, I was more interested in reading these books that my dark saint had brought down for me. In her generosity, she'd brought me three.

The Four Agreements by Don Miguel Ruiz.

A Brief History of Time by Stephen Hawking.

And *69 Million Things I Hate About You* by Kira Archer.

The agreements I got, just looking at the contents it seemed like something that would speak to my little vigilante vixen. I'd also chosen that one to read first, mainly because it was the shortest. I wasn't usually one for self-help type of books, but I enjoyed the philosophical background on that one.

The Stephen Hawking book was also intriguing because it showed depth and her desire to expand her knowledge on all things, not just murder.

But a romance? She just hadn't seemed like a romance kind of girl.

So, what the fuck did these books say about her collectively?

I didn't have time to work out my thoughts because the door opened at the top of the stairs. After days of being a model prisoner, I'd hoped they would at least leave the main door open so I could see into the rest of the basement.

They hadn't.

That was okay. I could be patient, especially since they were bringing me fresh clothes, gourmet food, and hygiene products. I'd stake my career on the fact that they didn't treat anyone else this well. If I had to guess, I'd say she wasn't prepared for me and didn't know what to do with me.

She was a vigilante killer after all, and I was an FBI agent...Ex-FBI agent.

The fact that I hadn't been let go for committing some type of crime was probably the only reason I was still alive. And I think she liked me a little. I hoped anyway. Our connection was too strong for her not to feel it.

I stacked the books up as the door rolled open, hoping to see *her* but expecting to see *him*.

Instead, I got Fletcher Reed.

Fletcher Reed in ridiculously large headphones. The kind I'd expect to see on some DJ from the eighties.

Well, what a great surprise. I laughed, but he just scowled at me before sliding a tray through the bottom and then going to work to unfold a card table. He set a laptop up and moved the banged-up metal chair in front of it so he'd face me.

When he looked up, his gaze moved back and forth between me and the tray. "Eat," he somewhat yelled. The fact that he couldn't hear himself so he was practically screaming at me was hilarious.

If someone two months ago told me where I'd be now, what I'd be doing and who I'd be doing it with, I would have laughed in their face. But here I was.

Standing, I stalked toward the bars slowly, a grin curving the edges of my mouth as we locked gazes. He gulped but kept his attention solely on me as I bent to pick up the tray. I thought about messing with him by walking backward to go back to the cot, but I would give him a break.

Adult conversation would be nice, and if he was my only option for the time, I didn't want to ruin my chances. Maybe he could give me some details on my dark saint if I played my cards right. Or maybe promised to keep certain details to myself.

Assuming she didn't already know.

The tray held another gourmet meal. As soon as I lifted the lid, the scent hit me and my stomach growled. I was going to have to step up my workouts in here if they kept feeding me like this. Who knew captivity could lead to more than the freshman fifteen I'd managed to keep off all these years?

With the exception of the first two days when I refused to eat anything, I'd eaten the meals they'd brought me down. As if I could earn, through eating and good behavior, another visit from my dark saint.

Maybe I needed another hunger strike?

I weighed that possibility against the creamy richness of the ravioli, melted mozzarella, tomato, and what had to be sautéed mushrooms. My stomach rumbled in anticipation of ecstasy. The garlic bread, also warm and fresh, added to the overall enticement.

Okay, if a hunger strike was necessary, I'd start tomorrow. A decision I applauded after my first bite revealed that the pasta pillows contained tender chicken wrapped in bacon. Fuck me, it was almost as good as sex.

That was pushing it, but I was closer to an orgasm with the food than I was with the lady of the house, so it would do.

For now.

The pop of a can top opening dragged my attention from the food as I took another bite. Reed took a long drink from an energy drink can and seemed very focused on the laptop in front of him. Only his eyes weren't moving on the screen.

I chewed the bite slowly as his foot tapped out an uneven rhythm. He was steadily trying to avoid me, but more than once his gaze cut over the top of the screen. The third time, I caught his glance and raised my brows as I made a point of taking another bite.

He scowled and opened his mouth, then clamped his jaw shut and *glared* at his screen.

Laughter shook my shoulders and I actually had to move the tray to rest on the bed while I grabbed a fresh bottle of water so I didn't choke. Awareness prickled over me. Reed was probably tracking my movements. Though it flew in the face of my training, I kept my back to him as I opened the bottle. Still chuckling, I took a long drink.

I returned to my meal without giving him a second glance. The weight of his stare made my grin widen. C'mon, Reed, give in to that pampered upbringing and need for a semblance of control. I savored the next bite, chewing slowly before following it up with a crunchy bite of the garlic bread.

Yeah, I was definitely going to have to add some pushups and crunches. Being stuck in this six by nine space had already left me restless. Then again, maybe she was fattening me up for the kill.

The mental image that conjured made me laugh for real, loud and long.

"What the fuck?" my audience demanded, his voice still pitched on the loud side. "Have you cracked in there, man?"

I raised my water bottle and glanced over at him, still smiling. His headphones were on so he probably couldn't hear me. Even if he could, he needed to work for the answer. I just saluted him with the water and went back to my meal.

The romance novel was starting to make a little more sense to me. Privileged overbearing asshole with an "assistant" who planned to drive him crazy by treating him badly after watching him tear through so many others?

Yeah.

A disgruntled harumph came from the other side of the bars and I grinned at my food. Yep, totally making more sense to me. I'd damn well toast her if she were here, as it was, I just saluted my dark saint to thank her for the insight.

Halfway through the meal I was taking my sweet time

enjoying, Reed cracked. I caught the movement from the corner of my eye as I was taking another bite of the garlic toast. Honestly, I couldn't say what was better—the food or the company providing my entertainment.

Probably the food, but I'd give Reed the benefit of the doubt.

"What's so damn funny?" The question carried an element of arrogance and a demand for an answer. With care, I paused to blot at my mouth with the provided napkin then glanced at Reed.

"Why do you care?"

"Just answer the question." Hostility and discomfort vied for dominance in his gaze.

"I'll make you the same offer I made her." I chose my words very carefully. "You want an answer, you have to give me one."

"Right, and Drew went for that." Reed snorted.

Drew. The name didn't quite fit her. No, but it was a name. That was more than I'd had before. "She most certainly did," I said. "Maybe she doesn't tell you everything."

He'd given me an answer whether he realized it or not, so I did him a solid and gave him one. I took another bite and let him chew on that thought.

"Bullshit," Reed said, irritation now ruffling the arrogance and the anger. "Prove it."

I laughed, for real. Cause, damn, that was funny. "You weren't present, how would I prove it?"

His teeth snapped together with a click, the headphones were in his hand and his finger tapped manically against it. The rest of him was still, but not that finger. Agitated didn't begin to describe it.

Taking another drink, I relaxed. He'd cracked once. My money was on him doing it again.

"I don't know." Fletcher's mouth twisted sourly around

the words. "Don't think this means you won this round, FBI man." He pointed a finger at me. "Or should I say ex?"

Grinning, I shrugged. "I haven't made it a secret that I've been kicked out of the Bureau." At least, not to my dark saint. "I also shared that when Drew—" just saying that name sounded wrong. She deserved a sensual name. Something that really rolled off the tip of your tongue during the peak of a heart stopping orgasm. Not something that was…cute and unisex—"came down to talk to me. You can ask her if you don't believe me."

His nose crinkled, but he didn't say anything.

Which made me wonder…

Either he didn't want to ask Drew because he didn't want to come across as weak, or…she wasn't here to ask. A shot of excitement speared through me. "You can't ask her because she's on a job, isn't she?"

"Wipe that insane smile off of your face," Fletcher said as he paled. "I'm not answering shit for you."

Which, paired with the way his blood was finding a different home other than his face, was answer enough. So, I did him another solid. "I was kicked off the team for being too reckless."

I wouldn't tell him anything of substance that I hadn't shared with her yet, but she already knew these details. And if he felt better about why I wasn't with the FBI anymore, he may be able to trust me a little bit.

"Oh great," he grumbled and tapped furiously against the keys. "We had to bring a dangerous man with a death wish into our house."

Chuckling, I kept my mouth shut. He wasn't exactly wrong. But he wasn't right either. "How did you get hooked up with Drew?" Nope, the more I said it, didn't make it more palatable. "From what I know about your family, you'd be more likely to be a target than an accomplice."

He stiffened. While I let him work through his own

thoughts, I finished off my meal, groaning in satisfaction as I pushed the tray away. They definitely didn't skimp on the portions here. I patted my stomach and turned back to Fletcher Reed.

"Not me. I tried to throw my apple so far from the tree I landed in an entirely different grove. If you know anything about me at all, you'd know I don't associate with them." He chugged the last of his energy drink as if it could provide some much needed liquid courage.

I didn't know this man very well, but I'd say copious amounts of caffeine wasn't what he needed. He bounced in his seat, his gaze constantly swinging between his screen and me, and there was a slight sheen of sweat on his forehead. If I didn't know any better, I'd think he was a drug addict, except I just watched him down an entire can of pure caffeine, and I suspected being here with me made him nervous.

So why had they put him on babysitting duty? More and more, I believed he was the only one left in the house.

"Is that why you burned your apartment?" I asked nonchalantly. I didn't give one fuck about it, but my curious nature wanted to know what could have provoked him to burn everything down.

His eyes widened and he ran his hands through his brown hair until parts of it stood on end. Then he smirked. "I've been estranged for a while. But periodically I like to put even more space and barriers between me and those dickheads… That's what you know I did," Fletcher said more to himself than to me. He sagged, like he was finally getting comfortable with me.

Or he was relieved.

Which meant there was something else in his past. I perked up. I really did love puzzles, and that might be what connected him to Drew. The urge to call him on it was strong, but not stronger than my desire to build a connection.

"I get fucked up families. My own parents were more than

toxic to each other, and me, when they were together. In fact, I can barely stand to look at my mom, and I'm fucking thankful she left me with my dad when she split." I'd take my tray over to the bars later, but if I stood up now, I ran the risk of scaring him. He was just too skittish.

Squinting one eye, he tried to hold back a twitching smile. And failed. "Is this you trying to bond with me? As your kidnapper?"

"I know you're not the dangerous one here. And I could give two fucks about that. I'm more interested in getting out of this cell." I made a show of looking around the small space. "What's it going to take to get out of here?"

This time, Fletcher was the one to double over in laughter. "Oh man, that was good. But I'll be straight with you. It's either going to take death or a natural disaster. That's just my own opinion."

Well, shit.

RICK

A GROAN ESCAPED me as I flexed a hand on the steering wheel. The wet heat of Vienna's mouth wrapped around my cock was almost too much, but I wouldn't peel her off me for anything. She had one hand fisted around my base, pumping me even as she sucked against the tip, and then slid me into her throat like I was her favorite treat.

All the blood in my body pulsed down to where she sucked me. More than once, I swore I was going to come, and then she'd back off until I was only shaking. Then, and only then, she ran her tongue around my tip until I was half-mad from it.

I'd pushed the seat back as far as I could, not willing to let her hurt herself on the steering wheel. I braced my free hand on the side of the passenger seat. It was the only way to keep from fisting her hair and fucking up into her mouth. As it was, my hips gave an involuntary shudder and I thrust deep into her throat.

"Shit," I swore, but instead of gagging, she hummed a sound that had my balls tightening up. Even in the dark of the car with only a hint of light from the dashboard to illuminate her, I could make out her eyes as she looked up at me. One more bob of her head as she slid her hot palm along me and then she relaxed her jaw and nodded.

"Thank you, beautiful," I whispered as if it were a fervent prayer and arched my hips. She braced her hands against my thighs and met my thrusts. Every push took me into her throat. The dig of her nails told me to increase my pace and she took all of me with such exquisite care I was ready to burst. "Vienna."

The strain of her name was the only warning I could give her before all the heat gathering in my balls let loose and I came with a shout. She didn't pull off, taking me into her throat so I released in jets that she swallowed until I sagged in the seat panting.

The lip smacking sound she made, along with another hum before she pulled off of my dick, had me shuddering all over again. "Hmm," she said, lifting a finger to the corners of her mouth as if looking for traces of my cum. "My compliments to the chef."

A laugh swelled up in me, bursting out of the warmth fisted in my chest.

"I definitely want seconds."

Now, she most assuredly was teasing me. I wrapped my hand around her nape and leaned forward to meet her lips in a hungry kiss. She met the first thrust of my tongue with a stroke of her own before she half laid over my chest. Her nipples were hard beneath the thin silk camisole top she wore.

I wanted to free them from their imprisonment and suck on them until she squirmed. But the pressure of her fingers on my chest had me slowing the kiss. I tasted myself on her tongue and I'd never found the idea of that even remotely appealing before.

There was nothing about Vienna I didn't enjoy. Even tasting my own cum on her lips. She bit down on my lower lip and I groaned as I loosened my hold on her. She gazed down at me, the image of an earthy goddess in the darkness of the car.

"Later," she promised me. "But you, my sweet Rick, you deserved a reward for a job well done."

I smiled at her. "Being with you is all the reward I need." And I meant it. Never in a million years would I reject her as a lover. It exceeded even my deepest dreams, but I reveled in being at her side, protecting her, helping her—just being with her.

The only thing missing right now was Fletcher. But he was safe at home and as long as he didn't do anything foolish...

I sighed.

"I know," she soothed me with a rub against the center of my chest. A vibrating sound intruded and everything about where we were and why we were here rushed back in. "Duty calls."

She wiggled back over into the passenger seat and picked up one of the burner phones she'd pulled out of the duffel bag we'd gotten from Satchel. With some regret, I tucked my dick away and did up my jeans.

Currently, we were parked in the dark of the trees at the far end of a rest stop. We'd pulled over here when Vienna had to leave a message for our next target. She stared at the phone. It had a series of numbers on the screen.

When she'd directed me in here, the last thing I'd been expecting was a "reward." My face warmed at the playful smile that had curved her lips and the sensuous heat of her mouth as she brought me right to the edge of orgasm over and over.

I swore my dick twitched at the mental imagery. She let out a little sigh. That sounded less than happy. I glanced at her as I got my seat back into position.

"Everything alright?"

"Yes," she said, tapping the phone gently against her lower lip. "He's moved the location for our meeting."

She'd mentioned dropping in earlier and security. "Do you know the new location?"

"Unfortunately." She pursed her lips. "We won't be the only clients likely to be there. It's far more public than I care for."

I nodded, waiting for her to make a decision. Another sigh escaped her and she studied me for a beat. I met her gaze without hesitation. Whatever she needed...

"We need to call Fletcher," she said. "We're going to be late getting home."

"All right. He was fine when I checked with him earlier." I'd done that right after we'd pulled over. "How late should I tell him?"

"A few hours, we can't give him more than that. The site Martin picked is another hour up the road."

"But we're not going to meet him there."

"No," she told me, a swift grin easing some of the thoughtfulness in her expression. "We're going to get into position to follow him and then I'll cancel."

"We'll follow and pick a new location after he's left."

Her proud smile was all the answer I needed. Retrieving my own phone, I called Fletcher and put it on speaker while I started the car and she programmed in the address of where we were going. I'd left plenty of meals for both Fletcher and our guest, but it wouldn't hurt to make sure Fletcher remembered to eat too.

———

"Pull into that house right there," Vienna pointed to a dilapidated house up on my left. What was once probably pristine white paint was now a dirty dishwater gray, peeling by the handfuls. The driveway was cracked with more dandelions poking through than there was concrete. The one thing in our favor here was the tall wall of overgrown shrubbery. That would provide partial coverage from the road.

Trusting Vienna wouldn't have us pull in here without good reason, I shut off the car, so our idling lights didn't draw attention in case someone drove by. Except, this was a deserted road. Houses were sparse, but the trees were plentiful.

The sounds of the car bubbled to a stop as the engine shut down. I rested my hands on my lap while Vienna typed away on her phone, switching between burners.

"The meeting place is about ten minutes from here at an old casino. I canceled. The convenience here is this road is the only way in or out. So, he'll definitely come through here." She grinned over at me and I couldn't help returning it.

"So why aren't there more cars coming through?" I glanced at the road, which had been empty the entire time we sat here. Casinos were usually packed with constant traffic because of their long hours. "And what about this house?"

Vienna glanced at the windows that were clouded with dirt and grime. No one had lived here for a long time. "This place is condemned. I checked the records as we were driving. No one will come running out shouting for us to leave. And this car is old enough that it doesn't stand out to people passing by." She swapped her phone out again. "As for why there aren't very many cars parked on the road, for the most part, any patrons attending the casino will stay overnight. It's an exclusive pleasure club that fronts as a casino. Only people with connections, people from the network who either need to meet clients there, or need a safe place to meet in general, tend to come and go as they please."

A pleasure club?

I frowned. I didn't like the idea of Vienna knowing about this pleasure club. "You've been there?"

She paused, glancing toward me. Her expression softened as she reached over and smoothed out the groove between my eyebrows. "Don't worry, I've never been there as a patron.

They don't treat women very kindly, in my opinion. Although, every woman is there willingly, which is the only reason it's still standing. Otherwise, Daddy would have taken care of it long ago." Then, she continued, probably just to set my mind at ease. "Daddy was the only one who ever went inside. I never have."

The amount of relief I experienced at her words was staggering. I'd heard of sex clubs before. Where they strung people up and allowed everyone to watch them during their sexual encounters. I couldn't imagine doing that with Vienna. In fact, I was pretty sure that was a good way to add mass murderer onto my conscience, because I was certain I couldn't allow strangers to see her like that.

Her delectable body was for my eyes only.

And Fletcher's, I added grudgingly. Yeah, okay, he had grown on me quite a bit. He just fit with us. Maybe because he was so quirky, and he didn't mind that I took care of him the way I took care of Vienna. Well...not the *exact* same way.

I brushed my fingers over the long column of her neck to let her know I appreciated her explanation. Vienna accepted my own quirks easily and while I knew they could be irrational at times, she always took time to explain when she knew something bothered me. I loved that about her.

"Okay, get ready. We took the long way around to make sure he would already be there by the time we parked. If I'm correct on who he's meeting and why, he'll be coming through here within the next thirty minutes." She twisted in her seat to watch the road.

I didn't have to ask her what kind of car he drove. I'd done most of the preliminary research on John Martin and he had a taste for the finer things in life. His current ride was a bright canary yellow Ferrari LaFerrari. The cost alone was over a million, even though it was one of the more affordable supercars.

What it wasn't was lowkey. Even with dim moonlight,

we'd see him coming from a mile away. I turned my head, resting the side against the headrest to watch the road. Within fifteen minutes, a bright yellow car flew past. Vienna excelled at what she did, and she never failed to impress me.

Shit, I wasn't sure we'd be able to keep up. She opened her mouth, but I was already turning on the car and backing out of the driveway. "I know. I'm on it."

She grinned over at me. "I never doubted you for a minute."

The warmth of her approval was the best feeling I think I'd ever experienced. Second only to sliding deep and bare inside her body. That was absolutely at the very top.

Now it was time to hopefully get some of the answers she'd been looking for. "Did you set another meeting?"

"Yes. In two days. I don't want him looking for us tonight."

Considering I didn't want to get the attention of the Ferrari or its driver, I hesitated about turning on the headlights. At the same time, I didn't want to get us into a wreck.

"You can turn the lights on up here," Vienna said, her voice calm and steady. I hit the switch as we blew past a side street that I hadn't even noticed was there but like the road we were on, it wasn't exactly in the best repair.

"We didn't lose them, did we?" I hated the idea of letting her down.

"No." Her confidence bolstered mine. "Martin is predictable. Daddy once described him as reprehensible, but reliable. His shipments always arrived on time. He always sets his meetings at the same place. He travels the exact same routes. He has only two homes he prefers and if he's shifting meetings to the casino, he's still living at the house in Monroe."

I frowned.

"You don't like him." Considering he'd wanted Vienna to meet him at a sex club, I wasn't all that fond of him myself.

She shrugged. "Take a left at the next street." Then she blew out a breath. "I don't feel one way or another about Martin. I am, however, suspicious. Daddy didn't trust many people. In fact, I could count on one hand the number of people I am certain he trusted."

I didn't ask.

"Once, I would have considered Martin on the list of those he trusted, or at least trusted tacitly. He doesn't pretend to be anything but what he is. A smuggler. He lives a hard life, he does hard business, he makes hard calls, and he charges hard currency."

Still wasn't hearing anything I liked. I took the next left smoothly and the old cracked road gave way to a slightly newer road, at least this weathered black asphalt still boasted white lines. More than the last road we'd been on. The buildings were still few and far in between. We passed what looked like some kind of old granary maybe.

"Why do you think he's not on the list anymore?" It went against my nature to probe her for answers, but there was an emptiness in her voice that bordered far too close to sadness.

"In a little under a mile, there's going to be a split in the road, take the right fork. Slow down, because we're going to take another right about a half-mile past that. It's gonna take us on a dirt road. But it heads back out to some vacation cabins. Martin's place is on the other side of that campground."

I nodded, but allowed myself a brief glance to the right to check her expression. The shadows only seemed to add to the emptiness in her face. When I slowed after taking the right fork, I reached out a hand.

She slid her hand into my palm. "I'm all right, Rick," she assured me. "I'm just thinking about Daddy and why he would have been looking into Martin."

The files she found at the storage locker. "You mentioned he had files on a number of the Network." She almost always discussed her father in the past tense. A part of me wanted to ask, but the rest of me wanted to respect her privacy.

"Yes," she murmured. "These files were different though. Information in them dated back years but it hadn't been collected over the years, at least—I don't think so. Daddy had his secrets. But this—this *feels* different. I don't have any other way to describe it. The way the information was collated and how he'd stored it, it didn't match how he did anything else."

"Your instincts are telling you that it might have something to do with what happened to him."

I noticed the worn sign that indicated a campground coming up on the right and slowed, turning in without letting go of her hand. The warning that the road would be dirt was appreciated because I took it carefully and the lights were on low.

"Should I turn the headlights off?"

"As soon as you see the first cabin." She squeezed my hand before she let me go. "And yes, I have been here before. When Daddy had to see Martin, I would explore out here. Sometimes, I found approaches to this property that his guards didn't even know about."

A hint of smug pride filled her voice and I grinned. "You plan ahead."

"Even before I realized why I needed to know this."

Still, I slowed down further because the dirt road had grown very uneven, and despite the dark, I didn't want anything to betray us. Not even a stray bit of dust illuminated by the tail lights. I avoided the grassier areas because it was tall enough for me to actually catch on fire with the undercarriage.

When I spotted the first cabin, I understood what she meant about it being closed and abandoned. It was practically falling down, the roof had half-collapsed inside of it.

Cutting off the lights, I slowed us to a crawl. It was another ten minutes before Vienna directed me to park near another dilapidated cabin. At least this one still had gravel. We might need to consider a more off-road type vehicle for the future.

But that was the future.

Canting my head, I looked at her. "What do you want me to do?"

"BE PREPARED. Martin is one of the few connections I've met in the network who prefers to have an active payroll. There will be guards and house staff. Guards are fair game. Especially his. I had Fletcher run checks on most of them just to confirm what I vaguely remembered Daddy mentioning. He chooses men who have records, or men he has information over to compel their service through blackmail." I took a deep breath. This was an info dump, but I wanted Rick to know that these men were different. "Fletcher found evidence the hired guards definitely involved themselves in the seedier sides of the smuggling *and* trafficking businesses."

Rick nodded, his face settling into a cold mask. "So, they enjoy their work a little too much."

"Exactly. Especially for Martin being a smuggler. They shouldn't be interacting with any type of questionable scenarios like what Fletcher found. So either Martin is in the know, and that's why Daddy started looking into him, or they're doing it under his nose. I mean, look at this place."

Rick looked out at the property as if he could see clearly through the darkness.

"An old campground that's not open anymore, although passersby would never know that from the vehicles that travel in and out. His lodge is something of a southern architectural masterpiece at the very back of this property. There are a lot of places his guards could do some shady things."

He nodded.

I already had a knife on my belt and a discreet gun holster under the blouse I pulled over the camisole, but I pulled a handgun and holster from one of the travel bags and handed it to Rick. "There's a silencer on here, but if we can avoid it, don't use this. Silencers suppress the sound, they don't stop it entirely." Then I moved the bag back under the seat.

"Got it," Rick said as he opened his door to get out, then he unbuckled his belt to slip the holster on. I followed him out of the car and we used as little force as possible to shut our doors. Sounds traveled in the backwoods, and doubly so at night.

Taking the lead, I pointed in the direction of Martin's house. There was an old barbed wire fence surrounding the place that was also electrified, but as long as nothing had changed, and I doubt it had—Martin played up on the abandoned aspect, and as we'd already determined, he was reliable—there was a spot three cabins back that had an easily scalable tree with a branch to the other side. The branch was only about four feet taller than me, meaning Rick could grab it to swing himself over.

I moved slowly, stepping on bare dirt patches where possible. Normally, I'd opt for a path that would hide our footprints, but today that wasn't necessary. Getting in quietly without alerting the guards was the top priority.

We found the path that led toward the cabins in the back. It didn't take us long to find the tree I remembered with the thick, sturdy branch leaning over the other side. Rick had stayed on my heels, mimicking everything I did perfectly. He was really picking up this work, and seemed empowered, like he was making a difference.

I was glad I'd helped him find purpose. Everyone needed one.

At the tree, I pointed, then hoisted myself up to the branch and swung myself over to the other side. I pointed at the fence and shook my head, letting Rick know not to touch it.

He nodded like he understood. Then with feline grace, grabbed hold of the branch, easily maneuvering himself over the old rusty barbed wire.

Motioning toward the house, we set off. There was still too much space separating us to see the lights of the house, but maybe in another five minutes we'd be able to make out any signs of life up ahead. Anticipation burned a hole through my stomach, knowing Martin was here. If all went well, I'd be one step closer to knowing who Red Death was. Why else would Daddy have had a picture of him in the storage unit?

We'd made it about twenty yards when voices reverberated through the trees as they moved closer. Guards. At least three of them from the sounds of it. And based on the racket they were making, they didn't expect to find anyone out here. Not coming from this part of the property.

Rick caught my eye and grinned. Tilting his head, he briefly closed his eyes to listen. When he met my gaze again he held up three fingers.

I smiled and squeezed his forearm to let him know he'd done a good job. If he was looking for bonus points to earn another reward, he was doing exceptionally well.

The spontaneity of warmth and affection surging through me had no place on the job. Unfortunately. I steadied my breathing, emptying out the emotion, bleeding it into a jar that I could safely store away. Work first.

We could celebrate later.

If we had a reason to celebrate.

Tracking the voices, I mentally debated efficiency versus security. If I were alone, I'd go for efficiency. I wasn't alone.

I caught Rick's eye, holding up two fingers I motioned to his eyes, then pointed to my back. A faint frown tightened his brow. The voices were drawing closer and we didn't have time for a debate or a hasty conversation.

He nodded once. Bless him.

The sharp firecracker-like echo snapped through the air, a flash of flaming phosphorus as the lit match touched the end of a cigarette. They'd revealed their exact location, and given me a way to track them.

Scent, sound, or sight.

I appreciated the effort.

Or lack thereof.

When they were not more than a dozen feet from us, but facing away, I moved. The dead grass and dirt strewn ground didn't echo with the sound of my steps.

A rustling snap turned the smoker around just as I reached them, but I jumped, leaping sideways. I caught the second man with my arms around his shoulders as I locked my legs around the smoker's head.

Using my own momentum, I took them both down in a roll. The tumble slammed the first man's head into the ground as the smoker twisted against the grip of my legs.

The cigarette sparked as it flew out of his hands, but I'd already let go of the first guy as I rolled with the smoker. A strike to his throat after I locked my legs and forced their air out of him, had him choking and gasping.

We were just completing the full tumble as I grasped his head, one hand on the top of his skull and the other on his chin. The last twist snapped his neck, and I was already tumbling back to my feet.

That was two of three. The third dropped with a vicious turn of his head. Rick let him go then moved over to deal with the one I'd knocked out. I didn't spare the man a second glance before Rick broke his neck.

After making sure the cigarette was out, I took apart the guns they were carrying. I wasn't leaving anyone or any weapon to come at us from behind. Rick pulled their phones, powering them off. We stripped away their ID before he moved them out of the way and into some of the thicker bush that had grown up around a fallen and diseased tree.

We would deal with the rest later.

Twice more, we had to remove guards as we grew closer to the house. Two pairs of two. The late hour—it was after midnight—coupled with their own comfort, made them easy prey. The fact Martin insisted on this kind of security was often treated like a vanity project.

He probably didn't think anyone would dare try to get at him directly. The dregs he forced into guarding him definitely didn't. How fortunate for us.

I didn't worry about cameras, though the route I took us on should have avoided them. If our host was lucky, we wouldn't need to worry. If he wasn't, we'd take the servers with us when we went and we still wouldn't.

The "grand" home boasted three main entrances, including one off the upper porch patio, another on the grand porch in the front, and the last through a far more ordinary kitchen door. His staff was not live-in.

A security box and a locked door were all that stood between us and Martin. I used one of the secure cards we'd lifted off the last set of guards as Rick fit in a key to the lock. As soon as the card reader flickered to green, he opened the door.

One dull lightbulb gleamed over the stove, providing the moderately-sized kitchen with enough illumination to navigate. Going perfectly still, I waited for thirty seconds to listen for what the house told us.

No sound of movement. No creaking floorboards. No thump on the stairs. No television or music. The distant, faint clunk of an air conditioning unit kicking on carried before the soft rush of air pumped from the vents.

Next to me, Rick waited. Did I want him with me or to

clear the place? Another mental debate. With me, would be better, at least close but also aware and on the lookout.

I slid off my shoes, one at a time and Rick mirrored my movements. He still had the backpack on and I tucked my shoes inside, then his. A bit of a tight fit, but socked feet were better right now.

Working off memory of the building plans Fletcher had pulled, I didn't bother with venturing out into the main house. Back stairs led from the kitchen and laundry room directly upstairs to the hall nearest the master bedroom.

A night light plugged into the wall a few feet from the mouth of the stairs let me see the outline of double doors. The wood flooring up here, sumptuous rugs, and even the molding were all expensive.

The construction of the highly-polished and ornate, dark wooden doors must have been decently thick, because the soft breathy gasps and moans accompanying slapping flesh hadn't been audible before I got right to them. Dropping a gloved hand to the doorknob, I turned it.

Unlocked.

I pushed the door in, but John Martin wasn't currently fucking some unfortunate partner. No, he was sitting naked and sprawling under the oversized monstrosity of a canopy bed with his mediocre dick in his hand while the light from the porno playing out on television flickered over him.

Well, one upside to the situation—he definitely wasn't packing.

"What the fuck! Drew?" Martin's face twisted up in enraged confusion as he hastily reached for the sheet to cover his groin. What a sad little tent he made.

Stepping in behind me, Rick shut the door quietly. I glanced over to the TV in time to see a very hairy bush paired with poor video quality fill the screen. Martin apparently liked seventies porn. Then the shot panned out to show a faded flower pattern couch.

"Rick, please turn that off." I turned my attention back to Martin, who seemed stupefied at my intrusion. When my gaze collided with his, he got some of his wits back. Scowling, he reached for his nightstand. "I wouldn't do that if I were you, Martin."

Blowing out a breath, Martin froze, then reluctantly leaned back against his pillows. "I haven't seen you in at least five, maybe seven, years. I damn sure haven't talked to Thackery in that time. Why are you barging into my bedroom unannounced?"

A slow smile curved my lips as I heard what he didn't say. When either Daddy or I visited someone in secret, they typically didn't live to speak about it. If Martin truly had been on Daddy's list of trusted confidants at one time, he would have known this. And from the look on his face, he did.

Which begged the question, what happened between them?

"I recently came across some very interesting details about you, Martin..." I let my soft accusation hang between us.

Martin was at least Daddy's age, but where Daddy had kept good care of himself, ate well and worked out, Martin clearly lacked that motivation. As a smuggler, he must not have seen any reason to stay strong and fit.

His white hair was thinning on top, his jowls hanging heavy as he panted from nerves, or maybe fear. I studied every tell and twitch as he watched me in return.

"If you think you're going to bait me, girl, you'll be disappointed. I don't play those games." He shot a quick look at Rick, who after pulling the plug on that C-rated porn film, stood as a silent sentry next to me. Rick's face was calm, his body relaxed with his hands hanging by his side.

I was impressed Martin didn't ask who he was. He would know Daddy never worked with anyone. His lack of curiosity only made him more suspicious.

"I don't like games either. What I do like is information."

That I needed to get without sharing too many details. I'd prefer to do this the less messy way. When things got bloody, it opened up opportunities to leave DNA behind.

Normally, I might have taken Martin back to the cells in the basement, but with Mr. Morgan in residence, that was the less ideal option. It was better to keep him far removed from everything I did until I knew what to do with *him*.

"So, what's it going to be? Are you going to shoot me without telling me why I'm on your shit list?" He bared his yellowed teeth like I would be intimidated. I wasn't.

"Okay, then I'll ask you a direct question and we can go from there. Who is Red Death?" I took one step forward, and Rick followed suit, except moving toward the other side of the bed.

Martin's brows lowered over his milky brown eyes as he pressed his lips together in the perfect image of confusion. "I've never even heard that name before. How the hell would I know who that is? Are you sure it's even a person?"

That gave me pause.

Based on the evidence I'd found surrounding Daddy's death, and the small amount of information he'd left behind, I'd worked off the assumption that Red Death was a person. But what if it was something bigger than that? I filed that thought away for later. For now, I needed to focus on what Martin wasn't saying as much as what he was.

"I'd like to believe you, Martin. You were once close with Daddy," I said in a conciliatory manner, and he started to nod like he'd play up their connection to save himself. "But you're not anymore. You haven't been close with Daddy in some time and that places a great amount of suspicion on your head."

"Our fallout wasn't anything to do with me. Thackery was the one—" he clamped his mouth shut like he hadn't meant to say that. Now we were getting somewhere.

I walked around the bed, skimming a gloved index finger

over the loose covers. "That isn't a story I've ever heard before. You know how Daddy likes to keep things private. But I'd really like to hear it. How satisfied I am with your story could affect the outcome of our visit today," I encouraged with a sweet tone of voice.

Martin messed with the blankets and sheets, pulling them higher up his plump body. I was at least glad to see the tent had disappeared. "Look, I know that sounded like our falling out was a bigger deal than what it was, but there's not much to tell. We had a difference of opinion on how we ran our operations. Thackery had a very strict code and he never deviated from it. I liked that about him. Respected it, even. But it wasn't my code."

I narrowed my gaze on his sweating, ruddy face. The closer I got, the harder he struggled to keep his composure. Men who were innocent didn't react that way.

"What is your code?"

His jowls shook when he gulped. "I'm a business man first and foremost. Profit is what I'm after, always. You and Thackery should both know this." He tossed up his hands in exasperation.

"Hmm. Still no idea who Red Death is? Or what Red Death is?" I asked, making sure to cover both options. He averted his gaze, but not before fear flickered in his eyes.

Gotcha.

Whipping my gun from the holster, I thumbed off the safety and pointed the muzzle directly where his soft dick lay under the blankets. His hands shot up and Martin held them still, most likely not wanting to provoke me.

"Red Death?" I repeated.

"I—I..uh. I—"

"Five seconds, then you'll have no reason to watch porn," I stated coolly.

"I don't know, okay? I've only heard whispers. Nothing concrete. I thought it was a place from what I've heard."

Now that…that didn't make sense at all. I was absolutely certain Red Death wasn't a place.

"What did you hear?" My heart picked up because while I wasn't sure I could trust Martin's intel, this was still a breadcrumb to follow. Behind every whisper was a sliver of truth, and when I had collected enough pieces I could start to see the big picture.

"Only that the price was too high for me. I had been asking about a service. I—I uh, I had wanted to secure a location for a revenge game."

"And where have you heard about Red Death?"

Martin's hands shook as his voice trembled. "One time. I only heard about Red Death one time, and it was from a man I haven't seen in at least three years. I haven't needed his skills and he was also a shady mother fucker," he rasped, a bead of sweat rolling down his temple.

"Who is this man?"

"The Vanisher," he rasped.

The next name on my list. Convenient.

"Tell me about the revenge game," I suggested, because he was still hiding something and I wasn't leaving until I knew everything.

"It's not important," he protested, his gaze fixed on my hand, well, probably more on the gun in my hand.

"Then it doesn't matter if you tell me."

He grimaced.

Oh, yes, I saw that too. "Five," I began. "Four…"

"All right," he swore. "Sheezus. You're fucking crazier than your old man."

That was almost sweet. "I'm still waiting."

THE CALL some eighteen and a half hours after they left didn't bode well. Granted, Drew usually messaged Rick if she messaged anyone when she was off on a "job" and we weren't with her. Being here by myself was a first for me. To pass the time, I'd been making myself useful.

I'd finished up a couple of jobs, added a cool two million to the slush fund, set up cameras on a half-dozen of the houses in the little "abandoned subdivision" we called home. One push of a button and I could check several angles outside. Something I tested a few times since I'd finished because it was oddly quiet without Rick here.

Worse, because Drew wasn't here either. Weirdly enough, that was why I'd taken the laptop down with me when I fed our guest. At least he was company, even if he wasn't the kind of company I wanted to keep.

I know what you did.

I mouthed the words. Dick. He knew I'd torched my apartment. Big. Fucking. Deal.

As it was, the phone call had proven disappointing. They were going to take longer. It couldn't be helped. Martin had tried to change the location of their meet, which meant Drew would have to deal with that and him. Rick wouldn't leave her. There was some comfort in that thought.

Searches ran on the screen. The latest reports on Sandra

Jane waited on my laptop for Drew to look at when she returned. I'd downloaded every clip of her I could find. I'd thought deep diving her was boring and a waste of time, no, that was practically cracking the Da Vinci Code compared to listening to her interview people, discuss her theories, or her research—or kill me please—her information on one of the greatest serial killers of all time.

The Judge.

I hadn't even fucking heard of the Judge. How could they be the greatest serial killer of all time? It made no fucking sense. Pinching the bridge of my nose, I shoved out of the chair and walked over to get another energy drink. I'd already pissed a river twice today, what was one more? Besides, I wouldn't sleep until I knew they were safe.

Might as well stay useful. Listening to Sandra Jane drone on and on about The Judge, his secret cases and how he delivered death as part of his sentencing, sounded like it had all the right elements to be a movie of the week suspense.

They still made those, right? Probably not. Netflix film then. Only, they needed a way better point of view character than her…

"…Casey Morgan's private files include several key witness statements and formerly unreleased links to other unsolved cases the former FBI Agent attributed to the Judge."

I nearly spat out the drink as I choked on it. Air and liquid did not belong going down the same pipes. Twisting, I glanced at the screen and the clip it played.

Morgan.

This reporter had files from a former FBI agent?

Ten minutes later, I'd relistened to that clip four times and had Channing Cash Morgan's file open along with his credit history, personal history, college transcripts, and the obituary for one Michael Casey Morgan, FBI agent for over thirty years prior to his "retirement" and death. He was survived by one son and his ex-wife.

How did this reporter get Morgan's files on the Judge? And did it have anything to do with Drew?

I glared at the screen then at my silent phone. Drew and Rick wouldn't answer if they were working and sending a message for anything less than life or death was not advisable.

Goddammit, I had to go talk to the former Fed in the basement.

Again.

Jogging down to the basement, I thought hard about how I wanted to approach this. I wasn't an interrogator, that wasn't in my skill set. Now hacking, movie trivia, and making Drew come? Absolutely.

Pulling information from a trained professional who could probably withstand torture? Not so much. So, I needed to outthink him. Or hell, maybe if I mentioned it, he would be so outraged this young grasshopper had his dad's files.

He wouldn't know she had his files, right?

Shit. What if she was his girlfriend or something? A friend of the family? I stopped on the bottom step, then pivoted to run back up. Wait, no. Even if that was the case, it was better that I found out.

I shook my hands out to my sides, releasing the tension, as I approached the sliding door that hid the cell from the rest of the basement. When I opened it up, I half expected to see Channing at the bars because he just seemed like the Pennywise type. Especially after that last time.

But he wasn't. He was sitting quietly on the cot with his hands folded between his legs while he watched me. The three books Drew gave him were stacked neatly on the foot of the cot, like he didn't want to disrespect them by setting them on the cold concrete.

I bet he'd already read all three. He seemed like the scholarly type. If that scholarly type also lived in the gym and ate nails for breakfast. It wouldn't surprise me if he fancied himself Clark Kent with a superhero alter ego.

"Do you have a girlfriend?" I pointed at him as he started to smile.

The smile died to be replaced by a combination of startling confusion and a touch of horror.

"I'm not hitting on you. I don't swing that way. And even if I did, you'd have really stiff competition with Mr. Clean. Just…Do you have a girlfriend? A mentee perhaps that's on the younger side. I already know you don't have any sisters or cousins." I loosely gripped the bars as I waited for him to answer.

My breathing was slightly elevated and my palms were sweaty. I belatedly realized what a nutjob I came across as. I shouldn't have had that last energy drink. Oh well, there was nothing to do about it now, except make the energy useful as the caffeine worked its way out of my system.

"Are you asking for our lady friend?" A hint of smugness leaked through his calm and pleasant facade. Because like, no one was that happy when they were a prisoner. Yet, yesterday he'd acted like he was on some kind of solitary retreat where one goes to find themselves. Even after I cut down his hope to get out of the cell.

I scowled. Good thing he showed that interest to me and not Rick. I had a feeling my new bestie would not entertain anyone's attention on our lovely death angel. Not that I liked his interest either, I was just sure I had better impulse control than the big guy.

"No. Answer the question or I'm going back upstairs." I stepped back, crossed my arms, and tapped my foot.

He sighed like I was the biggest pain in his ass. "No. No girlfriend. I'm not really relationship material, if you know what I mean. And no friends outside the Bureau, at least on the young side. Why do you ask?"

Hmm. This was why I wasn't an interrogator. I should

have had an appropriately vague response on the tip of my tongue. *Wouldn't you like to know* wouldn't go over very well, I imagined.

Honesty was the best policy, right? If I gave him some truths, maybe he would share truths in return. Oh hell, hadn't that been his game he had wanted to play last time? A truth for a truth.

"Let's trade truths. I'm ready now." I waited until he nodded before I gave him a truth. In case he decided he didn't want to play that way anymore, I didn't want to give him a freebie.

"Go for it," Channing said with a huge smile as he scooted to the edge of his cot. This was likely the most exciting thing to happen to him in days. Except for Drew's visits apparently. I'd have to ask her what they talked about. Not that I was prying or anything like that, but to fact check him.

Yeah right, Fletcher. You want to know if she flirted with him in that sexy, lethal way of hers.

"There's a woman on the television and online mentioning your dad's name." I waited to see if he would react. He did, just not the way I thought he would.

Expressionless, Channing just shrugged. "So?"

"So?" I eyed him. "Some chick is discussing your father and his *cases*, along with his case files, personal notes? Agenda? And you're just 'so?'"

Yeah, I wasn't buying that.

Sitting forward, he rested his elbows on his knees and clasped his hands as he studied me. "Reed, believe it or not, agents and former agents actually get mentioned in everything from cold cases to active ones to documentaries. Some woman mentioning his name isn't even a blip on the radar."

"Right, so there wouldn't be anything in his private journals that would be worth discussing?"

His expression didn't shift. Either he had the best poker face on the planet or he had no idea what I was talking about.

As it was, he just said, "You asked for a truth for a truth. I gave you one. If you want another…"

I scowled. Dick. "Fine. Ask."

"How'd you meet Drew?"

Of all the questions he could have asked me, that was not the one I expected. I blinked. "Business." Technically true…

"But?"

Yeah, nope. "Business. So, about his private journals?"

Channing exhaled. "What private journals and files he had, I inherited when he passed away. There isn't—" Then he paused.

Uh huh. I zeroed in on that hesitation. "There isn't—?"

"What kind of business did you meet on?"

"Why do you care?"

"Not your turn to ask the questions." The asshole grinned.

I debated my answer. "She saved my life. Happy?"

"How is that business?" Was he for real right now? Some of my outrage must have shown because the former federal jackass grinned wider. "You said you met her on business. What kind of business involves saving your life?"

"The kind that isn't mine to tell. Discretion, it's a thing."

He continued to stare at me until I swore he could see inside my skin. Or maybe he just wanted to. Finally, he nodded and leaned back, folding his arms. "I care because she interests me."

"I didn't—" Fuck. I had.

The man grinned. "What kind of work are you doing these days—at least the part you can talk about?"

"Data collection." Because that was a part of my work. "Who else has access to your father's files and journals?"

The smirk on his face wiped away. Yeah, thought I was going to let you distract me, didn't you? Not just another pretty face over here. "No one."

"Ehhh. Survey says you're lying. Don't pass go, don't

collect two hundred dollars. You want to try that answer again?"

"No one else *should* have access to them."

"Except?" Because there clearly was something he wasn't saying.

He met my stare. "Discretion."

I rolled my eyes. "That means your mother."

A twitch, barely there and gone again. But there. Right eye. The corner of it.

"So, would she give your father's journals to a reporter?"

"It's not your turn."

"Yeah, you lost your turn when you lied. Tick. Tock."

Rolling his head from side to side, Channing cracked his neck before he stood. I didn't move from right in front of the bars as he walked toward me.

"She could," he admitted when he was within arms reach. "Does Drew need me to find out if my mother gave away the journals?" Another twitch to the corner of his eye. Oh, he was not happy about this news.

Glee threaded through me. This was all useful information. "I'll let you know," I said to the last. This close, there was no mistaking anything about his appearance from his sandy blond hair to his blue eyes. The guy needed a shave, but he also had a thousand yard stare that I would never want to see across the table from me in an interrogation room without an attorney present.

You know, fuck that, without Drew present. "What do you want with Drew?"

Tag, Channing. You're it.

The irritation leaked from his face as something like amusement filtered in. "If you remember right, she kidnapped me. You should ask her what she wants with me." He smirked.

Hell, he had me there. But he must have thought I was an idiot not to see that he had some sort of Stockholm syndrome or something. The way his eyes lit up when he asked about her. Even now, those blue babies glittered. Although that could be because he thought he won that round.

"But!" I pointed at him. Shit what was with all the pointing? I forced my hand down. "You were the one who walked out clapping like you'd just found Pamela Anderson jogging toward you on a long stretch of sand, not a day older than her debut role in 1992."

He raised his arms to grip the bars, and I flinched. Hell, that wasn't even that fast. I needed to get a check on my responses where this guy was concerned, or I was going to make him think I was afraid of him. I wasn't. Not even a little bit. It was the caffeine. Maybe Rick had a point. Wait, not the point right now.

"So…*You're* the one who knocked me out," he said slowly as he tucked his chin. That didn't cause goosebumps to erupt over my arms. Those were from the sudden draft in the basement. This was a drafty basement.

My eyes widened. "Drew told me."

He laughed, shaking his head. When he glanced at me with a crooked grin, I stepped back. I was within reaching distance after all, and the last thing I needed was for this guy to knock me out against the bars. I was slender, I didn't need him trying to fit me through the slot so he could hold me hostage.

"I was very good at what I did. And my father was also very good at what he did. Part of what makes us so great is that we're trained to see what people aren't saying with their mouths. That's how you solve cases. You, Fletcher Reed, need to work on your body language. You told me ten different ways you were the one who knocked me out. That's a freebie."

Well, shit. It wasn't like I didn't know I had a terrible poker face. I spent the majority of my time behind the computer screen and not interacting with people. Fuck knew I avoided my family like the plague. "Okay, fine. I was with Drew that night. You still haven't answered why you're so interested in her."

We both had tried to lie. As far as I was concerned, we were back on a level playing field.

He shrugged, rubbing a hand over the thick beard. "The woman is a complicated paradigm. Who wouldn't be intrigued by her?"

"Mmhm," I hummed. There was truth in that, but it wasn't the whole truth. "How did you know she was going to be there that night?"

"I'll tell you the same thing I told her, I didn't." He smiled. "What's the case the reporter is focusing on?"

"How do you know it's a specific case?" I narrowed my gaze on him, making sure to hold my body completely still. *No tells now, mother fucker.*

"You just did. You kept your eyes open unnaturally long." He tried to suppress his grin, but he failed. I didn't believe he tried that hard.

Would Drew want him to have this information? Would I get anything else of value if I told him? I should at least try. If Sandra Jane was enough of a problem for Drew to ask me to look into her, then chances were, it had something to do with this case.

"The entire interview was around the Judge."

Channing's face turned to stone as he straightened. "What was the interviewer's name?"

"Why are you suddenly interested?"

He tilted his head, the heat of his glare as he studied me made me feel like an ant under a magnifying glass. In the desert.

"You know what, it's not important." He turned and walked back to the cot, dropping down like the conversation was over.

That was probably a good idea. Because I had a feeling I just fucked up, and I wasn't even sure how.

VIENNA

NEARLY THIRTY-SIX HOURS after we left, I pulled the car into the garage to park. Grit stung my eyes. My arms, legs, hell all of my muscles ached. Except for my ass. It was numb. Rick had handled the majority of the driving but the call on Martin had taken far more time than I expected.

It had also lasted longer. With a gentle hand, I reached over to touch Rick's thigh. His eyes snapped open. I waited a beat to let him reorient himself. The interior lights of the garage offered enough illumination for me to enjoy his smile when he registered where we were and who I was.

"You should have woken me." The mild reproach was adorable.

"I was fine to drive." I patted his leg and left it at that. I'd needed to think too. Martin's information was a lot to chew over. How much was fact? How much was fiction? How much had been him telling me what he thought would save his life?

As Daddy would say, sleep on it. Then think it through. So, that was what I needed to do. Rick hadn't asked me anything about Martin's comments or explanations. All he asked was, what did I need him to do?

My lower back popped as I climbed out of the car. I needed to walk around a little, then shower, have a glass of wine and then sleep. If I could. I'd half-expected Fletcher to rush out to greet us, but he may not have heard us come in.

Rick removed the bags from the trunk. "Do you want me to take these up to your room?"

"Please," I told him as I grabbed my backpack. A phone began vibrating in the pocket. A part of me wanted to ignore it. That wasn't acceptable. "I'll be inside in a moment. Can you check on Fletcher?"

When we'd called to tell him we were on the way back, he'd seemed very distracted. Rick nodded. "I'll throw him in a shower if he needs it. And get some food ready for us. You need a real meal before you sleep." The last sounded a little bit like a command, but layered in concern.

I smiled. "Thank you, Rick." I waited for him to go inside before I pulled the phone out all the way and checked the screen. Frowning, I hit answer. "Yes?"

"Lily…" The sigh over the line spoke volumes. "I expected to get your voicemail."

Filing that statement away, I leaned against the car. "What's wrong, Reuben?"

He went quiet. Weariness swept over me, I didn't have time for games but history and loyalty were worth something to me, so I waited him out. "Sorry, Lily. I'm going dark for a bit."

I straightened. "How long is a bit?"

"Could be a month. Could be longer. I know it's short notice. Not really telling anyone else but—well, you know the issues that have been happening."

Yes, I did. Far more intimately than he did. Then again, he hadn't said a word about Bailey. Business was business. "Do you have a place to go?"

"Wouldn't tell you if I did, you understand."

"I do."

"Be safe, Lily. Watch your back."

"I always do." Then because he hadn't hung up, I exhaled

around the pressure on my chest. Goodbye was awkward. Not something we usually did. "Try not to gamble on your vacation."

A sharp bark of laughter escaped him. "Now where's the fun in that?" He didn't wait for my answer, just hung up. The number would be dead. When—if—he came back, there would be a message sent through another contact point.

After I erased the phone, I powered it off before sliding out the SIM card. It took no time to smash it with one swift strike of a hammer. I had the tools lined up neatly on the wall. After I scraped the dust and debris into the trash, I headed inside.

No disposer meant I'd have to take care of any future bodies myself.

Thinking of all the ways that would add extra work onto my plate, I headed inside. Rick wasn't in the kitchen where I expected him to be. After weeks of him living here, that seemed to be the one place I could always find him. He must still be checking on Fletcher. Interested in seeing how Fletcher was doing myself, I headed toward the study, pausing only to hang my backpack on the banister heading upstairs.

Low voices carried through the shut door. I knocked twice before pushing it open. Even though this was my house, I had given Fletcher the use of this room as his own and wanted to respect it as such.

Their words stopped abruptly as soon as I stepped in. Rick had his arms crossed, his jaw clenching as he stared Fletcher down. My little pincushion looked wrecked. He had dark circles under his eyes, his hair was a mess and his shirt was crumpled. That might even have been the shirt he was wearing when we left. We should probably be thankful it wasn't stained with two days worth of food.

"I was just telling Fletcher it was time for him to take a shower, then we'd eat a nice meal together," Rick said, but it wasn't a suggestion.

Fletcher tossed his hands up. "I told you big guy, I was waiting for you guys. I'll shower after I talk to Drew." He looked at Rick, raising his eyebrows as if to say *do you mind*? From Rick's continued scowl he very much did mind. "Also, who cooks dinner at ten at night?"

"That's fine," I said as I waved a hand and took a seat on one of the spare chairs. I was battered. I'd rather just hear the update so I could get a full night's sleep. "Rick, do you want to start the food so we can go to bed soon?"

He hesitated, glancing between Fletcher and me. "I'd rather hear the update, if you don't mind?" Rick's voice was soft, like he wasn't sure if I would object. "Can we all move to the kitchen?"

I sighed, and Fletcher fidgeted with the arms of his chair while he twisted from side to side. "Yeah, that's fine."

"Fine, fine. Let's take this party to the kitchen. I could use a glass of wine to wind down anyway." Fletcher was up and out of the office before I made it to my feet. Rick quirked a brow, but I shrugged. He did seem off, but I had no idea why.

In the kitchen, Fletcher had two glasses down and was already halfway through opening a new wine bottle. "So, Sandra Jane. First order of the evening," he started without looking at either me or Rick.

What had happened over the span of thirty-six hours to get his back up so high? I should check the caffeine stash in the house. He could have over done it. Actually, I'd have Rick check it. He knew where all of Fletcher's hiding places were, and I knew he'd already cut it in half a few times.

"Yes, Sandra Jane, investigative reporter." I took a half full glass from his hand and leaned back against the counter, making sure to stay out of the way as Rick started pulling pre-cut veggies and eggs out of the fridge.

"From what I can tell, she's squeaky clean. Twenty-six years old. Practically a babe when it comes to that industry. She's had a couple decent breakthroughs on clearing up old cold cases, but that's it. Sandra Jane has impeccable credit, driving record, and school attendance. When she was in school that is. As far as the world's concerned she's a perfect, upstanding citizen who does her best to put the bad guys away." Fletcher took his time putting a stopper in the wine, then cleaning up the mess of the wrapper and cork. When he finally brought his gaze to mine, I thought he'd have a revelation for me.

"And?" I prompted impatiently. I was dragging and needed to get to bed sooner rather than later.

"Nothing. In my experience, when someone's that clean, there's something big and nasty they're hiding in the closet, like a weird fetish, childhood trauma, or crime. But with Sandra Jane, she's as clean as they come. I also cross referenced a few of my resources and no one has any information on her that's not squeaky clean." He started to open his mouth then stopped, shooting a glare at Rick. When I glanced over, Rick was busy whipping up omelets and pulling the bread out for toast.

What was with these two tonight?

"Okay, that's good enough for me…for now. Did anything happen while we were gone?" I sipped the wine, enjoying the full-bodied sweetness rolling around my tongue. It went a long way toward easing my tension.

"Well…" Fletcher cast his gaze toward the ceiling and twisted his lips to the side like he really had to think about it.

I lowered my wine glass. "Pincushion?" The nickname slipped out and he glanced at me. Despite the earlier agitation and the shadows beneath his eyes, he seemed almost genuinely forlorn. "I know you're tired, we all are."

Honestly, I probably wouldn't have pushed for the information, but he had seemed so insistent. All at once Fletcher grimaced.

"You're exhausted," he said, narrowing the distance between us. At this distance, at least I could tell he had showered even if he hadn't bothered with changing his clothes. "I'm sorry. I should have just waited until tomorrow except…"

Hand half-raised as though he'd meant to touch me, my little pincushion hesitated again. This wouldn't do. I caught his fingers in my free hand and pressed his palm to my cheek. Yes, I could smell some of the chips he'd eaten earlier, but there was a faintly orange stain on his shirt—not his hands.

Relief bled into his eyes and some of the tension binding him up like so much corded wood eased. "I talked to the Fed."

Behind him, Rick stiffened as he settled the pan on the stove. Despite the lightness of the action, the faint bang of metal on metal carried. Affection vied with annoyance. Rick wanted to protect me, maybe Fletcher had mentioned talking to Morgan earlier and Rick wanted to wait until morning.

Clearly not an option if it was bothering Fletcher so much. I kept my attention on the man directly in front of me. Both of us held wine glasses we were somewhat ignoring. The tendrils of his dark hair escaped the confinement of the bun he'd dragged it up into, as though with an impatient hand. The same one that had probably gone to rake through it and pulled tendrils free.

He sighed. "I know Rick said I didn't have to talk to him, and I did actually wear headphones the first couple of times I took down meals. I just… I had some questions."

"About?" I kept my tone mild. Fletcher's emotions were all over the place, but my calmness seemed to help him relax. That was important. The warmth of his hand on my cheek and the way he shifted the touch so that he could press two of his fingers behind my ear had me tilting my head as much as his height did.

"He wanted to play a truth game. You know a truth for a truth, and I wanted to ask him about something I'd seen in one of Sandra Jane's reports."

I waited.

Fletcher seemed at war with something, but he finally bowed his head and moved a little closer until he could rest his forehead to mine and after he put his wine glass on the counter, he settled his now free hand on my hip. "I probably should have waited for you, but I wanted to get you all the information. Especially if it involved his girlfriend or something."

"Does our guest know Sandra Jane?" Something unfamiliar unfurled within me at the suggestion. Our guest and the reporter? They were dating?

The rich scent of grilling vegetables and eggs wreathed the air. Exhaustion vied with the need for knowledge and my stomach pinched. Rick had been right about us needing a meal. But the discomfort moving through me had nothing to do with hunger or the long car ride or even the endless hours without real rest.

Not sleeping while on the job was a habit. Fletcher grimaced. "I'm sorry. This is a terrible way to welcome you home," he said. "It can probably wait."

"Tell me," I sighed as I set my own glass on the counter and curled my hands over his shoulders. "Now that I know there's something more you want to share, I won't be able to get to sleep anyway."

He closed his eyes and kissed the tip of my nose as if in apology. "Shit. I'm sorry. I dangled the proverbial carrot in front of your face then tried to yank it back. I hate when people do that to me." Scooting forward he molded his body to mine and twined his arms around me in a tight grip. I didn't say anything, I just let him hold me. He seemed like he needed it, and I had missed him too.

After a few moments, he stepped back, leaving his hands on my hips. "Our friendly neighborhood Fed doesn't know her."

Relief swept through me and I relaxed further. Given the

nature of why she'd hit Uncle David's radar, I didn't want to believe Mr. Morgan was working with her. Or worse, involved with her. I'd watched a brief clip of her interview from last year, and she seemed too tenacious and pretentious for who I would picture him going after.

"But… I've been watching all of her interviews and her most recent, mentioned a late FBI agent named Casey Morgan." He paused, waiting for my response.

I blinked, the fog in my brain dissipating as I realized what this meant. The journalist had a connection to Channing Morgan, whether he knew it or not. That could mean so many things. I'd have to question him myself on if he knew her.

"In fact, he seemed irritated that she had the journals. When I questioned him on how she could have gotten them, he wouldn't really say, except that he had inherited all of his dad's personal items. He did allude to his mother possibly having access."

"That's troubling." I picked up my glass to take another sip of wine while I mulled this new information over.

"That's what I wanted to tell you. About this possible connection. For what it's worth, he genuinely seemed unhappy that she had them," Fletcher added as if that would make me feel better.

I nodded. This wasn't something I needed to act on tonight. Sandra Jane wasn't going to solve the mystery of the Judge overnight, and Channing Morgan wasn't going to escape either. I'd revisit this once I was rested.

"Food is ready," Rick said, his tone soft and soothing as he slid the plates across the counter. "Eat here or in the living room?"

"Here," I said, moving to stand at the island. Tonight wasn't for a long meal and conversation. This was fuel to fill the body before we climbed into bed.

We ate in silence, and once we were finished, I headed up to take a shower while Rick and Fletcher took care of the dishes. The hot spray of water went a long way toward loosening up the tight muscles from spending so much time in the car. I probably spent a little too long in the shower but when I got out, I was in a much better state of mind.

Rick was turning down the covers as I stepped into the bedroom, his hair wet and clad only in a pair of boxer briefs. He'd probably taken a quick shower in one of the other rooms. I stepped up to the other side and stopped. Fletcher would probably sleep much better if he slept here with us. The difference I'd noticed in him the day after I'd slept with him was astounding, and he looked like he could use another full night of rest.

"Would you…" I started.

Shooting me a tired smile, Rick shook his head. "I don't mind. I'll go get him." He pivoted on his heel just as a quick knock came at the door.

"I know you're all probably exhausted. I am too. It's too damn quiet without either of you here," Fletcher called from the other side of the door. "I'd…I'd uh…Do you think there's room for me—" his words cut off as Rick opened the door.

Fletcher nearly fell through, but Rick steadied him with a hand to his chest. "I'll take the side closest to the door," Rick informed him as he came back to the bed. His hair was also wet. He probably felt like he should clean up before joining us, which was a good thing. Where Rick was in his briefs, Fletcher wore boxers and a T-shirt. The sight of them ready for bed pulled a smile to my lips.

The side closest to the door was usually my spot. But with both Rick and Fletcher, it did make sense I'd take the middle. Fletcher grinned at Rick's back as he came around to where I was. "I knew you liked me, Big Guy."

We settled in with Rick pressed against my side as Fletcher draped a loose arm around my waist. With both of them close, I slipped further into sleep quicker than I ever had before. I didn't even mind the extra body heat.

HEAT, like that on a summer's day in the south of New Mexico, blanketed my back. I swore I could tilt my head back and the sun would blind me. As it was, tilting my head back only earned me a nuzzling kiss at my throat and a hand drifting up my abdomen to cup a breast.

That snapped my eyes open to the gray light of pre-dawn in the bedroom. We hadn't drawn the curtains when we went to bed, but the shades kept the light muted. The massage of strong fingers moved over the shape of my breast.

A shift in breathing and the very real evidence of two erections pressing against me from either side gave me all kinds of ideas. I was completely surrounded, enveloped in them—sharp pleasure jolted through me as Fletcher pinched the nipple he'd been caressing and twisted it gently. The fabric of my shirt wasn't much of a barrier.

Rick's slumbering face filled my vision as I rolled my hips back and ground them against Fletcher's dick where it pressed right against my ass. The faintest push of the piercing was different where the tip rubbed on me. A delicious shudder went through me. Oh, I had enjoyed that piercing.

With a series of hot, open-mouthed kisses, Fletcher traveled from my throat to my jaw. He had his free arm beneath my head and the moment I half-twisted, he wrapped it around me and then our mouths collided.

Morning breath be damned. The combination of alternating caresses and pinches against that one nipple, the warmth of his arm curling around my head while he plundered my mouth with his, filled me with a kind of dreamy euphoria.

Moaning softly, I sucked on his tongue when he went to retreat, playfully trapping him as I teased the piercing. Oh, I still wondered what that would feel like on my cunt.

The bed moved next to us and I cracked my eyes open mid-kiss to find Fletcher gazing past me. Fresh warmth pushed up against my front. Rick's erection prodded my belly and I twisted to find him staring at me, and then Fletcher, then back to me.

"Do you want me to watch this time?" He rumbled in a voice thick with sleep. An unspoken 'or' dangled off the end of that question. Yes, I wanted Rick's eyes on us, but I wanted more than that.

Fletcher loosened his grip as I shifted, but I caught his hand before it could leave my breast and clasped my hand over his as I stretched toward Rick. His eyes seemed to glow in the half-light, the intensity of the blue had my cunt clenching all over again.

I locked my lips over his as I continued to grind against Fletcher. His muttered, "Thank fuck," was nearly lost under Rick's demanding growl. I let go of Fletcher's hand to reach behind me and in between grinding against him, I teased his cock through his shorts with my fingers.

Hot, thick fingers pressed under my panties, Rick's touch unmistakable and unhesitating as he massaged my clit. Fuck, I was already soaking. Another moan escaped me as I chased his fingers before he thrust two of them up into me.

Rick's thickness always pressed me so close to the point of pain, but the stretch of his fingers only echoed that sensation. Fletcher pumped against my hand then my ass as he continued to tease my breasts. He returned to my throat with more hot kisses as Rick plundered my mouth with his tongue and my cunt with his fingers.

Need writhed through me. I wanted them both. I skated my free hand up Rick's chest to his hair, then I fisted it. He bit down on my lower lip, almost a chastisement as I dragged my mouth from his. He pressed his thumb against my clit as he thrust his fingers upward and curled them.

The motion coordinated beautifully with Fletcher's torment of my nipples. Somehow, he'd gotten his hands under my shirt and I was writhing between his sharp, stinging pinches and twists, that he soothed with caring, massages of his palms. The contrasting and competing sensations swarmed through me, swelling that bubble of pleasure until it burst.

A startled cry escaped my lips as the most unexpected orgasm racked through me. Rick's fingers slipped away and I moaned, almost sobbing at their loss as much as the loss of Fletcher's fingers on my breasts.

Two pairs of male hands were on my panties and then they were ripping. What a magnificent fucking sound. "Fuck her," Rick ordered in a low voice that had my cunt clenching at emptiness even as a fresh rush of heat rushed to slick my already damp thighs.

"My pleasure," Fletcher answered. It was all the warning I received before he nudged the pierced tip against the entrance of my cunt. Someone curled their hand against my thigh, lifting my leg as Fletcher slammed into me.

A grunt and cry of pleasure escaped me as Rick's mouth claimed mine again. He didn't hold the wet kiss for long, pulling back and looking down the length of my body. I glanced down, following his gaze. Even though I could feel—reveled in the sensation—of Fletcher's thrusts and the strike of that piercing deep inside, it was something else to watch him taking me.

"Harder," Rick ordered. "Make Vienna feel it... she wants to feel you."

I lifted my eyes to find Rick's gaze on me again. It pinned me there, hot, needy, and demanding. I licked my lips as I curled one arm up and behind me to stroke Fletcher's hair. His hips pistoned forward with more force, the slam was enough to make me see stars.

"You can feel me, can't you, Drew?" Harsh and raw, it was an echo of my own need. I wrapped my free hand around Rick's cock. Bless him, he'd lost his boxer briefs somewhere and he pressed against my palm as he ripped my shirt. The masculine show of force was really doing something to me.

Fletcher lapped at my tongue, stealing my cries as Rick replaced his hands on my breasts with his mouth and then he sucked hard against one nipple, dragging it against his teeth. The unbearable tension expanded within me before it exploded. I came with a scream that seemed to drive Fletcher even harder, but his stuttering hips included hot jets of release flooding into me.

We clung there, suspended for what seemed like endless seconds as the pleasure crashed over me. The bump of his hips as Fletcher gave shallow little thrusts captivated me. It was like we strained to be closer even as he softened.

"Vienna." The demand in Rick's voice couldn't be ignored and Fletcher released my lips as I turned to find Rick staring at me, his lower lip wet from where he'd run his tongue over it. Like I was being pulled forward, I slid from Fletcher and then pushed Rick onto his back.

My cunt was already missing Fletcher, but I didn't slow as I straddled Rick, lined him up and with Fletcher's hands on my hips—we thrust downward and I took Rick in one fierce push that threatened to overwhelm me. The hot, hard length of his cock pulsed within me and I was right, his fingers really had nothing on his girth.

"Oh yeah," Fletcher exhaled as he ran his hands up my sides to my breasts. "How do you want her, Big Guy?"

Rick grunted and didn't take his gaze away from mine. Now that he was inside me, stretching me so completely, he seemed to have lost his desire to talk.

"Got it. Got it. Hell, this is so hot. I hope you don't mind, I'm going to take some liberties." Fletcher pinched my nipples and kissed up the side of my neck. Rick ran his hands up my thighs, digging his fingers in where they met my hips.

I sucked in a breath from all the sensations. So many hands…

Fletcher shifted until he straddled Rick's legs and dropped his hands to my waist. I was rolling against Rick, but with Fletcher's interference, he lifted me almost to the tip, then slammed my back down.

My hands fell to Rick's chest as we both groaned from the unexpected friction. After a beat, Fletcher repeated the action again. Then again.

His shirt-covered chest pressed against my back as he murmured against the crook of my neck. "This feels good doesn't it, Drew? Taking Rick's huge cock but at my pace. Have you ever thought about taking us both at the same time?"

Heat flared in Rick's icy blue eyes at Fletcher's words, and my pussy clenched around him. Had I thought about it? I was thinking about it now. Fletcher dropped one hand to circle the rosette and I squeezed Rick again.

"I bet you don't have any lube in here, do you?" Of course, he asked. I couldn't have answered him if I wanted to with Rick taking over our rhythm, using one hand over my lower stomach and one clutching the side of my hip to grind me against him in the most delicious way. Every slide of my clit over his cock ignited a new round of sparks in my core.

Fletcher was gone and back within seconds, flicking open a lid as he climbed back on the bed behind me. "I've thought about it. Since we first kissed, I've dreamed of what it would be like to share you with Rick in a position just like this. I've never done this before. It would be my first..." His hand pressed between my shoulder blades, guiding me down until I was chest to chest with Rick, who moved his hands to my back.

I caught Rick's lips in a hard kiss, amped up from the intense swirl of possession Fletcher's words erupted inside me. I wanted to be *this* first for him. I wanted this first from Rick too.

Cool liquid dribbled down my ass as a finger circled and pressed in. "I want Rick to hold you just like this while I slide into you from behind." He pushed his finger inside, alternating his own movements with Rick's, mimicking what it would feel like to have them both inside me.

Shit. The alien pressure was heating me up from the inside. This wasn't anything I'd ever wanted or thought about it, but with Rick and Fletcher, I needed it. I needed this connection to both of them at the same time.

I rocked against them as Rick swallowed all of my pleasure.

"Not today. We have to work up to this, but soon. Right, Big Guy?" Fletcher rubbed his other hand over my lower back, while he twisted and thrust into my ass.

Rick growled his agreement, sinking his tongue into my mouth, twirling it against mine as he started to buck harder underneath me.

"Oh yeah, fuck her harder. Just like that," Fletcher moved his free hand to the outside of my thigh, gripping me so tight it nearly pinched.

That crest was coming up fast as Fletcher pushed a second finger inside, scissoring and twisting.

I fell first, twitching and milking everything Rick had to give. My orgasm triggered his as his low growl turned into a deep groan. He pulsed as he spilled inside me, hugging me so tight to his chest I couldn't breathe. I didn't even care.

The time it took to come down was much longer than with Fletcher. With both of them working my body every sensation was more intense, overwhelming. Rick recovered quicker than me, content to rub soothing circles over my back as his hips flexed every so often, like he refused to give up our connection.

At some point, Fletcher left again, because he came back with a warm, wet washcloth, swiping away any excess fluid from my ass and thighs. "We can get you better cleaned up once Rick's dick decides to go down."

My face is pressed against Rick's neck, but his body stiffened. I could imagine the glare he shot Fletcher. And Fletcher's shit-eating grin.

"Hey, I'm not complaining. And now that I see how well Drew responded to that, I'd say a nice sandwich is in our future. What do you say?" He leaned down and pressed a kiss to my shoulder as he squeezed my ass.

I laughed, not able to muster up any irritation with Fletcher for being…him. The multiple orgasms went a long way too.

Pulling his hips back, Rick slipped out and slid me off to the side. He smoothed hair off of my face and kissed my forehead. "I'm going to go start breakfast and coffee. You stay here and rest as long as you want. If you're not down when it's done, I'll bring you a plate." He gave me one more lingering kiss to my lips and got out of bed. Fletcher was quick to finish cleaning me up before pulling the covers back into some semblance of normalcy.

I shamelessly watched Rick slide his briefs back on over his taut ass, and belatedly realized Fletcher was still naked from the waist down. When he noticed my attention, he looked down and cursed.

"Shit, I forgot I had a T-shirt on. At least you were facing

Rick the whole time. That would have been unsexy if you'd been facing me in just a sleep shirt." He had his boxers on in record time. "I need to check on a few things in the lair. Thank you. For letting me sleep with you two last night, and for the spectacular morning festivities," he whispered through a grin and pressed his lips to my cheek. The circles beneath his eyes were gone, and there was a lightness in his expression I was happy to see. Inviting him in with us had been the right thing to do. For many reasons.

Once they were both gone, I stretched. I could never go back to sleep after I woke up for the day. As it was, the post coital haze was already slipping away as too many thoughts vied for my attention.

I couldn't decide if I wanted to check in with Uncle David first, or go down and see Mr. Morgan. They were both equally important, and I wasn't looking forward to either.

That was what I told myself.

Tilting my head back against the pillows, I stared up at the ceiling. No matter what I did, I needed to shower first. Uncle David could wait. Shoving the blankets back, I rolled out of the bed. I glanced at the rumpled covers and smiled. Rick would want to deal with the sheets and everything later and I kind of wanted to savor the wildness of the morning.

Decided, I left it and wandered into the shower, loose-limbed and relaxed. Yes, Uncle David could wait. Shower. Breakfast with the boys, then Mr. Morgan. Business could wait just a bit longer.

Just a bit.

CASH

BREAKFAST CAME courtesy of the big guy, who collected the dinner tray and dropped off the breakfast one. He gave me a once over, then said, "I'll bring everything down later for you to wash up."

"Yep." I didn't bother with going for more conversation. This guy wasn't going to crack. Besides, I wanted—*Drew*—yeah, she deserved a far sexier name than that. "Can't wait."

I called the last as he closed the door and the sound of his feet on the stairs told me he wasn't sticking around.

Two days. At least two days they were gone. I couldn't tell time by anything but the meals. Most days I got two, the first day they were gone, I got three. Maybe because Reed hadn't been aware of the big guy's breakfast schedule.

What the Hell had Reed called him? I couldn't remember the precise wording, but the big guy was an excellent cook. Something I was already intimately aware of. Speaking of which, I gave the bristle of my three-day's growth of beard a good scratch before I claimed the new tray.

Hot fluffy pancakes, grilled sausage, scrambled eggs and a cup of milk and another cup of orange juice. There was even butter and maple syrup, but only a spoon to eat with.

That amused me.

I cleared the plate in no time, washing most of it down with milk, then set the orange juice to the side. After I moved the tray back over to the bars, I used water from the sink to wash my face, hands, and mouth.

After, I stripped out of my shirt—because why get it sweaty?—then went through the morning training regimen I'd worked out. After breakfast, I would stretch. Then a hundred pushups, followed by a hundred sit-ups, followed by jumping jacks and lunges. Some days, I actually added burpees. It wasn't the perfect regimen and sometimes it had downright fucking sucked.

But I needed to keep up my stamina and my strength. I sure as hell wasn't getting out of this cell on my good looks and my charm. Not yet, anyway.

I'd just moved into lunges when the soft sound of a step got my attention. I was a little flushed, and my breathing wasn't as even as I would have liked. "It's a little early for my bath," I commented when the door swung open. "You said this aftern—"

The rest of the word died unspoken. My dark saint had returned. She stood there, head cocked as she gave me a once over. The lack of expression didn't give me any insight into her opinion on my physique.

That was fine. I'd worked miracles with less feedback.

She wore a pale, cream-colored button-up sleeveless top. It was tucked into a high-waisted pair of black pants that I would have called yoga but these looked like they'd been painted on. Her cute little feet were bare, as were her toe nails.

The soft fall of her hair gleamed, even in the shitty lights down here. Then there were her eyes. Fuck me sideways, I'd never forget those golden-brown eyes, no matter what happened. They made me think of everything from a faerie to a wolf shifter, and I didn't really go for that fantasy crap.

Except Tolkien. That was classic. Not crap.

"Mr. Morgan," she said in that sultry, come hither voice and my dick stood right the fuck up to attention. That was the problem. She was darkness, light, and desire all rolled into one perfect little package. My dark saint. "I presume you have finished your breakfast."

It wasn't a question and since my tray sat right there by the bars, I didn't see a need to address it. Instead, I resumed my lunges. "Welcome back. Good trip?"

She cocked her head and didn't go for the chair. Disappointment hit at the thought that she wouldn't be staying long. Maybe if I teased her enough with information, she'd want to stay. Or not. While she looked in a decent mood, I didn't get the feeling she enjoyed that type of relationship.

"What gave that away?" She lifted one sharp eyebrow as her lips tilted up in an alluring smile.

Okay, this was good. My dark saint wasn't trying to hide that she was gone. Maybe it meant she was trusting me more, or it could mean she never planned to let me out. I was focusing on the bright side in this particular scenario. I'd been a good prisoner after all.

"Your boy, who brings the food down, was gone. He consistently brings the food. I get the feeling he takes pride in that and he wouldn't miss an opportunity to do it if he was here." I wiped the sweat off my brow with my forearm as I stalked close to the bars. I didn't touch them. I didn't want to risk scaring her like Reed, but I also didn't believe she scared easily. She wouldn't, she was too confident in who she was and her role in the world. It was written all over her plain as day.

Her gaze drifted down and I brazenly flexed my abs. What was left of them after all this good food anyway. Luckily, I'd just finished my workout, so I had the swoll going on. She lingered over the defined muscle before slowly bringing that mesmerizing gaze back to mine.

Gotcha. She wasn't as unaffected as she'd like to act. I'd have to start leaving my shirt off. And working out more. Hell, it wasn't like I had anything better to do. I'd just have to convince the big guy to let me shower more often. And bring deodorant.

"I take it you were treated well?" She crossed her arms. The move pushed her tits up and it took an act of God not to look. I didn't need her to think I was hitting on her. That would be very counterproductive to my goals, unless she blatantly hit on me first.

Grinning, I grabbed the bars above my head, making sure to continue tightening my muscles, just in case she was curious. She wasn't. Damn it.

"Yes. Mr. Fletcher Reed was a great host. He brought me food. Kept me company…" I hesitated, not sure how far I wanted to push her. Especially as her expression cooled considerably when I said his name. "And gave quite a bit away."

Drew stepped back, and I lost my grin.

"How do you know his name?" Suspicion shrouded her entire being, even if she didn't show any physical signs. It was all in her eyes.

"Do *you* know who he is?" I had thought, as at least one half of the Judge, she'd have done better research on the ones she let into her house. Then again, she hadn't shared much of herself with them, so I could have been wrong, as much as it pained me to admit.

Unsurprisingly, Drew didn't answer.

"A truth for a truth," I started, and kept going. This would hopefully be good enough intel that she would be compelled to play. "That man's family is notorious for their wealth and their fame. Not all of it is from legitimate sources. As part of that family, there's probably very few in certain circles who wouldn't recognize his face."

"And what circles are those?" The chill of her words bit at me.

"Law enforcement for one. The upper echelon of society

for another. Now your turn, beautiful Drew. What's your truth for that payment?"

Saying her name was a gamble. I didn't like it for her name, but fuck it. I'd already told her Reed gave a lot away. Her expression didn't even flicker. "I didn't agree to your game."

"True," I said, tipping my head when she locked gazes with me. "But you're not walking away and you're not dismissing me." Just staying wasn't enough. "Tell me something true. I'm in a cell and not going anywhere fast. Who am I going to tell what you tell me?"

She snorted. Not a delicate, gentle snort. No this was a full-on derisive go fuck yourself kind of snort. My kind of lady. I grinned.

"You're not half as clever as you think you are," she informed me.

"Story of my life, pretty lady, story of my life. But you're still here."

"For the moment."

"Accepted."

But we were at an impasse. No matter how much I craved the way her gaze had flickered over me earlier, now I needed to batter down that barrier before she finished erecting it. She was already shutting me out.

"If you can't figure out what truth to tell me, let's call it answering a question."

"Why would you believe any answer I gave you?"

"Because if you were just going to lie, you would have done it already. I've given you plenty of opportunities to lie to me. You haven't. You haven't chosen to answer or tell me anything, if at all. But you haven't just flat out lied to me."

The corner of her mouth curved upward and something like amusement flickered through her eyes. "Interesting observation."

"I'm full of a lot of them."

"You're full of something."

I chuckled. "I could say something crude."

"But you won't."

No, I wouldn't, so I just nodded my head.

She glanced away from me, her expression thoughtful. The distraction allowed me a solid view of her profile, the slight upturn to her nose, the softness of her chin, and the curve of her cheek. Even the corded muscles of—was that a hickey?

Then she glanced back at me again. "Two questions."

I raised my brows. "Clarify the terms and be specific please. Also, that's not a question."

"No," she said slowly, amusement bleeding into her expression. "It wasn't."

Good. We agreed.

"For clarification," she continued. "I will answer two questions. And only two. Choose your questions wisely. I do not believe you will receive this offer again."

You don't, huh? I didn't say that, but I considered my options. Pushing away from the bars, I let her have my back as I walked over to reclaim the orange juice. After uncapping it, I took a sip. The sweetness of the juice combined with the tart was kind of a nice change from all the water.

Though, the forced clearance of coffee and alcohol was probably something my doctor would appreciate. Instead of hurrying me along, Drew waited patiently as I debated what I wanted to ask.

"First question," I said finally. "What's your name? Your real name."

"You don't think it's Drew?"

"That's not an answer. Then I don't have to tell you that." I grinned. "Before you go, 'well then why did you call me that, Mr. Morgan?' in that sexy as fuck voice of yours, I said it because I like talking to you. Consider that a freebie."

The half-smile curving her mouth became a full one, just

briefly, but fuck me. It was so worth it. "Vienna," she said finally. "My name is Vienna."

Vienna.

Oh, that was so much better than Drew. Fuck, I didn't even care *why* Reed called her that. But Vienna made me think of the mystery and allure of the Alps and the jewel of Austria. I'd never been much for traveling outside the country, but I had actually been to Austria as part of an international law enforcement cooperative.

"I like that." I nodded. "It's a beautiful name for a beautiful woman."

That got a roll of her eyes.

"Not my best work."

The bland look made me grin. Narrowing the distance between us, I walked up to the bars.

"Second question."

She waited.

"Reed has no idea you're one half of the Judge. Does the big guy? Or are you lying to him too?"

A bomb might as well have dropped between us. Because she was no longer accessible to me. Her expression completely shut down and I almost rushed to take my question back. But that wasn't my style, and every interaction with her was a learning experience.

From the way she reacted, I expected her to turn around and walk that pretty ass back up those steps. But she didn't. So, a win?

"You said you believe I'm part of the Judge. What do you know about the Judge, Mr. Morgan?" Her voice was like a whip being struck between us.

I decided to answer because as much as I learned, I still didn't want her to be angry with me. Then she would forget about me down here. "You're the definition of a vigilante killer. You only attack those who have wronged society and, due to their political or affluent standing, have avoided justice."

"What kind of character do you think the Judge would have?"

Oh, fuck. This was a trick question. A high moral standing with the exception of a fuckton of gray areas. Which didn't bother me, I practically lived in the gray area. But beautiful Vienna could be offended depending on how I phrased it. "The Judge would have a strong moral compass to save so many lives."

When in doubt, go vague. It worked in many situations.

She nodded, slightly mollified, but her full, pouty lips were still pinched. "Both of my men know exactly what it is I do. And that is all you need to know."

Ah, but that was cutting corners on the answer. I tilted my head, having too much fun to let her get away with it. "I had quite the conversation with Reed. He may know you take down the bad guys, but he doesn't know you're part of an infamous duo of serial killers." Which made me think there was no one else in the house. Where was the other half?

She scowled when I labeled her, but facts were facts. Someone who committed a series of murders was a serial killer. "Don't you think that would matter to him? Even if he's not like his family, he may still wish to know the woman he's in bed with."

Her chest expanded on a short, but deep inhale.

So, she was sleeping with Reed... That was unfortunate. Were they serious or fuck buddies who benefited from each other's professional services? I just couldn't see someone like Vienna with someone like him. It didn't make sense.

If I had to choose between either of the guys, the big one seemed more like her type. He seemed like he could be a scary mother fucker if you disliked his cooking.

"I don't expect you to answer that question. I only get two and that was really more food for thought anyway...So back to—Does the big guy know who you really are?" I asked, lowering my voice so I didn't come across as demanding or abrasive.

Over the span of one moment, I witnessed what I was sure was an extreme moment of vulnerability for her. Something, given her strong personality I doubted many if any, ever got to see.

A plethora of emotions played across her features as she turned her head slightly to the side, while still keeping her gaze pinned to mine. Confusion, anger, surprise. Maybe a hint of righteousness and a spark of embarrassment. There were too many to name.

"No. He doesn't know of the Judge." Then, like I had hoped she wouldn't, she closed the door over the bars and left.

I had better get started on another round of sit-ups and push-ups. I'd add in some squats and mountain climbers for good measure. If I was going to get on her good side after royally pissing her off, she needed all the eye candy I could give her. Especially because she claimed both Reed and the big guy. "My men," she'd said.

Yep, time to increase the workout.

RICK

TODAY WAS a comfort food kind of day. If only for the fact that Vienna seemed a little off. I didn't like it and while food wouldn't fix it, I could damn well make sure it went a long way toward giving her a good experience.

And dining was an experience.

The previous morning had been amazing. While sharing Vienna had never been on my bucket list, I didn't hate it like I thought I would. Most men wanted to experience a threesome in their life, and while I didn't hate the idea, I thought I would have been more possessive of Vienna than that.

But when it actually happened, it didn't matter who was touching her. The only thing I cared about was how much pleasure she received. A Vienna in the throes of passion was a beautiful sight to behold, and I wasn't ashamed to admit, she lost herself to the pleasures of sex much easier and quicker with four hands and two dicks, instead of the typical two and one. And to see us wrapped around her small but strong body? My cock filled at the idea of a repeat.

Fletcher seemed like a kinky fucker, coming back with lube. Vienna hadn't mentioned it, but who takes lube on what they believed was a short stay without a partner?

Or had he hoped to sleep with Vienna all along? Of

course, he had. He was an irrepressible flirt at his apartment when she wouldn't let me kill him. I didn't mind so much now that she hadn't given me the go-ahead.

He strolled into the kitchen, and I scowled at him without any of the heat I might have given him a week ago.

"Hey now." He held his hands up. "I made sure to put the toilet seat down and I wiped up all the pee dribble you lectured me about last week when I used Vienna's bathroom this morning. Why are you looking at me like Jack could have fit on the door with Rose? And spoiler, he totally could have."

I had no idea what he was talking about, but my lips twitched anyway. "I was thinking about you having lube in your room and why you would have it."

Fletcher stopped next to me at the island and snickered. "Oh, that. I carry some everywhere, along with a few other items. I'd rather be safe than sorry."

"So, you weren't hoping to sleep with Vienna?"

"Oh, I absolutely was, and it was better than anything I could have dreamed up. You're not so bad yourself there, Big Guy." He slapped me on the back, then stole a cheese fry from the platter.

I laughed and he joined in. Yeah, this had been nothing like what I had expected when I first came home with Vienna, but I couldn't say I didn't enjoy it. Fletcher accepted me in his own way, just like Vienna did. That was something I never had before.

"So, are you trying to kill our cholesterol in one go?" He motioned to the plate of cheese fries with bacon and scallions on top, and the burgers I was putting together with sauteed onions and melted Monterey Jack. I also had chili on the side, if anyone was so inclined.

"No. I was hoping to give Vienna something to smile about." I frowned down at the burgers as I added lettuce and tomato to each one. We had to have *some* vegetables to go with the cheese and red meat.

Fletcher stepped closer and lowered his voice. "Yeah, she is out of it, isn't she? I don't think I've seen anything on her face except a dark thunder cloud since she went to see our friend downstairs." He straightened his shoulders and looked toward the sink, his hands twitching down his shirt. I wasn't sure what they were doing but it was a T-shirt. There were no buttons to mess with.

How suspicious of Fletcher.

"What do you think he could have said that upset her?" I asked as I put the top bun on each burger. Perfect. We were ready to eat now. I'd already sent Vienna a text about ten minutes ago letting her know it would be done soon. If I didn't see her in two minutes, I'd take a plate to her so her food wouldn't get cold.

"I have no clue," Fletcher said morosely as he dug his fingers in his hair and scratched the side of his head. It remained poofed up when he dropped his hand.

"You have some idea," I persisted. Fletcher was a ball of ecstatic energy. For him to be this beat down meant something happened.

"What did you say to him while we were gone?" I turned to face him fully.

"Big guy, it wasn't so much what I said. I think it might be what I didn't say…I'm really not fucking sure. He's smart as shit. I was mainly worried about Sandra Jane…" he trailed off.

I clocked Vienna's arrival without turning. She'd gone upstairs after breakfast, and closed the door to her room. I presumed to work but I didn't want to disturb her.

"Food smells good."

"Everything Rick does smells good," Fletcher announced and then he gave me a look. "Just, don't take that as an invitation."

"Wouldn't dream of it," I told him easily, then nodded to the platter with the fries. "Take that to the table."

"On it." He practically leapt into motion, so grateful for something to do. Vienna, glanced at me, studying me with a silent question in her eyes. I couldn't quite decipher it though, so I waited.

Finally, she asked, "What would you like me to carry?"

My first response was to say "nothing," but she wouldn't have asked if she didn't want a task. "If you could get the lemonade from the fridge, the glasses are already at the table."

"You made lemonade?" For a moment, a familiar spark filled those gorgeous tawny eyes of hers. My chest expanded and I smiled. That expression was exactly what I'd been hoping for.

"I thought it would be a nice change and it would pair well with the burgers and the chili."

She lifted out the pitcher with a little smile on her face and then paused to press a kiss to my cheek. "You spoil me, Rick."

"It's my pleasure," I told her, firm in that conviction. It had been since our first encounter in the alley.

Something like sadness touched that smile and I wanted to stamp it out. She opened her mouth as if to say something and Fletcher leaned around the doorway. "Big Guy, Hot Stuff, I'm dying of hunger out here and if I eat all those fries, Rick will get me before the heart attack does."

I frowned at the new nickname and Vienna gave him a very bland look.

"Not a fan of Hot Stuff?" He grinned, it was both cocky and playful. Vienna's soft laughter was a testament to that. I could live with the name if she was smiling again.

"Not really," she said after a moment.

"Okay, Drew, but—I'm still fainting from hunger and Rick took away all of my snacks."

"Good," she said and shot me a look of gratitude along with a smile. She didn't need to thank me for looking after Fletcher. I wasn't entirely certain how he'd survived this long, to be honest. His idea of diet was atrocious, he didn't work out regularly, and he drank far too much caffeine.

But he made Vienna smile and he wasn't a bad companion, so I would look after him if he wouldn't look after himself. It wasn't until we were all seated around the table that the weight of Vienna's mood blanketed us again.

Fletcher gave me a look then jerked his head at Vienna as if to tell me to do something. Though she'd done all the perfunctory motions of eating from loading up her plate to thanking me for the meal, she'd barely taken more than a bite.

A sigh escaped her. "Boys…"

Fear clenched like a fist around my heart and it was my turn to shoot a look at Fletcher. His expression mirrored my own worry, so we both looked at her.

"I need to talk to you both about something." Instead of continuing, she paused long enough that the need to go downstairs and throttle our guest began to grow. What exactly had he said to her? "Over the past few weeks, we've worked very well together. I believe."

"Agreed," I said just a half-beat ahead of Fletcher. But he nodded enthusiastically.

"We've also grown closer."

Not even a question. When I reached my hand out and laid it palm up on the table, the fact she took it immediately settled some of my nerves.

"I'm doing this badly," she said as though apologizing.

"Drew, you couldn't do something badly if you tried." Fletcher might be stretching the hyperbole, but I agreed with the sentiment.

"Tell us what we need to know," I said. "What you need us to know."

"I need to tell you about Daddy. Why we met… and what I've been doing. We've talked about it some. Danced around it. But I think you should know."

I nodded once. "I would love to know about your father."

Fletcher gave me an incredulous look, but the minute Vienna glanced at him, he gave her a small, if encouraging, smile. "Whatever you want to say, Drew. We're here."

She squeezed my hand once and blew out a breath. "A little over a year ago, Daddy died." The sadness in her voice shredded me. For the briefest moment there was a quaver, but she pushed on before I could say anything. "Or I should say, Daddy was killed."

Then she laid it out for us. Her father. His mission. The mission she'd continued, and the hunt to find his killer. All of it.

"So, Drew...I don't want to steal your thunder or anything, but we kinda already figured out what the mission was. Right?" Fletcher looked at me and I nodded.

I'd been doing a lot of her research for her, and I knew Fletcher had been working on something about a Red Death folder on the drive she brought home one day. There was a clear mission, and we'd had enough evidence to piece most of it together ourselves. She'd also made offhand comments to me about her father.

I wasn't sure what Fletcher had been told.

"Yes," she agreed, a little of her light returning since she started this entire discussion. "I know that. And I'm glad what I'm doing—what we're doing here, is something you both are fully aware of and on board with. I just felt the need to lay everything out for you. To give you a big picture of what I'm doing. Which you deserve if you would like to continue to stay with me."

I didn't like the sound of that, like we could leave at any moment and she'd let us. If she tried to leave, I didn't believe I could let her just walk out. From the look of utter abhorrence on Fletcher's face, he must have felt something similar.

"Hey now, no one said anything about leaving. I think when we crossed the bedroom barrier we became something different than we were before we walked in. Right, Big

Guy?" Fletcher flicked his gaze my way as if saying *help me out.*

Clearing my throat, I wiped whatever residual food away from my mouth. Mainly to get my thoughts together. "I would be devastated if you didn't want me here. I hope that's never the case."

She squeezed my hand and leaned toward me. "Oh, Rick. No, that's not where I'm going with this at all. I just wanted you both to have the full picture of who my father is—was."

I tilted my head. The way she said that made it sound like there was still something she hadn't shared. Because it was becoming second nature, I glanced at Fletcher, who had paled sometime in the last thirty seconds.

Bringing my full attention back to Vienna, I rubbed my thumb over her knuckles. "Who is your father?"

Fletcher choked on…his spit. He hadn't eaten or drank anything in ten minutes.

"Well, you see…Daddy is the Judge. If you've ever heard of him." Her voice was clear, concise and unwavering.

"Oh, I watched a documentary on him a couple weeks ago." Wait… The journalist that had been highlighted was a young woman. I snapped my head toward Fletcher who dipped his chin in acknowledgement.

"If you saw the most recent documentary that aired, our lovely Sandra Jane that I'm looking into was the star of the show. And she has our friendly Fed's father's journals." Fletcher nodded so hard I was concerned his head would fly off. "I think this is going to be a bigger issue than we thought." Already his gaze was bouncing toward the study and back, like he itched to go to work on said problem.

"The man downstairs said he didn't give them to her?" I asked.

"Correct, and I believed him. But we still have an ex-Fed in the basement who has a loose connection to an investigative journalist who is the chihuahua to end all chihuahuas when it comes to ambition. You need to pay her a visit," Fletcher said to Vienna.

"Wait. Storming in is exactly what Vienna shouldn't do. We have the man downstairs. We should be getting more information from him first," I argued. Running into anything was a bad idea. I'd seen that plenty from others in group therapy.

"Are you kidding? I just told you that man is smart as shit. And he's too happy to be here. If he wanted to snow us on his motives and what information he has, he could, easily. We should be looking at the facts and only the facts. Facts I get from my systems and resources. I'll call my cousin." He started to lift up from the chair but I stopped him with a hand to the shoulder.

"You just said you believed him," I growled. He was giving me whiplash.

Fletcher emitted an exasperated sound. "I also said he's smart as shit, and he's probably trained to lie through his teeth. I don't trust him."

"This Sandra Jane isn't going to storm the doors just because we realized who she is. Or that she's connected to our guest. We need to do our due diligence and—"

"Fuck waiting, Rick! This could be dangerous! This is big—"

"Stop!" Vienna's voice cracked through the room.

When I looked at her, I sat up straighter and dropped my head. Her face was flushed and her gaze narrowed to slits. She wasn't happy, and I belatedly realized Fletcher and I might be overstepping. We didn't make decisions for her. We definitely didn't talk around her like she wasn't here.

"Just...shut the fuck up. Okay? Sit down. Calm down. You're giving me a headache." She released my hand so she could rub her temple. "I've lived with this type of scenario my entire life. She's not the first, and won't be the last, journalist to try and figure out the identity of the Judge. And even if she did, Daddy—" she sucked in a breath, "he died. So, it's a dead end."

"You're forgetting you carry on his work," I whispered softly.

"Yes, but we're smarter than that. We take all the precautions necessary to cover our tracks, and we leverage the right resources in the Network." She mildly grimaced but didn't comment further.

"I could get behind all that, Drew. Except she's connected to an *ex-Fed* we have locked up in the basement," Fletcher said low with as much force as he could pack into his words.

"We keep going as we are. I have you both doing work for me, and some of it is about Sandra Jane. When I see a path forward, we'll take it. If we need to. For now, we keep digging up as much as we can." She laid down the law, and both Fletcher and I recognized it was not the time to push her. Not right now, when she looked like she could blow a gasket at any second.

"I'm sorry, Vienna. You know better than we do, how to handle this situation. We'll take your lead," I soothed, reaching out to caress her cheek with the back of my hand.

"Of course," Fletcher said through clenched teeth. I'd have to keep an eye on him.

"Lunch was amazing as always, Rick. Thank you," Vienna murmured as she rose from her chair and grabbed her still full plate. She dropped a kiss on my temple then Fletcher's and took her dishes to the kitchen. Without another word, she went upstairs and her bedroom door shut once again.

Everything needed to work out like she said it would. If there was even a chance she would get caught in any capacity, I was prepared to break all the rules.

I SURPRISED Rick when I went to a different garage in the subdivision and pulled out a different car. We'd been using mine a great deal lately and after our last trip, it still needed a full cleaning. It would also benefit us to shake it up. Besides, Mart's targets were usually found in more affluent areas.

"When should I worry?" Rick asked as he set my bag in the trunk of the sexy, sleek silver Acura. This car had been one of the handful of "splurges" Daddy had indulged me in when I'd seen it. A reward for a job well done, and a tool for future work.

Practical and pragmatic.

I hadn't driven her in over a year. The ache inside of me echoed the fresh pain. Picking the scab open and scrubbing it raw had left me—I didn't even have a word for it. Our guest in the basement had pointed out the boys didn't know who I was. Who my father was.

I'd rectified that. And they'd—stayed. The relief salting the discomfort helped, but I couldn't shake the unease that stalked my every waking moment. Not even the boys, with their tender touches and hot kisses, could fully chase it away.

Especially not when I came across them arguing not once, but twice in the two days since I'd told them everything. "I'll let you know," I finally said to Rick, because I hadn't answered him and he'd waited patiently. He deserved far more than my distance but the thick glass separating me from the world only seemed to deepen, not thin. "I'm meeting a friend."

His eyes narrowed.

"A female friend." I wasn't entirely certain why I felt the need to offer that bit of insight, but it settled him almost immediately. "She has a job for me. She knows what types of work Daddy and I do."

Rick nodded slowly. "So, she also knows your father?"

I smiled. "She did. I used to think they had a thing, but… nothing ever came of it. But when she needs our help, we go. Daddy didn't always agree with her choices, but he liked her."

Of that, I was certain.

"Can you trust her?"

I turned the question over in my head. "Yes." At no point had Mart ever given me a reason to doubt her. "But within reason. I trust very few people."

His brow furrowed. "I would prefer going with you." Before I could say anything, though, he raised his hand. "I would prefer it, but that's not what you need right now. With everything you told us about the Network, about the issues with it—is this woman part of the Network?"

"Tangentially," I admitted. "In fact, I think I'm going to tell her to keep her distance for a while." Reuben had seen the writing on the wall. Mart, bless her, probably would but she wasn't always interested in her own self-preservation. It was the one fact about her that had driven Daddy to distraction.

Also, the source of the three arguments I could recall them ever having. It was why she'd learned to fire a gun and handle a knife. Daddy insisted.

He had a point, she'd needed us far less after that.

"I'll be careful," I promised him. "I know how to look after myself. And…" I pressed a hand to his chest. "I will keep you apprised of my ETA."

Rick nodded, then glanced across the lot toward our

house. I parked the Acura two streets over, but we had a line of sight. Part of the reason I'd chosen this garage to stable her in. "I'll look after Fletcher and our guest. Do you know what you want to do with him yet?"

My lips compressed. Our guest. Mr. Morgan. Frustration edged under my skin. I'd let him get to me. I couldn't afford to allow that to happen again. As irritating as he was, I couldn't kill him for that. Sadly, releasing him wasn't an option.

The man made his pursuit abundantly clear. Now that he had my face and my name? No, I'd never be rid of him. A problem for another day. "I'm sorry, no," I told Rick. "You'll have to look after him a bit longer."

"I don't mind," he told me, gently. "Though I am tempted to use the hose on him for his next bath."

Surprise flickered through me. An image of our guest's all too seeing brilliant eyes as they focused on me with the keen intelligence and wit that promised he would never let this go flooded my mind. "Why?"

"Because he annoyed you." Rick shrugged. "It might also be fun."

The last made me laugh. Rising on my tip toes, I kissed him gently. "Be safe. No taking risks. I'll be back as soon as I can." He nodded, but there was no way to miss the hint of worry re-entering his eyes. "I will check in." Then I patted his chest and he moved to open the driver's side door.

Unlike most men, who would caress this car with their gazes and lust after her sleek lines and promise of wicked speed, Rick stayed focused on me. "Be safe," he repeated my earlier order. "I'll take care of the boys."

The boys.

Right, Fletcher and the guest. Better to not upgrade Mr. Morgan to any other status. Starting the engine with a push of a button, I blew Rick a kiss before accelerating out of the open garage. Then, almost against my will, I glanced at the rearview mirror.

In a span of weeks—a few short months—he'd changed my whole world. Jerking my gaze back to the road, I focused my attention ahead. Part of the reason I wasn't taking them was I needed to reorient myself back to the mission.

They had changed my world, but I couldn't afford for them to distract me from the work for too long.

I just… couldn't.

At best, it would delay the work.

At worst, it would get them killed.

The drive out to meet Mart was just what I needed. With old rock playing quietly in the background the silence allowed me to quiet my mind more than I had in days. I couldn't see my life without the *boys*, as Rick referred to them, but after so long of being by myself, I needed…

A minute. Alone.

When I pulled up to the entrance of the country club, Mart had added an alias for me on the guest list. Where Daddy and I constantly changed and evolved our IDs and personalities based on our jobs, for the most part, Mart operated under the same identity. Unless things got too hot, then she would do an abrupt change and move locations.

I'd asked her about it once, why she wanted to be so easily accessible. She'd responded, "Dollbaby, in the circles I travel in, these assholes are wealthy enough that distance usually isn't enough to get away from them. I'm too recognizable unless I were to do dramatic changes to myself. The only thing I love that my momma gave me was my hair." Mart had fluffed up her thick, healthy blonde locks. "I'm not cutting it or changing it. Besides, when these bastards get fleeced, they can't trace it back to me, so what do I care if I keep the same name?" She delicately shrugged one shoulder and pulled her full lips into a smirk.

That was just another thing Daddy had made a few snide

comments on. But at the end of the day, he didn't care what she did outside of giving her unsolicited advice.

The young guard at the gate didn't even glance at my ID as I gave him my name. He'd taken one look at my sweet ride and form-fitting tennis outfit and winked. "Have a great day and enjoy the amenities."

I laughed under my breath. Sometimes, people were so predictably blind to what they thought was in front of them. I was dressed nice, appeared as if I came from the same level of wealth as everyone else, so instantly I was accepted into their circle.

Parking at the clubhouse, I noticed Mart chatting up a few older gentlemen by the doors. Her coy smile and inviting body language had those men eating out of the palm of her hand. I would wager one of those men was her next target.

She glanced over toward my car where I was stepping out, and quickly waved off the men with a few soft words and a tinkling laugh. They watched her ass as she walked away, both murmuring to each other under their breath.

I grinned and shook my head. Mart had a talent. Not one Daddy would ever want me to cultivate, but a talent all the same.

"Honey pie," she purred as she stepped close, air kissing each cheek and tucking her fingers around mine. Staying close, her eyes sparkled as she looked me over. "Outside of the tension you're carrying in your shoulders, you look amazing. Something you're doing is agreeing with you."

"Thanks, Mart. It's great to see you too." I smiled so wide, I showed all of my teeth. I was happy to see her, it was rare I interacted with women on this job. But I also played up the part of a vapid friend.

"Let's grab lunch and I can fill you in on the job. Once we get the unpleasantness out of the way, I'd love to catch up." She looped her arm through mine and started walking us toward the doors.

This wasn't a club I'd been to. The last time I met her for a job, it was in Manhattan, which was an entirely different vibe. I subtly glanced around, noting the workers silently tending to the landscape, buffing any chrome, and cleaning the glass. They were so sure with their movements, I doubted the patrons noticed them at all.

Muted conversation filled with an air of self-importance surrounded us on all sides as we passed small groups of clustered men and women. Here, there was no rush, no sense of urgency. They were all just enjoying a day in their privileged lives.

Cool air washed over us, fresh baked bread scented the air as we neared the dining room. A young woman opened one of the double doors, wearing a sleek black outfit that was more sophisticated than the ground staff, but still marked her clearly as an employee. She gave Mart a genuine smile.

"Vicky, baby. I'm catching up with a dear family friend, can I get a private booth?" Mart asked.

That was what I loved about Mart. Even though she traversed the waters in this shark-infested pool with ease, she was still a decent person as far as I could tell.

"Of course, Ms. Truelove. Follow me." She grabbed two large menus etched on metal sheets and preceded us toward the back. Most of the people dining in were closer to the glass and the patio, but the private rooms were stashed away from sight of the general public.

The hostess showed us to a private room and filled our glasses up with cucumber-infused ice water before gently closing the door behind her. Mart immediately pulled a small puck from her bra and set it under one of the extra napkins after she clicked it on.

If the room was bugged, the device would disrupt the sound.

It seemed Mart was ready to get down to business.

"That's new," I commented as I picked up one of the

glasses and took a sip of the water. It was crystal clear, cold, and refreshing. The cucumber still made no damn sense to me. Then again, the reasons behind a lot of similar choices amongst those wealthier circles eluded me.

"It's not really that new," she commented, her smile genuine this time without the airs she put on outside. "But then, I suppose it's been a hot minute, hasn't it, Dollbaby?" She huffed out a little breath then shook her head. "You know Thackery. If it's not business..."

"... it's not worth discussing," I finished for her. The pang inside me rang so clearly. Yes, I did know my dad. Guilt clawed at me. I hadn't told Mart about him or what happened. I probably should have, but after Uncle David brought me the news and helped with all the arrangements, I hadn't really wanted to talk to anyone.

A knock at the door announced the arrival of the staff and I used the distraction to get my emotions back into their proper compartments. Mart was just *easy* to be around. As much as Daddy frowned at some of the conversations Mart and I had over the years, I genuinely liked her. Liked that she never put us in a position where we had to choose.

"Do you mind if I order for us?" Mart asked.

"Not at all." I'd had a rather large breakfast though. "I'm not terribly hungry, so something small?"

"Absolutely, you'll love their mushroom bisque. It's excellent, rich, and prepared exactly right." Then she glanced at the waitress. "Some wine for me, none for my girl here. Though she would probably enjoy the pomegranate spritzer and definitely bring us the fresh rolls with the bisque."

"Absolutely, Ms. Truelove." Then the waitress was gone and we were alone again.

"Pomegranate spritzer?" I just couldn't help it. "Should I worry that this club is a masquerade for Hades' realm and I can't get out?"

Tossing that gorgeous, thick mane of golden hair back,

Mart laughed. "Hand to God, Dollbaby, I just think you'll like the spritzer, it's not too sweet, definitely a little tart, but unforgettable. A lot like you."

I rolled my eyes and Mart let out a delighted little laugh. Yes, she enjoyed teasing me. Something else that had taken some getting used to. No one teased me. Well—Fletcher did.

And I liked how he teased me.

"Oh, I saw that smile. Don't think I won't be asking about it. But you are your father's daughter," she elongated the last few words with a chastising note. "So, I know better than to dive into the fun before we get the business out of the way."

"I appreciate that. And in the interests of our business, just a bit of advice—woman to woman?" It was the only way to phrase it and avoid digging deeper on the topic.

Mart raised her brows. "I love a good woman's advice."

"The Network's been having a few—service issues of late. New management. Supplier turnover. It might be better, for the near future, to veer away from anything involving them."

She considered me as she took another sip of her wine. "Never was much of a fan anyway. Let me know when it's good again?"

"Of course. Now, what do you have for me?"

The cheerful expression melted away, even her pale hazel eyes went a degree or two colder. "Have you ever heard of a man named Levi Ross?"

I shook my head and took another sip of water rather than answer.

"He's the third son of Antony Ross with his second wife, Lara Franklin."

Still not... "Franklin."

"Exactly, Darnley Franklin was a—con artist is probably the most polite term for him—who traded on people's faith to get in their pockets. He defrauded a great many people before the IRS shut him down."

"He was being investigated for murder."

"Sadly, no body, no crime." She shook her head. "Anyway, his ex-wife married Ross, who in turn adopted Levi. They told everyone he was the product of an affair."

"He wasn't." That was not a guess.

"No, but the whole action cleared the little pissbucket of the suspicion and scandal surrounding Daddy Dumbass, and he was once again welcomed into more advantageous circles. He's twenty-eight years old, he's never had a job, but he has a great many 'ideas' that he's putting together the funds for. He enjoys older women, particularly those with under-age daughters."

That was why I was here.

"He fleeces the mothers, seduces the daughters, and when he can't seduce them, he drugs and rapes them."

A knock announced the return of the staff with our lunch. We both went quiet while they delivered the bisque, the wine, the spritzer, and the fresh bread.

"Is there anything else I can get for you, Ms. Truelove?"

"No, darling Jason, we're fine for now. Just some privacy and if anyone is looking for me, you don't know when I'll be back."

He grinned. "I'll take care of it." Not once did he glance at me in speculation and his nod to Mart was kind, and honest. Yes, this was definitely one of the things I liked about her so much.

Focusing her attention back on me, Mart picked up her wine glass. "Patricia McCallum is a dear, if empty-headed, friend. If it had only been her money he'd taken, that would be one thing, but her daughter turned up pregnant. Her twelve-year-old daughter. I knew you'd be interested in Ross. That is for you, now let's talk about his basement we're going to clear out."

Hate flashed in Mart's eyes and I nodded. "Give me everything you have. I'll take care of it."

PARANOIA WAS A TERRIBLE THING...MOST of the time.

But I'd like to think my suspicious nature, especially after my teenage years, was what kept me alive and ahead of the game. Like that meme of the crazy-eyed, sleep-deprived man finding conspiracies and threads connecting everything and everyone, that was me. I thought about all the ways it could go wrong and contingency plans on how to manage the potential fallout.

Okay, maybe I wasn't as proactive as that. I just tried to be when the situation warranted it.

Staring at my computer screen into the beady little eyes of Sandra Jane, as she gave yet another interview on how much progress she'd made with the help of the journals, this was definitely one of those times that my paranoia kicked in.

Rick was unseasoned. He hadn't seen the seedier side of life and how underhanded people could be when they were trying to get their way. The only darkness he'd seen so far was what Drew had allowed him to see in the research he'd done. Which was completely different than a straight-laced woman willing to cut the throat of her best friend to solve the case.

I'd tried to tell him, on multiple occasions actually. But fuck, every time he shut the conversation down with an icy glare and a flex of his muscles. The big guy knew he was intimidating and played up on that until I slunk away scowling, determined to try and talk some sense into his block head another time.

It would all be so much easier if I could find something of the dirtier substance on the journalist. I was half-tempted to run down to the basement and engage Mr. Ex-Fed in another conversation. Except, that was a bad idea. I didn't know what I didn't know and clearly he knew things I didn't.

Learning my lesson from last time, I wouldn't be putting myself in another situation where I could fuck it all up. No, sir. Even if Drew hadn't made any waves about my conversation with him, I knew what he'd gained from me had to be what put Drew in a bad mood.

After her lunchtime revelation, I would bet my favorite system on the fact that he knew I was ignorant of the Judge. It hadn't mattered I'd suspected, I hadn't *known*. And he picked up on that.

Irritation with my stupidity kept my ass in the chair, while the fury directed at Channing made me want to run down to the basement and spray him down with the hose.

Rick had mentioned that in passing and it was a fantastic idea. A way I could get mine and stay ten plus feet away from the bars.

I turned my sound off and left my office. Drew might listen to some of my concerns if I could catch her without Rick around. Granted, he was always around, but it was time for him to be prepping dinner. If she was upstairs, I might be able to squeeze a few minutes in with her alone. I'd have to be quick, because I swore, it was like Rick had mom eyes in the back of his head and knew where I was in the house at all times.

He'd also cleaned out my caffeine stash when I was sleeping. Bastard. I hadn't said anything though. If I hadn't been so hyped up, I might not have confronted the Fed. My brain had just been so jumpy it made me crazy.

Tiptoeing, I glanced toward the kitchen. The clangs and bangs of pots and pans meant dinner was fully underway. Sweet. I slowly crept up the steps, using every wannabe ninja skill I possessed to go with zero noise.

I did pretty fucking good, if I did say so myself.

Outside of Drew's room, I lightly—so, so lightly—rapped my knuckles.

Her husky voice met my ears before she pulled the door open. Okay, so she wasn't talking to me. That was unfortunate. It meant someone else was cutting into my golden opportunity to talk some sense into her.

"Uncle David. I said I was going to take care of this my way," she said in exasperation as she waved me in.

By the skin of my teeth, I stopped myself from fist bumping as I shut the door so softly there wasn't even a snick. If she found it odd, she didn't say. She took her seat back on the bed against the pillows and pulled her laptop over her thighs.

"This isn't like you to be so worked up. She's only a journalist." She frowned and a small indentation appeared between her eyes as she read something on the screen. Drew also conveniently left out our friend in the basement and said connection to the journalist. "I know. I've been lying low. Of course."

Whoever this Uncle David was, he must have been speaking rapidly because her responses were one right after the other.

"What about the Vanisher?" She sat up straighter as she tucked her feet underneath her.

The Vanisher. I'd seen that somewhere recently…

I hesitated about moving over to the bed. Particularly when she seemed very focused on her call. Maybe I should—

She lifted her gaze from the computer screen and caught my eye, then she nodded to the bed. Maybe I should sit my ass down. Got it.

Moving around to the far side, I climbed onto the bed and moved over to sit next to her. Stretching my legs out, I crossed one ankle over the other and studied her screen.

Typically, that would be rude as shit, but she had invited me…

"I've never dealt with him directly," Vienna said. "Daddy did. A couple of times. He never wanted me at those meetings."

I could just barely make out the man's voice, older and definitely very familiar from the way he spoke to her. Well, that and the fact she called him "Uncle David." I didn't like him already. She exhaled a long, soft breath. It might not quite have hit "irritated" sigh, but it was close.

"I see."

In no language did those two words coming out of a woman's mouth mean anything good. Nope. If anything, the absolute *lack* of inflection in her voice worried me more than anything else. The Vanisher was on Dion's server. That was where I'd seen the name? Pretty sure.

Might need to revisit it.

Later, after this conversation.

"Yes, I said I would take care of the reporter and on my time and in my way."

The urge to take the phone and tell the guy on the other end to go get fucked surged through me. Throwing myself on the fire wasn't in my nature. I'd only ever done it once or twice in my life. Okay, three times. Twice for my cousin, him and his girl? I'd protected them.

The only other time had been when I'd gone into that warehouse at the port after Drew. I leaned my head back and studied her profile. The images on the screen flickered past and a part of me registered her looking at the file I'd been putting together, but it was how the light from the screen played over her face that obsessed me.

"Of course," she said. "Yes. No."

Another rapid fire set of questions.

"I'm secure." A soft laugh. "No, I don't need you to verify it for me. Daddy trained me well." Sadness marred her expression and my heart squeezed. For all I'd found that picture of her father fucking terrifying, Drew clearly loved him, and she clearly hurt over his loss.

Go figure, I got the fucking Stepford family on paper, dripping with wealth, and with nothing but ice in their veins. She got a serial killer, who looked like someone that would terrify Michael fucking Myers, and everything in her demeanor declared she'd loved him and he'd loved her.

"Goodbye, Uncle David. I'll talk to you soon. Yes, I promise." Finally, she hung up and exhaled another long sigh. Lowering the phone, she tapped the spacebar on the laptop and Sandra Jane's voice filled the silence.

Considering how many videos of hers I'd watched, I was pretty familiar with the content. I reached over and tapped the spacebar lightly. It paused the video and snagged Drew's attention. She gave me a tired smile.

The fact I recognized it as "tired" worried me more than anything else. "Hey…"

"Hi," she said, putting her phone down on the nightstand. It wasn't her normal phone. No, that was on the bed next to her leg. Must be a different one. She had a few. I filed that away as she turned back to me and leaned up to press a kiss to my lips.

My brain locked up at the first brush of her mouth against mine. All my good intentions and paranoia skipped off together. Sliding a hand into her hair, I tilted her head further to deepen the kiss. I drank in the contact like a sunflower in desperate need of the light that it turned to the flower next to it.

The weird thought vanished in a pop as she let out a soft moan and shifted to face me more. I caught her laptop before it could slide away, indulging myself in long, slow thrusts of my tongue on hers. Thrusts, she welcomed, then tried to capture as she sucked against my tongue.

Fuck, I loved kissing her.

With admirable restraint and reluctance, I should get a damn cookie, I broke the kiss and gazed down into her eyes. A hint of a real smile curved her lips and they were wet from my kiss. "Hi," she repeated.

"Hey," I answered.

"Did you need something?"

"Exactly that," I said. It wasn't why I'd come up here, but Vienna didn't need my paranoia. She needed facts. She needed evidence. She needed something solid. "I missed you."

Her gentle laugh washed over me like a caress. "I'm right here."

Yes, yes she was. I brushed my finger down her cheek. "Rick's making dinner. Can I get you anything? A drink? A massage? A hug?"

A hug? Since when did I offer affection like that? Who the fuck was I and what had I done with Fletcher Reed? I shoved that irritating little voice into the closet and locked the door.

"I need to finish reviewing all of this," she said with a sigh. "Or I'd take you up on all of that."

"Maybe later?" I offered. "I can go down and pull more reports, background, history—whatever you need."

Drew rested her head against the headboard and closed her eyes. "That might be helpful. Uncle David is on my ass about Sandra Jane, but he's up in tithers about the Vanisher too. I don't know where that came from and he won't say."

"Who is the Vanisher?" I asked as I stroked the side of her face. The woman was like crack. One touch and now I suddenly couldn't keep my hands to myself. "Actually, I'd rather know who Uncle David is."

Blowing out a long breath, she nuzzled my palm. "Uncle David is Daddy's closest friend. He's been around from the beginning. A lot of what I know, he taught me." She paused like she was deliberating what else to share. "He's the only one who really knew Daddy like I did, or as close as he'd let anyone else get to him." Her breath caught on the last word, and I pulled her to my chest.

My heart cracked right down the middle that she felt her grief so intense that it bled through in her voice. Drew was so tough she was like a layer of Teflon. But as much as I hated it, I loved that she felt safe enough with me to show this side of herself.

"And the Vanisher? Why is he important?" I rubbed her back. She drew in one shuddering breath, and once she let it out, I laid her back against the pillows.

"He's someone in the Network. I take it you've never heard of him?" Her golden eyes drank me in, and I damn near shivered from the weight of her full attention.

"No. I'd just started getting introduced to the Network when you saved me from that rat bastard. Mainly the people I did jobs for. The Vanisher never came up." I thought for a second she'd ask me about who I worked for, but Drew apparently valued privacy too much to pry.

I would have told her though. I'd share all my secrets if she asked it of me. Well, I'd try at least.

"He's something of an assassin. When he's contracted, he not only takes care of the person but erases everything about them, except for a photograph. From what Daddy had mentioned in the past, he's an arrogant prick." She shrugged. "He was also mentioned in the box we grabbed from the storage unit, so he's someone I wanted to look into anyway."

I thought about holding my tongue, but I was never very good at that. "Hmm. I saw a file for the Vanisher on Dion's servers. I'll pull that up and we can comb over it. We should probably go over the box again, just in case you missed anything. Oh—I can also call in some favors to—"

"Wait." Drew pressed a finger to my lips, her eyes full of

frustrated amusement. "Don't call any favors in. We don't need anyone outside of the three of us to know we're looking into him. In the Network, making waves is never a good thing. In fact, getting the Vanisher's attention is a sure way to become his next photograph. And I never want to see that happen to you because you spoke to the wrong people. Okay, my little pincushion?"

I grinned against her fingers. What a fucking nickname. As silly as it was, I loved that she gave me one. It made every-thing about who we were to each other seem…more. Shit, I really didn't recognize myself anymore.

"Okay, although I don't work with people with loose lips, I can understand your concern. I don't want to be a photo-graph either."

"Good. So, what you can do is continue looking over your systems, Dion's files, and Daddy's files. Run anything by me you think could be important and we'll make a decision from there." Leaning forward, she caught my bottom lip between her teeth, before sliding her mouth against mine in a wet kiss.

I. Fucking. Loved. Kissing. Drew.

"You could have told me to jerk off with a cheese grater slathered in Icy Hot, and I'd agree when you look at me this way. So, whatever you said, works for me," I whispered, pressing one more kiss to the corner of her lips. I couldn't resist.

She laughed, and it went straight to my dick. Okay, time to go, or I wouldn't get any work done. And Rick might be upset we left him out while he slaved over a hot stove.

"I'll let you know if I find anything. I'll start working on this now." I reluctantly pulled myself from the bed. At the door, I looked over at her and I was pleasantly surprised to see her watching my ass with a smile painted on that luscious mouth.

I gave it a little wiggle just to make her laugh. It worked.

Then I was gone, and all of the dark suspicions started

creeping back in. If this was my one job, I wouldn't fuck it up. I'd find everything there was to find on the Vanisher. And I'd keep working on Sandra Jane too.

She must have a dirty skeleton in her closet somewhere. If she did, I'd find it.

That was a promise.

VIENNA

MART'S JOB would take a couple of days. She also needed three or four days to set up her end. Ultimately, that would be a week. I wasn't comfortable with leaving Ross out there for the time being, but Mart assured me it took him time to line up a new target. Time she needed to get the access. Then I'd handle the transport. Once the artwork was cleaned out and in the hands of a mutual friend on the other side of the country—then I'd deal with him.

Rick would probably enjoy this job. Fletcher too, come to think of it. It would be something different. Transport helped supplement our income and paid for new toys and land. I'd taken fewer jobs in the last year or so. Mart's opportunity would pay twenty-five percent. A ridiculous fee, but then I was taking all the risk.

I'd do it for far less, but I really could use the money and she refused to hear otherwise. Uncle David had questions about the Vanisher. What did I know about him? Had Daddy kept any files on the man? What rumors had I heard?

Honestly, it was out of character for him. Then again, he had concerns about the Network. Concerns about those going missing or falling off the map. He wanted me to keep my distance. Of course, I agreed with him.

"Vienna?" Rick called as he nudged the door open. I had a bag on the bed. I'd been debating about what I planned to take with me. Already, I'd cleaned all of my weapons, sharpened my knives, gone over everything we'd picked up from the Satchel and divided it all into three new go bags.

Go bags I'd added to the closet downstairs. I'd also briefed Rick on a pair of lockboxes. Fletcher would need his own. I needed to set those up. "I'm still here," I told Rick as I returned to the closet. I still hadn't fully decided on my approach to Sandra Jane. But Uncle David's impatience had begun to bleed into his communications.

That meant I needed to take care of it now. Especially after the latest "news" broke.

"I take it you saw the news?"

I sighed as I flipped through three different outfits. Professional. Bar. Gym. All perfect for attracting male targets, a female target was different. I chose a white shirt and black slacks. Professional, but not trying to get noticed. "I did."

A three-quarter sleeve, A-line dress in dark gray went practically anywhere. It wasn't a little black dress, but it was far more versatile. Options. Options would be better. Carrying them out of the closet, I found Rick staring at the suitcase then at me. His expression wasn't difficult to read.

Sandra Jane's latest addition to the ongoing search for the Judge. A missing, former FBI agent and profiler once linked to the case. It was a bit of a scoop for her, a coup. Because even the FBI seemed to be getting in on it now.

A problem we did not need.

The struggle playing out over his face tugged at my heart. At the same time, he needed to get used to this. "I know you don't like it when I go…"

"It's not that," he said, frowning.

"No?" Because that didn't seem altogether honest.

"Well, it's not only that."

That was better. "Talk to me." I was removing the items from the hangers and folding them neatly. Without a clear cut plan, I would be making some of this up when I got there.

Nearing the bed, he took the dress and, following my

example, prepped it for packing with ease and neatness. The beautiful thing about that dress was it shook out wrinkles easily. "The reporter."

"I'm listening."

"She's not your usual target."

No. She wasn't. I added the items to the bag then returned to the closet. Casual jeans for a potential coffee encounter, paired with a plain, uninteresting blouse. Then running gear. That was one thing Fletcher had definitely discovered about Ms. Sandra Jane. She ran religiously.

It would afford me a good look at her.

"My concern is that you're going after someone who hasn't done anything to earn the attention."

I glanced at him. "What exactly do you think I'm going to do, Rick?"

The troubled look on his face bothered me.

"I...Don't know," he said, sounding lost. I hated that this situation, something that would have never come up if he hadn't met me, played on his mind and his conscience. Rick was such a good man. I wished he could remain innocent of this world for as long as possible, but that wasn't an option. As much as I couldn't stand that my work was changing who he was, he needed to have open eyes if we were to survive.

Hating myself for it, I pushed Rick into a corner, needing him to see why this was important. "Then what would you have me do, Rick? Would you prefer I wait to see what kind of evidence she truly has when the police are knocking down my door? Do you think we should put all those women and children at risk once we are no longer around to save them?" I gentled my words as much as I could, but Rick still flinched.

"Vienna," he pleaded, not a whine but so unsure of himself it broke my heart. "Of course, I don't want them at risk. But I can't stand the thought of you being at risk either. Maybe I should go." He stepped forward, hands gripping a pair of slacks.

I shook my head. "In time, maybe you could be the one doing these types of runs." Not likely. As much as he hated seeing me go, I recognized I'd have just as much of a hard time watching him leave for something potentially dangerous. In this, I had the training, experience, and instincts under my belt. Rick only had what I taught him. "But right now, I need to be the one to check her out. I'm a woman. I'm less of a threat, and would probably go unnoticed unless I approach her. You wouldn't have that advantage, and she's suspicious by nature."

He nodded, dropping his gaze to the bed. Poor Rick did not like what I was saying but he saw the truth of it. "You're sure you need to do this now?"

"Yes," I assured him, tucking the blouse in my hands neatly into the bag. Then I took the slacks he was currently folding and stuffed that in the bag as well. I tugged him closer to me until I could wrap my arms around his waist, tipping my face toward his. "I mentioned this to Fletcher, but my Uncle David is getting twitchy about Sandra Jane. If I don't follow through and take care of her, in the most humane and ethical way possible, he will. And he's much less circumspect than Daddy and I are. Than Daddy was." I sucked in a harsh breath at the slip. "All Uncle David sees is a threat. He doesn't see an innocent woman, even if she is making our lives difficult." I'd already explained who Uncle David was, and he would understand why that was the worse option.

Rick pressed his palms against my lower back and dropped his forehead to mine, breathing me in with something akin to desperation. "Okay, I don't like it, but okay. What are you planning? Talk me through this so I know what to expect. If I have a timeline, an idea of where you'll be, and your general plan, I stand a chance not to lose my mind while you're gone."

Sighing, I rubbed my chin against the hard planes of his chest. We'd talked about this already, the three of us. But I humored him because this was what he needed from me right now. "I'll check in. I plan to canvas her home. Fletcher has a file put together of her routines, her house blueprints, and a list of all known associates, specifically who she interacts with on a daily basis. I'll be gone roughly seventy-two hours. Maybe ninety-six, depending on how any interactions I have with her goes." That was only if everything went smoothly, but ideal situations were ideal for a reason. "I should be back in plenty of time to tackle Mart's job with room for a small break in between."

He deflated, practically sagging against me as he released a weary breath. "I'll miss you," he whispered.

"I'll miss you too," I returned, pushing to my toes to kiss the underside of his jaw. "I'll check in when I can. You'll take care of Fletcher while I'm gone? Make sure he remembers to eat and shower?"

"You know I will. I already moved all the caffeine to one of the other houses. I don't need him bouncing around while I'm worried about you...I'll take care of our guest too. You don't need to worry about anything here." He wrapped his arms more securely around my body, squeezing me to him.

"No one knows where this place is, but if the worst case happens, and someone comes while I'm gone, there's a hidden door in the basement with a safe room. It's not in the designs. No one would ever know it's there, and it's stocked with MREs and bottles of water. Take Fletcher and Mr. Morgan. Knock him out if you have to. There is a small cell inside the safe room you can throw him in." I told him how to access the door, and how to close it behind him so no one would ever suspect the basement was bigger than it was.

"When you're ready, come say goodbye to Fletcher. Just so you know, he's having second thoughts. When I left him, he was freaking out, going through his devices for anything that might help you."

I almost wanted to sigh. Fletcher seemed calmer about this

before, so what had upset him now? Or was it only that the time for me to leave closed in on them? So many things it could be. Admittedly, when I would leave for jobs previously, Daddy would only ask if I had everything I needed and remind me I had only so much time before he came after me.

It was a reasonable statement, based on my skill level and the types of tasks I undertook. His farewell followed more in the vein of the one I would give him if he had to leave me behind when I was much younger. Only then, Daddy assured he would call at bedtime. The only time I was to call him was if I was in any kind of danger.

He never left me for longer than three days. Seventy-two hours, almost down to the minute. I was the one who had to wait while Daddy went out to confront the monsters. Waiting could be grueling and it did odd things to the mind.

More often than not, he left on his own jobs while I was gone. But as I'd grown older and more independent, his solo trips didn't worry as much. Though they had still kept me on edge.

Had right up until the day he'd just not come home.

The burn in my chest stung almost as much as my earlier slip. "I'm coming down now," I assured Rick even as I closed my suitcase. Everything had been packed, I'd been delaying myself enough. The job had to be done. I would make the call when I got there.

Downstairs, I found Fletcher pacing back and forth in front of his system. He had a headset on and his hands moved in a faintly wild gesticulating pattern like he was preventing himself from throttling—someone?

"Fletcher?" I said softly, one hand on the door.

"Shut. Up." He snapped, but at no point did he look at me. So I didn't take offense. "I don't want to listen to your excuses. International press has access to a lot of different information, especially when they request it to do a follow-up story—shut up. I'm not done."

The level of command in his voice was extremely provocative. He practically growled as though he were dressed in one of those ten thousand dollar suits and stood in front of a company, like Morgan said his family owned.

"You can request it as background research. You know it. I know it. You know I'm not above a little petty payback if you don't do exactly what I asked for. No, it doesn't fucking matter why I need it. Maybe I want to jackoff to the high-definition quality of her voice. Fuck knows her dead eyes don't do it for me."

Now my eyebrows raised.

"Wow, maybe you do have a brain. Fantastic—what the fuck do you mean twenty-four hours? Why the hell am I paying you anything for twenty-four hours? Fuck if I wanted to take that long, I could drive there, write a program and hack it out myself."

He put his hands on his hips and glared up at the ceiling.

"Arrogance isn't what got you out of the shit when your grandfather cut you off. It wasn't what cleared your academic record to get into Oxford. It definitely wasn't arrogance that cleaned up the background check so that lovely girl you fell in love with wouldn't learn about your less than stellar background." He almost huffed a laugh that was incredibly unfriendly.

I'd seen Rick work while he finessed a machine, but this was something else. I liked this. My nipples tightened and I pressed my thighs together as he held control over that conversation.

"That's not a threat at all," he said in an almost buttery soft voice. "I don't break my word." His tense shoulders relaxed and he nodded. "Six hours sounds great. I really appreciate you going that extra mile. Consider that another point off your debt. I'll shave it as soon as the information is on the server I sent you. Right. Yeah, I know you love me. Who wouldn't?"

With that, he pressed a button on his keyboard and yanked the headset off. A faint jerk betrayed the moment he realized I was standing there. "Drew…"

"Hey." Setting the case down, I crossed the room and let him sweep me up into a hug.

"You're leaving already?"

"Yes," I told him as I rubbed his back. The taut muscles there felt like they'd been etched into stone. "The sooner I go, the sooner I can get back."

"I'm working on getting more…"

"Shhh," I soothed as I leaned back and he trailed off as I fixed my gaze on him. "I know you're doing everything you can and then some. But I meant what I said about not trading in favors."

"That was different."

"That's trackable."

"No," he said, his grin genuine and sly. "Trust me, on this one, no one will track it back to us."

Oddly, I had no trouble believing him. "I trust you. Do you trust me?"

He blinked, his delight at my admission faltering at my question. Then, he nodded. "I do."

"Thank you." Pushing up onto my toes, I coiled my arms around his neck and he met my kiss with a sweet gentleness that turned fiery almost immediately, before it cooled back to sweetness again, if edged with just a hint of fear. "Look after Rick for me."

He frowned. "Big guy's got everything covered."

"He does," I agreed. "He looks after all of us, but I need you to look after him now. Make sure he rests, he eats, try to distract him if he gets too worried. Don't provoke him if you can help it."

Fletcher's sudden grin warmed me. "But provoking him is fun."

"Just be good," I murmured and shook my head. They had been managing quite well on their own.

"You'll be careful?" One, simple question, yet it held so much depth and emotion.

"I always am," I said rather than promise anything else. "I'll check in when I can."

He caught my hand and squeezed it as I let him go. "I'll leave you a message if I find anything out. I know you don't like answering your phone but…"

"I'll have mine as well as the burner with me. Leave the message on mine."

"Yes ma'am."

He tugged me back for one more kiss. "Come back soon—please. Rick and I will both be waiting."

"Soon as I can."

Then I forced myself to let him go. I wasn't lying to either of them, but the ferociousness of the concern they both exhibited looped around me like a wild hug I was carrying away from the house. It followed me out to yet another car, not the Acura this time. Instead, I just got out the old Toyota that was bland, nondescript, and excellent on gas mileage.

The guys were outside when I pulled away.

On impulse, I blew them a kiss. They both grinned.

Get on with it, I told myself.

The sooner I got there, the sooner I could come back home again.

RICK

TWO DAYS.

It had been two days since Vienna had left to do her reconnaissance on Sandra Jane. The last forty-eight hours had been pure hell as everything seemed to test my patience. Although the house was cleaner than it had ever been. The floors shone, the gloss on the cabinets glistened, and I wasn't even sure these cabinets were the kind that were supposed to reflect like that. I'd just polished them to the point of reflection.

The windows were so clean, the house didn't appear to have windows.

I'd also spent a considerable amount of time organizing meal plans, prepping vegetables, cooking and freezing single servings for Fletcher in case I went on any jobs with Vienna. He could also use them for our guest, if needed.

When I wasn't locked in my own head, I sat with Fletcher in his study. I had needed the company, and remained quiet and out of the way while he worked. He didn't seem to mind, in fact, he relaxed whenever I took a seat, as if he needed the comfort too.

The last check in was supposed to be this morning. Two hours earlier.

Two whole hours.

Vienna missed it. But that wasn't terribly concerning,

given what she was doing. If she was out in public or had engaged Sandra Jane in conversation, she wouldn't be able to check in.

During her first jobs, she had hardly checked in at all, unless she was on her way back and decided to pick up some food. That she had made a concession to check in at regular intervals set my nerves at ease. I loved that she appreciated my quirks and did what she could to make me feel more secure with her.

Except...Fletcher was threatening to shred all the control I was barely holding a tight grip to.

"Big guy. I'm worried." Fletcher paced around the study, periodically glaring at the burner on the desk, willing it to ring. I wanted it to ring too. More than anything. My chest was starting to ache from going too long without hearing her voice.

I was trying to hold my shit together, but it was getting harder and harder by the minute.

"Why are you rubbing your chest?" Fletcher stopped in front of me.

Glancing down, my hand was almost tearing a hole in my shirt right over my heart. "I don't know."

"We should call her. Make sure she's okay." He stalked over to the desk, reached out to pick up the phone before pulling back at the last minute. Then he repeated the movement several times, clearly at war with himself.

"No," I said with more confidence than I felt. "Vienna knows what she's doing. She'll call when she can. I trust her." I raised my eyebrows, waiting for him to agree.

He bit his lip, then nodded while staring longingly at the phone. "Yeah, you're right. You're right." Fletcher scrubbed his face then worked his hands through his hair, using a hair tie to fasten it into a bun.

"She'll call." I sat forward, fisting my hands on my knees.

"She'll call." Fletcher agreed as we locked gazes.

———

Twelve hours later

"You should really eat," Fletcher said quietly as he picked at the Figgy glaze pork chops and garlic couscous. Over the course of the day, he'd gotten quieter and quieter. While I thought that would help, I started to miss the normalcy of his constant running commentary.

When he stopped, fear that something *was* wrong grew sharper, louder, and harder to ignore.

The quieter he got, the more anxious I became. If we didn't hear something soon...

I didn't know what I would do, but it would be bad. The pressure bubbling beneath the surface was bound to burst at some point.

I glanced down at my own untouched plate. "Do you think she's okay?" I grimaced, hearing the trembling strain in my voice. As much as I wanted to be strong for Fletcher, I didn't think I could for very much longer if we didn't hear from Vienna.

My entire body itched from the uncertainty. I'd never gone this long without talking to Vienna before. I needed her.

So much.

Fletcher hadn't answered as he moved the couscous in a circle.

Breathing became hard, and drawing a deep breath was impossible. "I need her to be okay. If something happened to her..." I paused, squeezing my eyes shut.

A hand landed on my shoulder and I opened my eyes to see a morose Fletcher leaning toward me. The outside corners of his eyes drooped, mirroring the edges of his mouth. "You know what. I'm sure it's fine. Drew knows exactly what she's doing. If she hasn't called, there's a reason." His fingers bit into my muscle and the small bite of pain helped. "I've been sleeping in my room. Why don't I sleep in Drew's bed with you tonight. God knows I could use more than a couple hours of sleep, and it might help you too. Just so you know, I'm not the little spoon."

He tried to grin, but it fell flat. Especially with dark purple bruises under his eyes.

I didn't even try to return it.

Suddenly, a nervous burst of energy exploded in my stomach. I needed to tire myself out. I needed to do something to take my mind off the fact that I hadn't heard from Vienna in twenty-four hours.

"We're not hungry. I'll put these in the oven and clean up. Then we're going to the gym." I stood, grabbing his plate and mine.

Behind me, Fletcher groaned as he pushed back his chair. "Fine, fine. I hate the gym, but we both need something to do right now."

Hopefully beating the hell out of the punching bag would bring some relief to my hopelessness.

———

Twelve Hours Later

The seventy-two hour mark came and went. I'd fed our guest. Taken him the materials to bathe along with fresh clothes. I'd even taken down three new books. More for something to do than anything else. He brightened right the fuck up at the sight of them. I'd brought down another case of water.

After Vienna's reaction to him that one day, I'd foregone juice or milk. I thought he'd earned a privilege. Clearly, I'd been wrong.

"So," he said as he settled on the cot with his food. "Any chance I could talk you guys into a cup of coffee? I planned to ask Vienna."

Everything in me stiffened.

"But she hasn't come back to see me." He took a bite of his food and stared at me, his smirk firmly back in place.

I didn't want her name on his lips. No matter what happened with him, at least before, he hadn't known who she was. His knowledge of Fletcher's identity was a problem. Vienna's?

No. He wasn't ever leaving the basement.

Not if I could help it.

Instead of responding, I stared at him and waited. As soon as he finished, I took the tray and closed the door. Fletcher was in the kitchen, phone in one hand and a mug of coffee in the other.

Even after the punishing workout in the gym, sleep had been elusive. Fletcher had taken the spot on Vienna's bed away from the door. Thankfully, he'd slept.

I'd dozed but every single sound woke me.

As I washed up our guest's dishes, I glanced at Fletcher. "You are only getting one cup this morning."

"I know," he said, not moving his gaze from his phone. "You should consider a nap."

I ignored that. Fletcher had gone to shower while I prepared the meal. Soon, the dishes were done and all that remained were our own omelets with toast.

Neither of us ate.

This wasn't acceptable. "Put the coffee down and take bites." Following my own orders, I picked up my fork and went to work. Fletcher spared me an impatient look, but for once he didn't argue. After setting the phone and the coffee mug down on either side of his plate, he kept looking at the phone as he ate.

It was aggravating the hell out of me.

"Staring at it is not going to make her call." If anything, it made me want to smash his phone. Then I'd have to clean up the mess. There wasn't even laundry to do. The sheets had already gone through the dryer. I just needed to fold and put them away. There were fresh sheets on the bed already.

Everything was ready for her to come home.

"I'm not staring at it, willing her to call," Fletcher commented. "Well, not much. I'm waiting for it to finish generating the report on logins to the game in the last few days."

Game? I frowned. "What game?"

"My game, Big Guy." Fletcher paused, straightening all at once and staring at me. "Oh, man, you're breaking my heart. Surely you remember my video game? Come on, the hottest app. Selling like crazy, doesn't charge a fortune for in-game bonuses? Tons of fun for the whole family and all kinds of quests to unlock?"

Sometimes, I genuinely wondered if Fletcher spoke the same language as the rest of us.

He put a hand to his chest, his tone mockingly aggrieved and melodramatic. "Rick, my buddy, my big guy, my pal—I thought we were really working on this communication thing. You're wounding me."

"Not yet," I said slowly. "Though it grows more tempting by the minute."

I'd been careful not to bruise him up during our "spar." Vienna enjoyed his pretty face. Or so she'd indicated. Bruising him would just worry her. No sooner did my thoughts turn to her then I tracked to the clock over the stove.

Another hour had passed.

Another day when she hadn't been in contact.

Three. Long. Hellish. Days.

With possibly one more to go if she stuck to the schedule she said she *might* have.

Might.

So many unknowns.

"Right," Fletcher said on a long exhale. "Game. C'mere, let

me show you how this works. Drew really likes it. So, you should learn how to play."

Why hadn't he said so? Another hour trickled past, slightly faster this time, as he introduced me to the game. It was not something I normally enjoyed, but I was grateful for the distraction.

Fletcher even managed to eat a few more bites of food. I did my best to focus though, if he needed me to enjoy his game then I could at least remember what he taught me.

———

Four Days.

"I told you not to call her," I said for what felt like the hundredth time.

"I'm not calling her," Fletcher protested. "I'm just trying to ping her phone. If I can ping it, I know where she is. You know, when it's on."

I sighed. "Vienna has rules for a reason."

"Wait, there's rules?" Fletcher blinked at me. Despite getting some sleep, he still had the look of a man on the edge. I got that. "What rules?"

Studying him for a moment, I frowned. Had she not told him…

"If there are rules, I need to know them," Fletcher informed me. "I do well with structure. Look, I even do the damn dishes if you don't get there first."

That was true.

"Yes, there are rules to any job she does. The five Ds, she calls them." Oh, no sooner had I begun to talk about them then I realized how much I needed to hear her voice. Repeating them from memory, I could almost imagine the huskiness as she dictated the rules to me that first time.

The rules for being with her.

Working with her.

Living with her.

"I'm listening…" Fletcher yanked me back to the present. Yes. Living with *him* too.

————

Five days.

Five. *Fucking*. Days.

Something was wrong.

There was no doubt in my mind that something had gone *extremely* wrong. I constantly watched the news. Even though Sandra Jane had been on the news and different morning shows almost non-stop, as if she were some new shiny object America was obsessed with, there were no news of attacks on Sandra Jane or any arrests on the Judge.

Nothing that should alarm me.

But still.

Vienna would never go more than three days without checking in. She should have been home yesterday at the latest. Vienna would have at least given us a heads up if she was going to be late.

I stood at the window, staring out at the road.

Today was sunny. A beautiful day with birds chirping in the trees surrounding the subdivision. It was picturesque, something out of a Thomas Kinkade painting, if he had ever painted an abandoned, modern gothic subdivision.

Yet, it was ugly.

Without Vienna the world was an ugly, terrible place.

Over the last few days, I'd hardly eaten when I didn't force myself, barely slept, and had lost the ability to quiet my mind. Even now, my body quaked with the force of questions pelting through my thoughts.

Where was she? Was she hurt? What was she doing?

Did she need me?

Most especially, did she need me, when there was

nothing I could do about it. Not a damn thing except for stare out this fucking window. It was pointless. Absolutely useless.

Still, I couldn't get my feet to take me anywhere else. Not when this was where I'd see her first if she did come back. The bleakness of the situation crowded me, and I stopped breathing. When my lungs burned and my eyes watered, I sucked in a damning breath.

I didn't want to breathe without Vienna.

Hard footsteps pounded down the hallway, and it was a miracle I slanted my head enough to see a wild eyed Fletcher flying into the room.

"Rick. We have to do something." He pulled at his hair as he walked in a tight circle. "Her phone is completely offline. I can't track her. If the app was at least running in the background on her phone, I'd be able to hack her location. It's off. It has to be. I've delicately tapped all my resources for any information that could shed light on where she is. Nothing. There's nothing, Rick! How can you stand there in the window when we can't *fucking find her*?" His worried tone ended in frantic yelling.

I grimaced. I was more than worried. I was dying inside.

Standing in the window was the only thing that helped.

"I don't know what to do," I admitted in a pained whisper. It hurt to know I had nothing to offer in the quest to find her. Before Vienna, I floated through life from one program to another with no real skills to assist Fletcher.

Just knowing he was searching the web and dark net for her and I couldn't help, tore at my pride. Everything Vienna had taught me to do, Fletcher had already done. I could handle it, pride didn't mean much when Vienna's safety was on the line, but Fletcher was running up against dead ends too.

"I'm going down to get the Fed." He spun on his heel to sprint toward the laundry room.

"No!" I grabbed his arm. "Vienna doesn't trust him. I don't trust him."

Turning to face me, Fletcher grabbed my biceps, squeezing as he stared me dead in the eyes. "Rick," Fletcher pulled in a short but deep breath. "Big Guy," he continued, his voice reed thin. "Something is wrong. That's not an assumption at this point. It's fact. I deal in facts and this one is a bastard of one glaring me in the face. I've exhausted every. Single. Resource. I can't find her. It's like she never existed." He paused, but if he was waiting for me to answer, I had nothing. Every word that left his mouth brought my fear to life and paralyzed my brain.

"We need help. We need someone who knows how to find people. We need someone with connections. We need someone who can do all the fucking things I can't." He gave me a small shake. "We need the Fed."

I found myself nodding and before I realized what was happening, we were running down the steps to the basement.

Then Fletcher slid the door open with such force, it banged against the wall and threatened to bounce off the tracks.

The Fed was lying back on the cot, his arm stuffed behind his head and one of the books I'd brought him open in his hands. When he saw us, he shot to a sitting position and tossed the book on the end of his bed.

Fletcher did all the talking. I was glad. As much as I wanted to take control of the situation, my tongue was glued to the roof of my mouth.

"Channing Morgan," Fletcher started.

The man lifted a brow, waiting for him to continue. He picked up on our fear and tension. He had to. It was a physical thing constantly choking me.

"Our lady friend is missing. We haven't heard from her in days. I don't—" he gasped. "I don't know what's happened except that something is very wrong. We need your help."

Like I was only a passenger in my body with no control, I watched Fletcher pull the keys from his pocket and unlock the main door to the cell. Absently, I wondered how he got those keys. Either they were my set or Vienna had given him his own.

"If you get her killed. I will fuck with your life so much, your grandchildren's grandchildren will feel it," Fletcher threatened. But it was empty. If Channing Morgan betrayed us, he wouldn't have access to his systems to fuck him over.

The barred door swung open.

Our guest dropped his chin as a dark, slow grin slithered over his face. Waves of piercing doubt crashed into me, but still I was frozen.

"Call me Cash."

EPILOGUE

VIENNA

THE NUMBNESS in my arms trickled into my consciousness. The painful nips and stinging of sensation trying to return. The muscles wanted to cramp, but my arms were at an unnatural angle. I couldn't move them to relieve the stress or the discomfort.

Piece by piece, the last few days began to surface. Following the target. Studying her. Tracking her meetings, who she talked to, where she liked to go. I'd been in and out of her place a half-dozen times. Nothing of the journals or the research materials were kept there.

Smart.

Then…

Somewhere a lock ground and the tumblers clanked. Pain thudded through my brain like thunder rolling with each piece I tried to put into place. My mouth was dry, my tongue seemed half-stuck to the back of my teeth. I couldn't feel my legs. The temperature was cool, too cool. The numbness in my arms might be the way I was bound, but my legs?

Were they zip-tied? It had to be zip-ties. There was no icy

sensation of metal or abrasiveness like rope. I couldn't so much as twist to test them though. Steps echoed through the darkness.

It was the first moment the fact I sat in darkness struck me. I was sitting in darkness. A hood was over my head. The cloth stuck to my face, like I was clammy with sweat despite the chill. It added a grungy odor to the air, but nothing medicinal.

The hood whipped off my head and light blinded me. I couldn't see a damn thing past it and my eyes teared almost in defense. Closing my eyes, I tried to give them time to adjust. Something had gone sideways.

This was why we had to do our homework.

"So," my visitor said and I cracked an eyelid open to try and identify them past the burning brightness. "Shall we try this again?"

The boys return in High Note.
Vienna's survival? Still TBD.

AFTERWORD

Well…

Right, so let's chat. From the beginning when Fletcher knocked Cash out and Vienna hog-tied him into the trunk, we knew Cash would spend the rest of the book in the basement. The question was, how would he get out?

Unlike in book one, where Cash's story ran parallel with theirs, in this one, he has become indelibly intertwined. But is he friend or foe? For Vienna, her personal code says she shouldn't hurt the innocent. But for Rick and Fletcher, protecting Vienna is more important than anything else.

Now she's missing and they need Cash's help. Whew, yeah, that little pucker feeling you have going on right now? Buckle up. It's probably going to become a lot more dangerous from here on out.

Yeah. Far more dangerous.

winks

See you next time. Don't forget to grab your copy and leave a review!

We are so excited for what comes next. What about you?

ACKNOWLEDGMENTS

We wanted to take a moment to thank you again for picking up First Chorus. We have been living and breathing with this story for more than a year. No book or story is conceived, brought to life, or allowed to breathe in a vacuum. Even when we're working on other projects, we're always talking about this one. Or the after it.

Or the one after that.

The #girlgang around us has been fabulously supportive with alpha reading, beta reading, comma cops (truthfully, I need help with this the most), and even a soundtrack to help us stay on target for mood.

Books are the source for community building online and off. They foster friendships in the form of shared interests, support groups (not kidding), and love of characters. It's not all that unusual to fist pump a character's success, to cry with them over a loss, and to burst out laughing at how life's little absurdities get to them.

Even better, when you see a community or family developing within the pages that you actively root for because on various levels, it provides the readers with an element of that same success. We live, viscerally, through the characters on the page.

As authors, this affects us as well. Our #girlgang is right there with us, cheering us on, grimacing, squealing, laughing, and at times wanting to give our characters a hug.

When we get yelled at for something that happens to our

characters, we know we did our job. We know you love them like we do.

Not going to lie, that feeling is the best. So we wanted to take this moment to acknowledge all of you for being on this journey with us.

Thank you.

xoxo

Heather and Blake

ABOUT HEATHER LONG

I *love* books. Not just a little bit, but a lot. Books were my best friends when I was growing up. Books didn't care if I was new to a town or to a class. They were always there, my trustiest of companions. Until they turned on me and said I had to write them.

I can tell you that my own personal happily ever after included writing books. I've always said that an HEA is a work in progress. It's true in my marriage, my friendships, and in my career. I am constantly nurturing my muse as we dive into new tales, new tropes, new characters and more.

After seventeen years in Texas, we relocated to the Pacific Northwest in search of seasons, new experiences, and new geography. I can't wait to discover what life (and my muse) have in store for me.

Maybe writing was always my destiny and romance my fate. After all, my grandmother wasn't a fan of picture books and used to read me her Harlequin Romance novels.

Follow Heather & Sign up for her newsletter:
www.heatherlong.net
TikTok

ABOUT BLAKE BLESSING

Blake is a hyper asian ball of sunshine, and she cannot be contained in one box. Prone to random bouts of spinning or hyper-focusing, she's also equal parts goofy, ridiculous, and random. It's funny that she writes so much dark romance. Her goal is to provide stories about characters you can't help but root for through thought-provoking situations, even if they're a little—a lot—morally gray.

TikTok

ALSO BY HEATHER LONG

82nd Street Vandals

Savage Vandal

Vicious Rebel

Ruthless Traitor

Dirty Devil

Shamelessly Loyal (Novella)

Brutal Fighter

Dangerous Renegade

Merciless Spy

Reckless Thief

Fierce Dancer

Dirty Dancer

Bay Ridge Royals

Shamelessly Loyal (Novella)

Battle Lines

Deceptive Truce

Wicked Surrender

Violent Chaos

Desperate Victory

BLOOD Brothers

Burn

Lure

Own

Blue Ivy Prep

Problem Child

Mad Boys

Party Crashers

Money Shot

Bravo Team Wolf

When Danger Bites

Bitten Under Fire

Cardinal Sins

Kill Song

First Chorus

High Note

Last Word

Chance Monroe

Earth Witches Aren't Easy

Plan Witch from Out of Town

Bad Witch Rising

Fevered Hearts

Marshal of Hel Dorado

Brave are the Lonely

Micah & Mrs. Miller

A Fistful of Dreams

Raising Kane

Wanted: Fevered or Alive

Wild and Fevered

The Quick & The Fevered

A Man Called Wyatt

Going Royal

Some Like it Royal

Some Like it Scandalous

Some Like it Deadly

Some Like it Secret

Some Like it Easy

Heart of the Nebula

Queenmaker

Deal Breaker

Throne Taker

Lone Star Leathernecks

Semper Fi Cowboy

As You Were, Cowboy

Shackled Souls

Succubus Chained

Succubus Unchained

Succubus Blessed

Shackled Souls (Omnibus)

STANDALONES

Kiss of Fate (w/Blake Blessing)

Taste of Karma (w/Blake Blessing)

I'll Be Home… (w/Tate James)

Overexposed (w/Tate James)

Switchboard Duet

Talk to Me

Don't Let Go

Untouchable

Rules and Roses

His Moonstruck Wolf

Thunder Wolf

Ghost Wolf

Outlaw Wolves

Wolf Unleashed

ALSO BY BLAKE BLESSING

The Collection

Snatched

Edged

Crazed

Bastard Brothers of Carnage Series

Addict

Convict

Killer

Psycho

Traitor

Mazza Series

Marks of the Mazza

Bonds of the Mazza

Secrets of the Mazza

War of the Mazza

Astrid Scott Series

Pretty Lies

Ugly Truths

Busted Dreams

Vivid Fears

Brittle Hope

Fragile Minds Duet

Fractured

Altered

Standalone RH Romance
Pin-up Girl

Standalone MF Romance
Full Glasses and Burju Shoes